The Shadow Games

The Shadow Academy Book One

Alison Ingleby

Windswept Writing

Contents

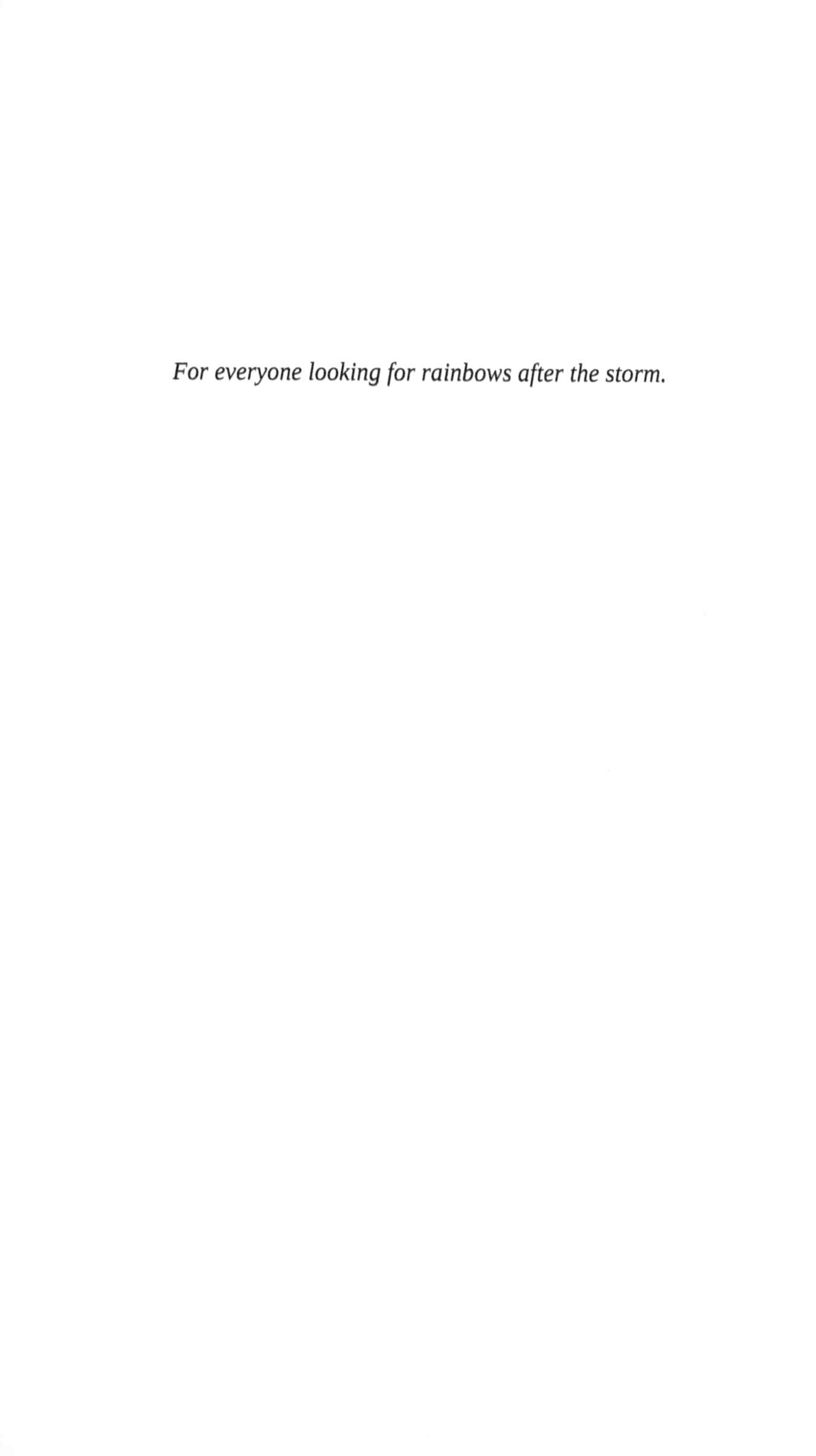

For everyone looking for rainbows after the storm.

1

Dragons

TODAY COULD BE THE best day of my life. Or my greatest humiliation.

In a few hours, I would find out if I had what it took to make it into the Royal Academy. If I passed their mysterious test, my family would be secure for life. Dad could retire without having to work himself into an early grave, and I would have achieved my dream.

If I didn't pass the test . . . Well, that wasn't an option I was prepared to consider.

I stood at the apex of our curved growing-yard, leaning as far out as the dome encasing it allowed. In the distance, through the narrow gulf between the towers of New Vegas, the white spire of the Royal Tower glowed pink in the early-morning sun. The lower part of the tower, the Royal Academy, bulged out, like a donut perched on a street vendor's spike. The tapered point above consisted of apartments for Academy members, official function rooms, and at the very top, the royal apartments of the king and his family. But royalty didn't matter to me. All I cared about was the Academy.

The families of Academy trainees were given a one-off payment equivalent to five year's wages. When my sister, Layla, was accepted into the Academy two years ago, the credits had allowed us to move from our old, windowless apartment to this one on the edge of the tower. Because of Layla's hard work and good fortune, we were better off than most lower-levelers, but my father still worked long hours to pay our bills, and I knew my parents worried about not having savings for the future. If I made it into the Academy, too, they would be freed of that burden. And I would become one of the most valued members of New Vegas society.

There was a lot at stake.

"Vesper," Sol called, his thin, reedy voice filtering through the orange trees behind me. "My dragon's lost its puff."

I took one more look at the gleaming white building, allowing my gaze to linger on its curves, before scanning the patchwork of blue sky high above, segmented by the metro trains that connected the towers. Then I turned to see where my little brother had got to.

Inside our garden-yard's dome, the light levels gradually increased to simulate the sun rising. The sun rarely penetrated this far down the towers, so the dome provided our days and nights, as well as the light for our fruit and vegetables to grow. I ducked between the two orange trees and found Sol sitting on the pathway between the tomato plants and the miniature fountain. Three toy dragons sat scattered around him, the fourth he held in his hands.

Sol gave it a despondent shake and looked up at me. "It's run out of puff."

"Well, we can't have that." I stifled a smile and crouched down in front of him. "Let me see if I can magic up some more."

Sol clung to his toy, reluctant to hand it over. It was the orange dragon—his favorite. Dad had saved up to buy it for his sixth birthday. If we'd run out of the cartridges that produced the fake smoke, Sol would be devastated.

"I'll feed him," he announced. "Can you get me some firestone?"

"Sure." I made a move to stand, but something in his eyes stopped me. "Are you okay, Sol?"

His little fingers tightened on the dragon. "Are there any dragons out there, Vesper? *Real* dragons?"

"I'm afraid not, little brother. They died out decades ago. Typhon was the last."

"And the biggest?" Sol asked excitedly.

I lowered my voice. "And the most *dangerous*. But yes, he was the biggest and strongest." I tapped the orange dragon's nose. "Though your Typhon is a friendly dragon, right?"

"Yes. He'll protect me," Sol said with the conviction only a six-year-old could have. Then his face fell and tears welled in his brown eyes. "I saw one last night. A big, black one. You were trying to talk to it, but it was angry and didn't want to listen." His voice rose until it was almost a squeak. "It was going to breathe fire over you, and then . . . and then I woke up."

I wrapped my arms around my little brother and pulled his thin body into mine, ruffling his dark hair. "It was only a dream," I said soothingly. "Dragons don't exist. It was just a dream."

He sniffed into my t-shirt.

After a moment, I pulled back. "Now, shall I go and get you some firestone? Then Typhon can chase the black dragon away."

Sol wiped his nose on his sleeve and nodded. "Thanks, Vesper."

I stood and glanced back through the dome just in time to see a silver pod zip past. It slowed to dock further along the tower.

That was odd. Silver pods were used by Guardians and Peacekeepers, but we rarely saw either down here.

I slid open the door to our apartment. Like most homes in the lower levels, it was compact, providing the bare minimum of space for four people to live. But it was a fraction bigger than our old apartment, and with Layla now living at the Academy, I had a tiny bedroom to myself. Her apartment was almost as big as ours. All that space for one person.

The sound of running water came from the small bathroom, mingling with my mother humming her "laundry tune" from my parents' bedroom. Mom had a tune for everything—cooking, cleaning, laundry. She said it made the chores more enjoyable.

I stood on my tiptoes to reach the high cupboard where Sol's toys were kept, once again wishing I was taller than five-foot-two. I was about to give up and fetch a chair to stand on when there was a click and hiss as the front door of the apartment slid open. There was only one other person who had the code for our apartment. I ran into the narrow hallway and threw my arms around my sister.

"Layla! What are you doing here?"

Layla was a fraction taller than me, and while Sol and I had inherited Dad's dark hair and olive skin, Layla got Mom's genes. Her brown hair was woven with strands of gold and amber, and fell in waves around her round, pale face. Having graduated from the Academy last week, she'd swapped her white trainee uniform for the light gray of a Guardian.

My sister grinned back at me. "Well, a little bird told me that someone"—she tweaked my nose—"aced all her exams."

My stomach flipped. "You know the results?"

"Unofficially." Layla shrugged. "They're all processed automatically before the final testing."

I looked down at my hands, nerves gnawing at my insides. I may have aced the academic tests, but that wouldn't mean a thing if I couldn't pass the Academy's test today.

The test nobody talked about.

My mother emerged from the bedroom, holding a pair of Sol's trousers. Her face broke into a smile as she caught sight of my sister. "I thought you'd be involved in the testing today."

Layla nodded. "Can't stay, but I wanted to come and wish Vesper luck." She glanced over at me. "Walk with me to the transport deck?"

"Sure. Let me get my things." I stumbled into my bedroom and leaned over my bed, closing my eyes and sucking in air. It was a good thing I hadn't had breakfast, or it would be making a reappearance right now.

You always feel like this before a test. Just breathe through it.

Light footsteps approached. My mother's scent, jasmine blossom and lemon, filled the air.

She rubbed my back. "You know, whatever happens today, we're really proud of you. The Academy isn't for everyone. You may even be happier in a . . ."

"Normal job?" I glanced up at her. *Is she kidding?*

A ghost of a smile crossed her face. "It's not so bad, you know."

But it would be. Anything less than the Academy would be a failure. Not that life was bad now. If I had done well in my exams, I should be able to get a decent job. But it wouldn't be the *same* as being an Academy member. And though I wouldn't admit it to my family, secretly, I wanted to prove that I was just as good as my sister.

"I just wish they'd tell us what to expect so I could prepare for it." I blew out a breath. "I don't see why the test has to be such a big secret."

"You can't prepare for it, Vesper. That's the point. It's . . ." She bit her lip and turned away, carefully folding Sol's trousers and placing them on my bed. "Well, anyway. You should be going."

Layla's laugh rang loud in the hall in response to something Dad said. "You nearly ready, Ves?" she yelled.

"Yeah. Give me a minute!" I called back, then turned to Mom.

She stared at me intently, her blue eyes scanning my face as if trying to memorize my features.

"Are you all right, Mom?"

My mother reached up to cup my face, tracing my cheekbones with her thumbs. "Of course. It's just a big day." She smiled, but it seemed kind of forced.

"I'll be back this evening," I said, as much for my benefit as hers. "Even if I get into the Academy, they let you come back to pick up a few things. I'll be fine, Mom."

"I'm sure you will."

As Layla's footsteps sounded outside the door, Mom pulled me into a tight hug. I guessed she was finding it hard to accept that I was no longer a child. I clung to her, feeling her reassurance wash over me—a warm blanket shielding me from the reality of the world outside our apartment. Her breath was hot on my ear. "Remember, everything the society does is for our protection."

When she pulled back, I stared at her, puzzled. "Wh—"

"Come on, Vesper," Layla said from the door.

My mother gave a small shake of her head. I forced out a smile before grabbing my bag off the bed and turning to my sister.

"Sorry. I was just saying goodbye."

Layla rolled her eyes. "You'll be back before you know it." But her voice also carried a thread of tension.

She stepped back to let me out of the room. I hugged my father, who waited in the hall, already dressed and ready for another day overseeing food production in the hydroponic factory. Laugh lines creased his warm skin, and his dark hair was threaded with gray. Every year, he looked wearier. He had worked so hard to support us all these years. My heart twinged at the thought that I might free him of that burden.

"Good luck, my little star," he said. Unlike my mother, his smile was easy and relaxed.

Layla was named for the moon, me for the evening star, and Sol for the sun. Which was kind of ironic given we rarely saw any of them from down here. We once took a school trip to the roof of Tower 14 at night to see the stars. They twinkled as if someone had thrown glitter across the sky. The sight had made me forget to breathe.

"Thanks, Dad." I glanced at the doors to the garden-yard. "Say bye to Sol for me? And can you get him one of those fire cartridges? His dragon's stopped working again."

"The rate he's going, that dragon will cost me a month's wages." But the smile didn't leave his face as he walked across the small living area to Sol's cupboard.

If I pass the tests today, Sol will be able to have all the dragon puff he wants.

The thought made me smile as I turned back to Layla, who held the front door open impatiently. "Let's do this."

Rush hour hadn't yet begun, so the travelators were quiet as we made our way to the nearest bank of elevators. Level 137 was family accommodation, and most of the people we did pass were dressed in the blue coveralls hydroponic staff wore.

We were a couple of streets from the elevators when a group of people stepped out from a side street. One, a tall woman with long, white-blonde hair, was dressed in the same light gray uniform as Layla. An older woman and two men wore the darker gray of the Peacekeepers.

They stopped at the door to an apartment farther up the street. The Guardian consulted a device on her wrist, then nodded at a Peacekeeper, who stepped forward and scanned the lock. He stretched out a hand, but before he could open the door, it exploded outward, sending him stumbling backward into his colleagues.

My heart jumped as the explosion rang in my ears. A girl ran out of the apartment, ducked under the arm of the Guardian, and sprinted down the street toward us.

Blonde hair whipped around a pale, drawn face. When the girl's blue eyes met mine, a jolt of recognition froze my feet to the floor.

Layla tugged my arm, trying to pull me toward a narrow side alley. "This way."

But I couldn't move. I searched for the girl's name. She was a few years younger than me, but I'd seen her at school and around the Level 135 recreation area. I had a feeling her mother worked at the hydroponic farm and her father . . . I didn't know what had happened to her father, but I was pretty sure he wasn't around.

Marissa. That was her name.

"Stop!" one of the Peacekeepers hollered.

Then something happened that left me wondering if my mind was playing tricks on me. One minute, Marissa was running toward us. The next, her body jerked, and she flew backward.

She must have gone at least fifty feet before she fell into a heap at the Peacekeepers' feet.

I blinked, struggling to believe what I'd seen.

She flew? But that's not possible?

Marissa sprang to her feet and flung her hands out toward the Peacekeepers. Nothing happened. She looked down at her hands, as if there was something wrong with them, then threw them out again.

The Guardian walked toward her, a soft smile on her face. "There's nowhere to run, Marissa." Her voice was gentle, yet firm, like a schoolteacher chastising a pupil.

Marissa spun around. Her eyes, wide with fear, met mine and she opened her mouth, but the Peacekeepers surrounded her, wrestling her to the floor.

"Come on, Vesper!"

Layla dragged me into the alley. She marched me through the network of backstreets that formed a grid between the main thoroughfares. In a dark passageway, she stopped, glanced around to check there was no one listening, and turned to me. Strands of dark hair clung to her forehead.

"What—"

She grasped my shoulders. "You didn't see anything, understand?" She gave me a shake for good measure. "A criminal was arrested. That's all."

I stared at her, perplexed, as a thread of unease wound through my stomach. "But Marissa's not a criminal. She—"

Layla's gaze flicked upward. I remembered the cameras that tracked our every movement. "She *is* a criminal. The Guardians are never wrong. You know that."

The intensity of her gaze unsettled me. I opened my mouth, but the flash of fear in Layla's eyes made me close it again.

"It's our job to keep everyone safe. Criminals must be removed to protect the society. Now, come on. We're late." She whirled around and stalked off.

"To protect the society," I whispered, trailing after her.

That was what we were taught from kindergarten. Guardians and Peacekeepers kept our society safe. As a result, crimes were so rare that this was the first time I'd ever seen the Peacekeepers on our level. And Layla was right. The Guardians were never wrong. Not like the system of juries and judges we studied in history class that let the guilty walk free while innocent people were locked away for crimes they didn't commit. If you committed a crime here, the Guardians *knew*. No one escaped justice.

But Marissa? I didn't know her well, but she never got in trouble at school. And she had looked so terrified, so confused . . .

I jogged to catch up with Layla. "What did they do to her? She flew fifty feet. That's not—"

I nearly ran into my sister's back as she stopped and whirled around. She grasped my arm, her fingernails digging into my skin.

"Ow!" I stared at her in confusion. *What's gotten into her?*

"Sorry." Layla smiled awkwardly and released my arm. "Look, just try and forget about it, okay? You've got more important things to worry about today."

I trailed after her, chewing my lip. I'd never seen Layla like this before—so closed off. If I didn't know better, I would have thought her afraid.

We took the elevator to the transport level in silence, then weaved through the streets to the transport deck. It was busier up here, the chatter of morning commuters and the hum of the pods a welcome distraction from my thoughts.

Layla glanced up at the huge clock hanging on the side of the tower. "I've got to run. You're meeting here, right?"

I nodded. There was a meeting zone to one side of the transporter deck and our class had been told to meet there at eight.

"Well, I suggest you visit the restroom before heading out. There's bound to be a queue when you get to the Academy, and if you don't go before the testing starts, they'll make you wait." Layla searched my eyes and smiled. "You'll be fine."

I swallowed and nodded again. I wanted to put my arms around her and draw on her strength, but I held back. Guardians were supposed to be aloof, emotionless. Hugging in public, even with family, was definitely not allowed.

As if she could read my thoughts, Layla took my hand and squeezed it gently. "Good luck, Vesper."

Feeling more confused than ever, I watched her stride toward the silver pods reserved for Academy members and graduates. My fingers closed around the slip of film Layla had pressed into my palm.

2

The Royal Academy

T HE PUBLIC RESTROOMS WERE empty, apart from a cleaning bot that whirled around my legs, impatient to be done with its job. I hurried to the end cubicle and locked the door. Inside, I sank down onto the toilet and opened my hand.

My fingers slid over the thin film as I clumsily unrolled it until my sister's scrawled handwriting became visible. I scanned the three lines, then read them again.

> *Whatever they show you, remember that everything the society does is for our protection.*

> *Destroy this note.*

> *I love you. L x*

My fingers trembled as I let the film roll up in my hand. What did it mean? Of course the society protected us, but why did my sister feel the need to slip me a secret note to say something she could—and already had—told me?

I unrolled the film again, my eyes focusing on each word, searching for some hidden meaning. But if Layla had meant to convey some subtler message, I didn't see it.

Footsteps clicked on the tiled floor and the door of the cubicle next to me swung open. A pair of smart shoes appeared under the barrier dividing the cubicles, and I heard a sigh as their owner sat down to relieve themselves.

Quickly, I searched in my bag for my nail scissors, then carefully snipped the film into tiny pieces. Standing, I flushed them down the toilet and made my way out of the cubicle. I placed my hands under the airblower, staring into the mirror as it cleansed my skin. My green eyes looked fearful, though perhaps that was just my imagination. I tucked my hair behind my ear and left the restroom, my mind whirring.

"Hey, Vesper!" A girl with dull brown hair and a freckled face waved at me from the meeting point.

I smiled at Lainey and hurried over. "Hey. How are you?"

She scrunched up her face. "Okay, I guess. Not looking forward to getting my results."

"I'm sure you did great," I said, trying to sound reassuring.

"What about you, Ves? Did you smash the exams?" Fergus punched my shoulder lightly, his hand lingering a little longer than necessary.

Heat rose to my cheeks. "I think I did okay."

He snorted. "That means you smashed them." He raised one hand in the Academy salute and affected a posh voice. "Ready to take your place at the Academy, Miss Rodriguez?"

"Shut it, Fergus." I scowled at him, but he grinned, unapologetic, and slung an arm around my shoulders.

"Don't forget us when you're in the white tower."

I shrugged off his arm, catching the look of consternation on Lainey's face. The three of us had been friends ever since elementary school, but in the past few months, something had changed. Words hung unspoken in the air between us, each of us knowing that if one person said something, they would start a chain reaction none of us were quite prepared to face.

But this couldn't go on for much longer. If Fergus did like me as more than a friend, he had to know that, as much as I cared for him, I didn't feel the same way. As for Lainey . . .

If you get into the Academy, you won't be able to see them anyway.

The thought sent a pang of regret lancing through my chest, but it was quickly dissipated by nervous energy. It wasn't as if I'd be banned from seeing my friends. I just wouldn't have as much free time.

"Did the nursery accept your application, Lainey?" I asked, trying to push thoughts of the Academy test from my mind.

Lainey's face broke into a smile. "Yes, as long as I pass my exams. They didn't say anything about the test today."

"Smithson didn't mention it in my interview, either," Fergus said. "I tried to get some information out of him, but he just closed up like an oyster." He snapped his fingers shut to demonstrate.

"Well, you shouldn't have been dumb enough to ask. He could have called the Peacekeepers on you. I thought you *wanted* to work for the mechanics?" Lainey gave him a mock glare.

Fergus shrugged off the comment with a grin. "It was worth a try. Don't you think it odd that no one seems to remember a test everyone has to take?" He turned to me. "Has Layla said anything to you, Vesper?"

I shook my head, avoiding his gaze.

It *was* odd that no one was allowed to talk about the test. Fergus had badgered Miss Reyes, our class teacher, about it all year, to the point that she'd threatened to suspend him if he mentioned it one more time. But she hadn't acted as if she was hiding some big secret. It was more like she was embarrassed to admit she didn't know anything about it.

"I guess we'll find out soon enough," I said, glancing over Fergus's shoulder. "Here comes Miss Reyes now."

"What are you going to do if you don't get into the Academy?" Lainey asked me as our teacher herded us into a group and began to register us.

I touched the back of my hand to the scanner Miss Reyes held out and waited for it to register my microchip. A green light flashed in acknowledgement. My teacher smiled and waved me toward the pod. "I'll figure something out."

"You don't have a plan B?" Fergus stared at me. "I know you're clever enough to get through the exams, Ves, but that's not all the Academy looks at. Remember Darren? I'm pretty sure he flunked finals, but for some reason, they let him in. He's training to become a Peacekeeper now."

I rolled my eyes. "Stop worrying, Fergus. It'll be fine."

My classmates had been busy applying for apprenticeships and jobs for months. I should have been doing the same, but that would feel like admitting defeat. Admitting there was a possibility I could fail.

I won't. I can handle whatever they throw at me.

My hands clenched at my side. I just wished I knew what the test involved.

Despite my nerves, a bubble of excitement welled up at the sight of the large gray transporter waiting for us. This would be only the third time I'd ever traveled by pod. They were more expensive than traveling by metro, but there was no metro link to the white tower. The only way to reach the palace and the Royal Academy was to fly.

Once inside the pod, I pushed past my classmates and led Fergus and Lainey to one of the large windows. There was barely a bump as the pod rose from the transporter deck. I gazed out of the window, watching Tower 14 recede into the distance, then peered down at the thick black smog that smothered the old city floor.

"What do you think's down there?" Lainey asked, pressing her face to the window.

"Down where?" Fergus choked out, his back to the window. His face was pale, his Adam's apple bobbing up and down in his throat as he stared resolutely at a point on the ceiling of the pod.

I stifled a smile, remembering the last time we'd traveled by pod. Fergus had tried looking out the window and promptly vomited on Lainey's shoes.

"Under the smog. Do you think the criminals they put down there survive?" Lainey asked.

In our history lessons, we'd been taught that New Vegas had been built on top of the ruins of an old city than had become unliveable. There were rumors that monster still roamed the streets, but they were just tales, dreamed up for kids to scare their younger brothers and sisters. If they had ever existed, they had long since been eradicated, like the dragons that had been prevalent in New Vegas until they'd gotten out of control. Even monsters could not live under the smog.

"No," I said shortly. "How could anything survive down there? There's no light, no water, nothing. That's why they throw criminals down there. It's a death sentence. It would be kinder just to kill them here, but—"

Fergus jabbed my ribs, stopping me. I glanced around and bit my lip as I realized the people around us had fallen silent. Miss Reyes's gaze found mine, her eyes conveying a warning. She'd have called anyone else out for what I just said, but I was her star pupil. She knew that a glance would be enough.

"Sorry," I muttered, ducking my head. It wasn't the first time I'd had to be reminded to hold my tongue.

Layla had said Marissa was a criminal. Would she be sent down to the old city floor? Surely, she couldn't have done anything bad enough to deserve that?

I found myself chewing my lip again. Getting distracted by someone else's problems was the last thing I needed today. Layla was right. I needed to focus on the test. Perhaps once I got into the Academy, I'd be able to find out what Marissa's arrest had been about.

"Vesper, look!"

I followed Lainey's gaze and gasped. The curved spire of the Royal Tower soared above us, piercing the blue sky as delicately as a needle through fine silk. Unlike the residential towers, which had garden-yards, transporter decks, and recreation platforms built into them, the surface of the white spire was perfectly smooth. This close, I could see the faint outline of floor-to-ceiling windows, tinted white to protect the privacy of the people inside.

It was dazzling, breath-taking.

A surge of longing caused tears to prick the backs of my eyes and I suddenly found it difficult to breathe. *I could be part of that world. In a few hours, I might be looking out from the other side of those windows.*

I tore my eyes from the spire to look down. Below us, pods landed and took off from the transporter deck located on top of the donut shape of the Academy itself. Aside from the transporter deck, the top of the Academy was covered with solar panels. The clear dome that protected the deck from the winds whistling around the towers retracted to let us through.

"Where do they grow their food?" Lainey murmured.

"Layla says there's a separate tower dedicated to growing food for the Academy and royal family."

A flash of green caught my eye. I nudged Lainey, pointing to a sunken area among the solar panels where a series of tiers formed a bowl around a central patch of grass. "Check that out! It beats the Level 135 recreation area any day."

Lainey's eyes widened and she opened her mouth to reply, but at that moment, the pod dropped through the dome and gently touched down on the blindingly white transport deck.

We disembarked and had our microchips scanned again. An Academy trainee led us down a set of stairs set into the transporter deck, along a short corridor, and into a large circular hall filled with rows of chairs. About half were already occupied, some people chatting with their friends, others nervously glancing around. A line of windows was set into the top of the room, though as with the windows on the outside of the tower, they were tinted so we couldn't see through them. Below the windows, the walls were covered in a gray fabric.

"I'm afraid we're going to have a bit of a wait," Miss Reyes said as we sat down. "There are restrooms in the far corner, and you can help yourself to drinks from the machines." She motioned to a pair of drink dispensers set into the wall. "When they're ready for us, you'll be called in alphabetical order. Keep an eye on the board for your name."

The holoscreen on the far wall displayed the school name, followed by a list of people. As quickly as a person's name disappeared from the list, a new one appeared at the bottom. They were currently on Tower 3, Level 25.

I sighed, realizing Miss Reyes hadn't been exaggerating. It stood to reason that they'd start with the upper-level kids and work down. No one really cared if lower-levelers were kept waiting.

Food was brought out at midday, and my schoolmates crowded around it. Catching the disparaging glances thrown our way by some of the other school parties, anger and embarrassment burned in my stomach. It wasn't as if any of us were starving—no one starved in New Vegas—but it was rare to be able to eat until our bellies were stuffed.

Wait until I get into the Academy. I'll show those upper-level snobs who look down their noses at us from their luxurious penthouses that we are just as good as them.

In the Academy, it didn't matter which level or tower you came from. Everyone was equal.

By the time our school name flashed up on the board, my stomach was a bundle of nerves. Lainey was one of the first to be called. Ten minutes later, my name was added to the list.

"Good luck," Fergus said. His mouth stayed open as if he wanted to say something else, but he stopped himself. Color tinged his pale cheeks and a lock of sandy hair fell across his forehead.

I stood and rubbed my palms on my pants. "You too."

Then I took a deep breath and walked toward the door leading to the test rooms.

3

The Test

"**L**OOK FOR THE ROOM with your name above it," one of the Peacekeepers said as he motioned me through the door.

I nodded and tried to smile, but it quickly fell from my face. My insides felt like a ball of wriggling snakes, and hot and cold flushes alternately pulsed through my body. I wish I'd grabbed a drink in the main hall, but it was too late now. Instead, I licked my dry lips and tried not to retch as my stomach churned.

The short corridor led to a larger, slightly curved hallway with evenly spaced doors, each with a name illuminated above it. I walked along, my footsteps muffled, the corridor blanketed in silence, and suddenly felt very alone. I passed twelve doors before I found one with my name above it.

Lucky number thirteen.

Swallowing, I wiped my palms on my pants one more time and brushed the back of my hand over the entry pad. The door swished open.

A young woman looked up as I walked in. "Vesper Rodriguez?"

"Yes."

She smiled and motioned to a padded chair. "Please, take a seat."

The woman wore a blue-gray uniform with two wavy lines on her shoulder. The uniform color indicated she was a Technician, the third class of Academy graduates, but I had no idea what the symbol meant. I wasn't really sure what Technicians did, only that it had something to do with keeping the city running. Mind you, I didn't really know what Guardians and Peacekeepers did, either. There couldn't be enough crime in New Vegas to keep all of them busy.

The chair and the desk where the Technician sat took up most of the small room. The walls were covered in the same gray fabric as the hall. Close up, it seemed like some type of carpet with fine ridges embedded in the surface. What looked like a giant helmet was suspended above the padded chair. Wires led from the device down the legs of the frame and into what looked like a large computer on the woman's desk.

I sank down onto the cushioned chair and warily glanced at the device above my head. "What is that?"

"A virtual reality device," the woman explained.

"Is that the test?"

"We monitor how you respond to what you experience in a virtual reality simulation. This isn't like an exam. There's no right or wrong way to do things. It just depends on how your brain reacts." She smiled again, obviously trying to be reassuring, but her words just sent another jolt of fear through my veins.

No right or wrong way? Then how am I supposed to know how to pass? A dull ache began in my head, and I rubbed my temples.

The woman frowned. "Just try to relax, Vesper. It won't take long."

She lowered the device until it encased my head. I closed my eyes and focused on breathing through my nose, trying to combat the feeling of claustrophobia.

"Ready?"

"Yes," I croaked.

When I opened my eyes, I was no longer in the test room.

I stood on a low sand dune in a desert landscape. At my back were more dunes, but in front of me, the sand merged into rocky ground scattered with low bushes and cacti. The sun beat down, hot enough to burn my skin, and when I looked down, I saw I wore a thin, white dress. Sand trickled between my toes as I shifted my weight from foot to foot to escape the heat.

What is this?

I looked around, but there were no other people or any sign of human habitation. The only sound was the hissing of sand blown across the dunes by a faint breeze.

Except that *wasn't* the only sound. A faint rattle reached my ears, like the noise made by the shaker toy Sol had as a baby. When I found the source of the noise, my blood turned to ice in my veins.

A rattlesnake.

I stumbled backward, my feet scrabbling for purchase. Sand cascaded down the dune toward the snake. It hissed angrily and moved toward me, lifting the front part of its body into the air. I'd never seen a real snake, but I'd seen footage of them on documentaries. It was positioning itself to strike.

Adrenaline fizzled through me as my brain screamed at me to run. But I knew if I ran, the snake would strike.

It's a simulation, I reminded myself. *Whatever it is, it isn't going to kill you. They're just seeing how you respond.*

I closed my eyes and tried to calm my breathing.

This isn't real. This isn't real.

When I opened my eyes again, the snake and the desert were gone.

I now stood on top of Tower 14. The dome encasing the viewing platform was gone, and a strong wind whipped my hair back from my face. At first, I felt an odd sense of disappointment that it was daylight—I wanted to see the stars again—but then my feet began to move, carrying me to the barrier surrounding the platform. My hands closed around the bars, the cold metal burning my skin. Then I began to climb.

This isn't right.

I tried to climb back down, but my muscles refused to obey me, my hands and feet continuing upward as if I were a puppet controlled by invisible strings. I clenched my jaw and tried to temper my rising trepidation as I reached the top of the barrier and looked down into nothing.

Hundreds of feet below, pods zipped around the city like fireflies, and metro trains rushed between the towers like peas blown through transparent straws. Wind buffeted my body, threatening to send me over into the void.

I tried again to wrestle back control of my body, but I could barely keep myself upright, let alone climb back down. Panic rose in my throat. *I am going to die,* I realized, just as a gust of wind caught me and I toppled over the edge.

Fear took over. Not fear of death, but fear of the pain that precedes death. I plummeted so fast that my lungs felt like they were flattened against my chest. Air was ripped from my mouth.

My heartbeat thundered in my ears as I whistled past the first pods.

With a jolt, I remembered.

This isn't real.

I closed my eyes and smiled.

For a moment, I thought that was it. My eyes opened into darkness and I blinked, wondering if I was staring at the inside of the virtual reality helmet. As my eyes adjusted, I realized it wasn't totally dark. I could see faint lines on the wall. My foot bumped against something hard and I reached down, feeling the floor rise in front of me in regular steps.

I was in a stairwell. Probably a service staircase, judging from the rough concrete and the outline of pipes above me.

Was I supposed to go up or down?

I decided on up, running my hand along the wall as I placed my feet gingerly on each step, grateful that the boots I wore gave some protection from stubbed toes. I strained my eyes and ears, but all I could hear were my footsteps and the dripping of water. All I could see was darkness.

A scream broke the silence, followed by a cry for help. It sounded far away, but the cry was so familiar that I found myself breaking into a run, stumbling up the stairs as quickly as I could.

The stairwell lightened, and I moved faster until I reached a landing, seeing two doors leading off it.

"Sol! Where are you?"

My brother's scream answered me. I pushed open the right-hand door, letting it swing shut behind me. Service lights illuminated a corridor lined with ventilation ducts. It felt as if I were in the very depths of the tower.

I ran down the corridor and through another door. Sweat trickled down my neck. "Sol?"

This time, his cry was louder. Three paces brought me to a solid door with an access pad to one side. I pressed my hand against it, but the light flashed red.

"I'm coming, Sol!" Frantically I looked around, my gaze alighting on a metal fire extinguisher.

Wrestling it from the wall, I slammed it repeatedly into the door. On the fifth try, something gave. I slammed my shoulder into the door and fell into the room beyond.

It was sparsely furnished with large glass doors leading out onto a small balcony. The doors were open, letting in the noise of cargo pods transporting goods between the lowest levels of the towers.

I bolted across the room and through the doors, my gaze caught by a tiny pair of hands clinging to the balcony rail. But as I reached out for them, my hands hit an invisible barrier.

"Sol?"

My brother's eyes, wide with terror, looked up at me. He dangled from the balcony, his knuckles white on the narrow rail. A warm breeze ruffled his brown hair. Fifty feet below him, the dark smog clouds that separated New Vegas from the old city floor swirled ominously.

"Vesper? I-I can't move." His voice was barely a squeak.

One small hand slipped. Instinctively, I lunged for his arm, but again, I met the same resistance. I ran my hands over the invisible barrier, searching for any weakness. I found none.

"This isn't real. This isn't real," I chanted under my breath.

But Sol's fear was.

"Vesper!"

His gaze met mine. As his fingers began to uncurl from the balcony rail, I felt something crumple inside me. I slammed my fists into the barrier, but it was no longer there. The momentum of my blow carried me forward, and my fingers trickled over Sol's skin as his thin arms slipped through my grasp.

I clung to the empty air and screamed as my brother fell into the void.

My fingers dug into the cushioned arm of the chair, hair clinging to my sweaty forehead. As I reached up to brush it away, my hand hit the hard casing of the virtual reality device. Slowly, it rose above my head.

I blinked as the testing room came into focus. The Technician was white as a sheet, but she quickly recovered her composure and turned back to her desk, reaching for a cup.

"Here. Drink this." She held the cup out to me. It trembled in her hand. "It will help calm your system down."

I sipped the drink, the cool liquid soothing my dry throat. It tasted slightly sweet, and almost immediately, I felt more relaxed. I drained the cup and handed it back to the woman.

"Did I pass?"

Her fingers flew across the screen in a blur. "I'm not really supposed to tell you, but I will say you had a very strong reaction."

My heart leapt. "So I did pass?"

The woman turned to look at me. "Whenever you're feeling ready, you can leave. Turn right out the door and continue along the corridor until you're stopped. My colleagues will direct you from there." She turned back to her computer and brought up a list of names.

I pushed myself up out of the chair and stood, feeling slightly unsteady. My clothes were damp with sweat and my neck stiff, but my heart rate had returned to normal, no doubt due to the relaxing properties of the drink. The only lingering effect of my experience seemed to be a dull headache.

The corridor was empty, but I followed the woman's instructions and walked along it until two Peacekeepers blocked my path. They directed me into a room where perhaps thirty young people waited.

"Vesper!"

Seeing Fergus, I hurried over to him. "What are you doing here?" On impulse, I gave him a hug, needing some reassurance that I was back in the real world. His eyes were bright and, as usual, his face was split in a cheeky grin, but his cheeks were flushed. Like me, he'd been sweating.

He shrugged. "Well, presuming you passed the test, it seems I did, too. Though I can't say I enjoyed it very much."

I opened my mouth to reply, but at that moment, there was a loud cough from the front of the room. A tall woman with slicked-back black hair and honey skin waited for us to fall silent. Her uniform was a shade darker than the gray the Peacekeepers wore, and the embroidery running across her shoulders and arms set her apart from anyone else. Although I'd never seen her in person before, I instantly recognized her and quickly sat down.

"Welcome. My name is Saskia. I am Director of the Royal Academy."

And the king's daughter. The third most powerful person in New Vegas, after the king and the crown prince, Saskia's older brother.

"Firstly, let me apologize for the experience that you have just been through. I appreciate that it was traumatic, but let me assure you, it is the only way to identify those with the potential to join the Academy." Her smile broadened. "Which, I'm delighted to say, you all have."

A murmur of excitement rippled around the room. I caught Fergus's eye and grinned.

"Some of you may have a slight headache at the moment, which is completely normal. The test activated new abilities within each of you, and it will take you some time and a lot of training to be able to control your powers. That is why you will be confined to the Academy for the next two weeks. It's for your own protection, as well as the protection of other citizens."

Saskia paused and looked around. "There is just one further formality we have to go through before I can officially welcome you as Academy members."

My heart sank. *Another test?*

As if able to read my thoughts, she smiled. "Don't worry. This isn't like the other test. It's a lot less painful." The director's grin faded as she turned serious. "Academy members and graduates have a very important role in our society. We are responsible for keeping the society running, eradicating crime, and making New Vegas a peaceful, safe place to live. I must be sure that every person in the Academy is committed to upholding our societal values. Those of you who are will find a warm welcome and a new family here in the Royal Academy."

Her gaze slid over each of us in turn. Perhaps it was my imagination, but I felt her eyes linger on me. I smiled, desperately wanting this woman to like me.

"If any of you do not believe in our values . . ." A frown creased her brow for a fraction of a second before the smile reappeared on her face. "Well, let's hope that *won't* be an issue."

4

Abandoned

W E HAD A MUCH shorter wait for the second round of testing. After ten minutes, I heard my name called and followed a slim, dark-haired Guardian into a small room. I didn't know what to expect, but apart from two chairs facing a screen on the wall, the room was empty.

"Sit down, Vesper," the man said. "This shouldn't take long. I just want you to watch the images on the screen."

I sat down on the hard chair. "That's it?"

He nodded and smiled, taking the other chair. "That's it."

Puzzled, I looked up at the screen. My eyes took in the images flicking across it, but my mind was distracted, going over the director's speech in my mind. She said the test had triggered abilities . . . What did that mean? I didn't *feel* any different. Then an image of Marissa flying backward appeared in my head. No one could jump that far and at that angle. It was as if she'd been thrown, but none of the Peacekeepers had been close enough to touch her.

"Vesper, concentrate please."

I started, but the Guardian just smiled and nodded at the screen.

My cheeks flushed. *You're not there yet. Don't blow it now.*

I took a deep breath and stared at the screen. A series of short video clips showed recordings from the camera feeds embedded around the city. The first few covered recreation areas. I watched children playing in sandpits and adults wandering on pathways lined by palm trees.

Then the screen flickered and a video feed from one of the hydroponic farms appeared. I recognized the room, or at least one like it, from the tours we'd gone on at school. Row upon row of potato plants, ready to be harvested. There was a sudden movement on the screen, almost too fast for me to catch. I blinked and shook my head, wondering if I was seeing things. The footage rewound and the same clip played again, slower this time. There was a blur, then a man appeared in the room, grasped the stalks of two potato plants, and yanked them out. He glanced around fearfully, the plants dripping water onto the floor. Then in a flash, he was gone.

But that's not possible?

The footage played again, frame by frame. I kept my eye on the time indicator at the bottom left corner, wondering if the video footage had been edited. There were no jumps in the counter, yet it was impossible for someone to just *appear* like that in the room.

The screen switched to a camera feed from a courtroom. The same man stood there, minus the potatoes. He hung his head as a Guardian sentenced him for theft and exiled him to the city below. The courtroom was empty, apart from a woman holding a baby and a child of about five who clung to her coat. The man and woman exchanged a look. Tears sprang to my eyes because the look was not one of guilt or admonishment, but pure love.

I bit my lip. He had only stolen some potatoes and by the look of him and his wife, they needed the food. Food that the society should have provided for them.

But I didn't have time to dwell on this thought. A new image appeared, and my eyes widened in disbelief. A boy in his early teens with bright red hair stood cornered in what looked to be some kind of service corridor. Blue sparks flickered around his hands like tiny lightning bolts, but they didn't seem to be hurting him. His eyes were wide in fear as three Peacekeepers approached. Before they got close, a man ran out from a side corridor to stand between the Peacekeepers and the boy. His red hair was threaded with gray, and he wore the blue overalls of a factory worker.

"Don't hurt him! He doesn't know what he's doing. He didn't mean any harm." His voice was panicked as his gaze flitted between the three Peacekeepers.

"Please step aside, sir," one said. "The boy is dangerous and must be taken away for everyone's safety."

The man hesitated. "What will happen to him?"

"He will be taken to the Academy for testing."

"But he's only twelve!"

"Nevertheless, you must see that he is dangerous—"

The video feed flickered and cut out, but not before I saw bolts of lightning shoot from the child's hands.

I stared at the static on the screen, then turned to the Guardian. "What happened to the boy?"

"He was brought to the Academy," he said. "He was taught to control his ability and eventually became a Peacekeeper himself."

"And his father?"

"His father attacked the Peacekeepers trying to take the child away and threatened to come to the Academy to fetch him back.

As a result, he was taken in front of a Guardian and sentenced
—"

"To the city floor," I murmured.

"Yes."

Just because he wanted to protect his son? I didn't say the
words aloud. I knew questioning the society was wrong.

But how is this right?

"That will be all, Vesper."

I jerked my head and looked at the Guardian. "I'm done?
You're not going to ask me any questions?"

He shook his head. "No. Let me accompany you to the
waiting room."

He seemed kind of dejected as I followed him down the
corridor to a small room where three people sat. "Wait here.
Someone will be with you shortly." He turned and walked out.

"Did you pass?"

I turned to look for the voice's owner.

A tall, gangly boy with a cloud of curly hair raised his hand in
greeting. "Or was your Guardian as tight-lipped as ours?" He
gestured to the room's other occupants—a slim Asian girl,
whose long hair hung down over her face, and a bored-looking
redhead.

"He didn't tell me," I admitted. "I don't think I did anything
wrong, but I'm not really sure what they were testing, either. Did
they ask you any questions?"

The gangly boy shook his head. "Nope. We all just got told to
watch the footage on the screen." He shrugged. "Maybe they
were testing our reaction to it?"

"Perhaps." I took a seat, wondering if my body language in
the testing room had given away my thoughts. But I'd been so
careful to keep my expression neutral and my body relaxed. A

flush of guilt ran through me. Where had those thoughts even come from? If someone was a thief or danger to others, they *should* be banished to the city floor.

"How long have you been waiting?" I asked, trying to compose myself.

"Feels like hours," the red-haired girl grumbled, tugging at her perfectly coiffured curls. Her clothes were expensive and her accent polished.

"Daria was one of the first to go through the test this morning," the boy explained. "They must be processing us in batches. I've only been here ten minutes. I'm Aidan, by the way."

So Daria must be from the upper levels. That explained her haughty attitude. And Aidan was a lower-leveler, like me.

"I went through the first test just before lunch." The Asian girl's voice was so soft, I could barely hear her words. Her eyes flitted nervously around the room. "My name is Shui."

"I'm Vesper." Worry niggled inside me. There were only four of us. The director made it sound like everyone passed this test. Shouldn't there be more people in the room?

The door opened and another gray-clad Guardian walked in. Following her was the last person I expected to see. A person I never thought I would set eyes on, let alone meet.

Prince Cayden. The king's grandson and third in line to the throne.

Even Daria seemed shocked, but before any of us had time to respond, another figure strode into the room. Saskia had returned, and she didn't look happy.

"Please, take a seat," she said, though the comment was clearly directed at Cayden, who stood frozen at the front of the room. A slim Peacekeeper and a stocky Guardian silently entered and took up position in the corner as the door clicked shut behind them.

I'd only ever seen the heir to the throne on the holonet, mainly during festival time when the royal family made a point of getting out and about. Not that they'd ever made it down to the lower levels of Tower 14. He looked younger in person, and I felt an unexpected pang of sympathy at the confusion on his face. But he quickly composed himself. Brushing back his dark blond hair, he took a seat right at the front.

"I'm afraid I have bad news," Saskia said without preamble. Her face was tight, and her fingers squeezed the lectern in front of her as if it were some kind of stress ball. "Although you all demonstrated the natural ability we look for in Academy members, the results of the second test indicate that your commitment to our values and the laws of our society is questionable."

Her gaze moved to each of us in turn—everyone except Cayden. "This is, without question, the worst part of my job. But you must understand that in order to keep our society safe and for citizens to trust us, there can be no doubt as to your loyalty. There is also no question of you returning to your families to choose a different career path. Without proper training, your abilities make you a danger to society."

Her words washed over me. The thread of worry that had tied my stomach in knots tightened. Tears of shame burned the back of my eyes and I dug my fingernails into my thighs, hoping the pain would stop me from throwing up or, worse, crying.

I failed. Years of work, hours spent preparing for the exams, and never once did I think I would fail.

How can this be?

It was only then that Layla's hastily scribbled words came back to me.

Everything the society does is for our protection.

Did my own sister think I'd fail this test?

Your commitment to our values and the laws of our society is questionable.

I glanced down at my clenched fists. I *was* loyal to the society. I believed in protecting citizens and eradicating crime. There must have been an error in the test.

"So if you won't let us into the Academy and we can't go back to our families, where *do* we go?" Daria asked. Unlike Shui and Aidan, who looked terrified, Daria and Cayden each wore a calm, resolute expression, as if this was all some terrible misunderstanding that would soon be cleared up.

The corner of the director's mouth twitched, giving me the impression she'd been faced with this reaction many times. "You will be taken down to the city floor. Your parents will be told there was a tragic accident, that you had an undiagnosed heart or brain condition and reacted badly to the test. They will be compensated and permitted to hold a memorial service for you."

We sat in stunned silence.

Cayden was the first to react, exploding out of his chair. He stood stiffly in front of his aunt, his fists clenched at his sides. Although they were related, they didn't look much alike. Cayden's father was the son of King Alexander's first wife. When she'd died, the king had taken Saskia's mother, Adrienne, as his second consort.

"There has obviously been some mistake, Director," he said stiffly.

"I'm sorry, Cayden." Saskia gave him a sad smile. "There are no exceptions to this rule, even for you."

"I believe Grandfather would disagree." The prince's words were pure ice, but Saskia didn't quail.

"It was your grandfather who put the rule in place. I double checked, but I had a personal note from him confirming his decision."

With that, the fight seemed to go out of Cayden and he sank into a chair, his face pale. Something flickered across Saskia's eyes as she looked down at him. Pity perhaps? Or sorrow?

Daria wouldn't give up that easily. "Surely he didn't mean for you to condemn his own grandson. Your *nephew*."

Perhaps she thought that if she could ally herself with the prince, she would also be saved. I didn't blame her. My mind whirred. Even if I'd had a few bad thoughts, I hadn't *done* anything wrong. How could I be a threat to society?

"Please, sit down," the director said coldly. "I would hate to have to restrain you."

Daria tried to step toward her, but her leg stopped in mid-air. Her brow furrowed. I could see the tension in her body, the way she strained against . . . nothing.

I glanced over at the two silent figures in the corner. The Guardian stood passively, her hands clasped in front of her, but the Peacekeeper stared at Daria, his expression focused.

He's stopping her. Somehow, he's preventing her from moving.

Daria's eyes widened. "What . . ."

"Sit down, Miss Rothschild," Saskia said smoothly.

Reluctantly, Daria obeyed, shooting the Peacekeeper a look that clearly conveyed her wish to personally skin him alive.

The director released her grip on the lectern. "You will be escorted down to the city floor and given provisions. Good luck." She nodded to the Guardian, who opened the door. Gray-clad figures filed in, and the small room suddenly felt crowded.

"Wait!" I was on my feet before quite registering the fact that I'd spoken.

The director paused on her way to the door. "Yes, Miss Rodriguez?"

I took a deep breath, feeling everyone's eyes on me. "I believe there has been some mistake with the test. I am loyal to the society. I would like a retest, please."

Saskia gave me a tired smile. "I'm sorry. The results of your test were quite clear."

"How? I haven't *done* anything wrong. I haven't *said* anything wrong. I . . ." My voice trailed off as the realization struck me. *My thoughts criticizing the society were all in my head. The Guardian in the room knew what I was thinking. How is that possible?*

"Your results were clear," Saskia repeated. "I'm sorry, Miss Rodriguez." With a brief nod, she turned and left the room.

"Follow us." A Peacekeeper grasped my arm firmly, yet gently.

In the end, only Aidan fought his captors. He got in a few decent blows before they did something to him, and his eyes rolled back into his head.

I felt numb as the Peacekeeper guided me down a short corridor. "Where are we going?"

"We're taking you to the transport hanger," the Guardian accompanying me replied. "There are pods waiting to take you and your friends down to the city below."

They're not my friends, I wanted to say, but it seemed pointless. Her final words scrolled through my mind, like the news headlines that crawled across the bottom of our holonet screen. *The city below . . . The city below . . .*

The place they sent criminals to die.

The corridor seemed to close in around me as we walked. I stumbled. A hand reached out to support me, but I shrugged it off. My heart pounded in my ears as I fought for breath.

I was dimly aware that we'd entered a large space filled with noise but it was only when the footsteps accompanying me stopped that I tore my gaze from the floor and looked up.

A silver pod stood in front of me, its door open. A gentle nudge from behind encouraged me forward, but I resisted, turning to look around. A short distance away, Cayden approached an identical pod, the Peacekeepers and Guardian standing outside it bending their heads in a token of respect.

Shock rippled through me as I caught sight of the Guardian designated to take him down to the city below. As she raised her head and turned to follow him into the pod, she caught sight of me and her eyes widened.

"Layla!" I started running toward her, but I didn't get ten paces before invisible hands pulled me back. I landed in a heap at the Peacekeeper's feet.

Layla made a move toward me, mouthing my name, but the Guardian who'd accompanied Cayden into the hanger placed a hand on her arm. The man looked from Layla to me, then said something to her. My sister shook her head violently and tried to push him away, but the man's grip was firm. Whatever he said next made her sag and go still, as if the fight had been sucked out of her.

I was pulled to my feet and dragged the remaining distance to my own pod. "Layla, please! I haven't done anything wrong. The test didn't work!"

But my beloved sister, who bandaged my cuts and bruises when I'd hurt myself as a kid, who held me when the nightmares woke me, who gossiped with me about boys and taught me how to apply makeup, just stared at me as if she no longer knew me.

Then I was shoved inside the pod and the door closed, forever cutting off the world I had known.

The City Floor

I SAT IN SILENCE as the pod left the hangar. My body felt numb. I had no words to beg for mercy, no energy left to fight for my freedom.

How could this have happened?

I had always believed that if I worked hard enough, I would succeed. Failure was never an option. I had been so close, but somehow, I had let my dream slip through my fingers.

Perhaps if Layla hadn't visited this morning, if I hadn't walked with her to the transporter deck and seen Marissa's arrest, I wouldn't have thought to question what I'd seen on the screen. Somehow, it felt easier to blame someone else for my misfortune. I brought my knees up to my chest and hugged them.

"There's a bag of supplies for you." The Peacekeeper sitting across from me pointed to a small backpack next to my seat. I eyed it, wondering if there was anything in there that would keep me alive for more than a week. Not if the little I'd heard about the city below was true.

"What's it like down there?" I asked in a small voice.

He exchanged a glance with his colleague. "We don't really see much of it," he muttered. "We just drop people off."

The Guardian sitting next to me placed her hand on my knee. I supposed the gesture was meant to comfort me, but her touch made me flinch. "When we leave you, your abilities will return," she said. "You must learn to control them if you are to survive."

I stared at her. "My abilities? You mean like that . . . that thing the Peacekeeper did to me?"

She smiled sympathetically. "People have different abilities and different strengths. In time, you'll learn what yours are."

That's assuming I survive long enough.

"Why can't you tell me? Surely it doesn't matter to you once you've left me to *die*?"

Neither the Guardian nor the Peacekeepers answered. I glared at them, daring them to meet my gaze and wishing I could give them a taste of their own medicine. I looked down at my hands. Could I throw people around? Have sparks fly from my fingers?

The headache I'd had since the first test was now a monotonous ache, like a tight band squeezing my skull. I picked up the backpack. "Are there any headache pills in here?"

"There are painkillers, but you won't need them once you're down there," the Guardian said.

Another cryptic remark.

The Peacekeeper farthest away from me turned to a small screen and control panel on the wall. "We're approaching the barrier. Slowing down."

The pod didn't have large windows like the transporter pod I'd taken to the Academy, but there were a number of small round portholes. I peered through one, surprised to find we were already near the base of the towers. Faint twinkling lights from the lowest levels pierced the gloom. I wondered what time it was. Judging by the rumbling in my belly, I'd guess late evening.

This morning, I had imagined myself watching the sunset from inside the white spire of the Academy. I had almost *felt* the giddy excitement of visiting home to pick up my things, seeing Mom and Dad's proud smiles as they hugged me goodbye, pictured myself in the white trainee uniform, a single crown adorning each shoulder.

I tasted blood in my mouth. The pain from where I'd bitten my tongue was a welcome distraction from the agonizing thoughts of what I had lost.

The pod inched down into a dark fog that swirled around the windows, blocking the towers from view. The lights dimmed, and I sensed the Guardian next to me shift uneasily in her seat. Tension filled the air, seeping into my skin, and I shivered, though it wasn't cold. If I was going to die, I'd rather it be sudden and quick, not this drawn-out torture that had every bone in my body jangling with fear.

"What's the holdup?" the Guardian asked. There was a slight edge to her voice. Clearly my captors weren't any keener to be here than me.

"Just waiting for acknowledgment," the Peacekeeper replied. A light on the control panel pulsed green. "Right. Here we go."

The pod hummed and continued descending. The Peacekeeper had mentioned a barrier, but I couldn't see anything out of the window except the thick black smoke that separated the towers above from the city floor below.

Then suddenly, the tension inside the pod eased. I frowned as my head throbbed, realizing that for the past few seconds, my headache had disappeared. Now it was back with a vengeance.

The Guardian let out a sigh of relief and rolled her shoulders. "I always hate that part."

"Get ready, Miss Rodriguez," the Peacekeeper across from me said. "We're not hanging around."

When I didn't reply, he picked up the backpack from the floor and shoved it into my arms. Then the pod door slid open and a hot wind rushed in. My long hair whipped around my face, stinging my eyes. I blinked frantically, trying to make out what was outside the pod, but everything just seemed dark.

"Jump!"

"What?" I turned to the Peacekeeper.

He smiled, not unkindly. "Jump. And good luck, Miss Rodriguez."

I gaped at him. How far were we above the ground? Perhaps this was how I was going to die and the backpack was just for show. A long fall, then a quick death.

"Now!" the Guardian snapped.

Someone shoved my back. I reached out for the pod door but was too slow. I screamed and my stomach lurched as I fell into the inky blackness.

I was wrong about the long drop.

My body slammed into the ground, knocking the air from my lungs. After a moment of shock while I gasped for breath, my nerves sent a red alert to my brain that I'd banged my knee. I bit my lip and squeezed my eyes shut to stop myself from crying out. Gradually, the pain subsided to a dull throbbing and I opened my eyes to look around.

It wasn't quite the pitch blackness I'd originally thought. As my eyes adjusted to the dim light, I began to make out vague shapes and outlines. There were even lights in some of the buildings, glowing faintly in the darkness. And if there were lights, there were people.

Perhaps it isn't as dead down here as I thought.

I gave my knee a prod, and reassured that there was no real damage, climbed to my feet. There was no sign of the pod or anyone else. I didn't know if that was a good or bad thing. The air was warm and muggy with a sour aftertaste, like the compost bin in our garden-yard. My hands trembled with adrenaline as I fumbled with the fastening on my backpack, hoping the Guardians had found enough kindness in their hearts to give me a flashlight.

A wet snuffling noise stopped me in my tracks. I froze and peered into the shadows around me. There was a faint scratching, like a fingernail running along a tabletop, then the snuffling picked up again. When a pair of blood-red eyes blinked out at me, a squeak escaped my lips before I could clamp them shut.

Rats!

I scrambled backward, trying to put as much distance between me and the *thing* as I could. We had rats in the towers, of course, but they were small, brown things that scuttled through the ventilation shafts and ran at the first sight of a person. Whereas this must be the size of a cat, and rather than running away from me, it crept closer.

The eyes glowed as the creature observed me. Probably debating how tasty I'd be and how much of a fight I'd put up if it decided to take a bite.

I plunged my hand into the backpack, pushing aside a water bottle and candy bars until my fingers, slick with sweat, felt the smooth plastic of a flashlight. The bright white beam of light cut through the darkness, illuminating the creature in front of me. I nearly dropped the flashlight. It *was* a rat. Or at least what a rat would look like if you pumped it full of steroids and implanted red lenses in its eyes.

Its thick tail swept across the floor, causing a cloud of dust to rise around it. I took a step back. The rat scuttled forward, stretching out its long nose and sniffing the air.

"Go away," I told it, waving my arm in what I hoped was a threatening manner. "I'm not worth bothering with."

The rat seemed to disagree. The scratching of its claws as it moved closer sent a shiver racing down my spine. I waved the flashlight at it, the beam bobbing in the dark, but it just blinked its red eyes and thumped its tail on the ground.

I swept the beam to one side, wondering if I dared point it down at my backpack to look for a weapon. The light found a second pair of red eyes, then a third. I swallowed, trying to control my rising panic as I slowly hooked the backpack over my shoulder. I was about to run when a voice stopped me.

"You should switch that off, you know. They're attracted to the light, and if you keep it on, other, worse things will come hunting."

It was a male voice with an odd accent. From his tone, he was amused about something.

Probably me.

"What if you're just waiting for me to turn it off so you can jump me?" I asked, trying to search for the voice's owner while simultaneously keeping one eye on the rat that was now just five feet away. It was useless. I couldn't look in two places at once. Plus, the dazzling beam of my flashlight had ruined my night vision.

"If I'd wanted to attack you, I'd have already done it."

I jumped as the voice spoke right into my ear. His warm breath tickled my neck, and a spark of anger ignited in my stomach.

How dare he sneak up on me.

"Now, will you *please* turn that thing off? Or I'll have to bag this little chap for dinner."

"You *eat* rats?"

"What's wrong with that?"

A hand closed around my wrist, making me squeal.

"Stop it!"

"Stop what?" I was confused.

Before I could protest, the man slipped the flashlight from my hand and switched it off.

"You're hurting my head," he growled. "I should have known you were one of *them*."

"One of who?" I blinked frantically, bright spots dancing across my vision.

I sensed the man pull back and reached out, catching hold of a muscled forearm.

"Wait. You have to help me."

He grunted and began to pry my fingers loose. "I don't *have* to help anyone. And right now, you are putting me in danger. The slavers will be here any minute."

"The slavers?"

Giant rats. Slavers. What other horrors did the city floor hold?

A scream ripped through the darkness.

"Sounds like they've found one of your friends already."

"They're not my—" I stopped. "How do you know there are others? How do you know who I am?"

The man sighed impatiently. "Because every year around this time, a handful of you get dumped down here. Frightened kids who've no idea what they've been thrown into. You're ripe pickings for the slavers. I thought we had another few days or there's no way I'd have answered your call."

"My call?" I echoed.

"You screamed. Loud enough for the entire city to hear. Now, if you don't mind, I'll be going before they turn up. Don't look so glum," he added, as though he could see the expression on my face in the dark. "It's probably better this way. You'll survive longer with a faction than you will on your own. I'm sure the Sirens will pay a high price to get their hands on you."

He yanked his arm from my grasp and stalked off.

Frightened kids? I couldn't see how old the man was, but he didn't sound that much older than me. My mind was still in shock, and I'd already forgotten half of what he'd said.

Calm down, I told myself. *There must be a way up to the towers from down here. Once I'm home, I'll be safe. I can talk to Layla. She'll know what to do about the test results.*

First, I needed to get home.

I stumbled after the man, my eyes still adjusting to the dark. All I could make out was the faint outline of a tall figure, perhaps six-foot and well-built. He seemed to be favoring his right leg. I gritted my teeth. I really didn't want to beg for help, but right now, I didn't have a choice.

I closed the distance between us and grabbed his arm. "Can you show me how to get back up to the towers?"

He snorted and shook me off, not bothering to pause. "There's no way up."

"There must be."

Ten minutes in this place and that was all I had to cling to. There must be some way I could get home.

The man didn't answer.

"Fine." I matched him stride for stride, hoping that the street was clear of obstacles. *Is it always this dark down here?* "I'm coming with you."

That stopped him. "No, you're not. I—" His body stiffened, and I sensed his anger turning to fear. "They're coming. Run."

He took off down the street, moving surprisingly fast given his limp. I followed, trying to ignore the part of my brain that screamed running in the dark always ended badly in horror movies. He obviously knew the street better than me and gradually, his footsteps began to fade into the distance. Gasping, I halted and glanced over my shoulder. A faint purple glow moved toward me, sparking and crackling like a live electrical wire. Within seconds, it was close enough that I could make out an odd kind of pod, flying perhaps ten feet off the ground. Sparks of electricity flickered around it, briefly illuminating a window on the front of the vehicle, and I caught a glimpse of a dark-skinned man, teeth bared in a wild, terrifying grin.

I ran.

My heart pounded in my ears as I pumped my arms, willing my legs to go faster.

"Yeee-haw!"

The man's war cry echoed around me, the air seemingly on fire with the purple light. Something stung my neck and I reached up, my fingers finding a small dart embedded in my skin. My brain barely had time to process the pod hovering over me before my legs collapsed and darkness claimed me.

6

Elan

W HEN I OPENED MY eyes, purple sparks still danced across my vision. I blinked, wondering if I'd taken a knock to the head. Rubbing my neck, I felt a twinge of pain where the dart had pierced my skin.

The dart.

I sat bolt upright and looked around. Purple lightning crackled around the metal bars of the cage that surrounded me on five sides. The floor beneath me was dirt-covered concrete, cold and dusty under my fingers. My mouth felt parched, and as I sucked in a breath, something tickled the back of my throat, causing me to cough.

"Vesper? Are you okay?"

I turned toward the sound of the voice and spotted Aidan's frizzy hair through the bars of the cage.

"I think so." I slowly got to my feet, wincing as my body protested against its recent rough treatment. I felt like one big bruise.

"Woah. Don't touch the bars!" Aidan said quickly as I reached out. He grinned ruefully. "Take it from me, it hurts."

"I'd have thought iron bars would have been enough," I muttered.

"Is the prince awake yet?" Aidan asked, nodding behind me.

I glanced over my shoulder to see Cayden slumped on the floor in a cage next to mine.

"Don't call him that," Daria hissed from a cage on the other side of Aidan's. "I bet they don't know who he is. If they find out, they'll hold him hostage."

"Well, at least they'll keep him alive. Besides, it doesn't seem as if the king wants him."

I pictured Daria rolling her eyes. "You don't know that."

I left the two of them bickering and walked to the front of the cage, close enough to the bars that I could feel the crackle of electricity in the air. The hairs on my arms rose and I shivered, though the room was not cold. A single light hung from the cracked ceiling, casting a dim light over the cages arranged in a semicircle around a pair of double doors. I counted them, the simple task helping calm my thoughts. There were ten altogether, eight with metal bars, six of which crackled with electricity, and two that appeared to be constructed of thick plastic.

I was a prisoner, but at least I wasn't alone.

Daria had turned her back on Aidan and now sat in the center of her cage, legs crossed in the lotus position, back ramrod stiff. In the cage next to her, Shui was curled in a ball, trembling. She looked so young, though she had to be eighteen, the same age as the rest of us. I wrapped my arms around my ribcage, wishing I could go over to comfort her.

The two cages next to Shui were dark and empty. My gaze slid over the double doors and the plastic cages. At first, I thought they were both unoccupied, but as my eyes adjusted to the dim light, I noticed a small figure sitting at the back of the second cage.

My eyes widened. "Marissa?"

"Hi, Vesper." Her voice was dull and lifeless, her hair matted to her head.

"What happened? You were arrested . . ."

There was a pause, then she nodded. "I got hauled up in front of a Guardian, then they dumped me down here for the slavers to pick up."

"Why aren't you in a cage like ours?"

"Because she's a leccy," a voice growled.

My heart skipped a beat. What was *he* doing here?

My eyes drifted to the cage on the other side of Cayden. The man slouched in the center of his cage, arms folded, the tension in his shoulders betrayed his unease. He wasn't as old as I'd assumed. Perhaps twenty or twenty-one. Scruffy, dark hair framed a face that was a little too long to be called handsome. His skin looked tanned, though given the smog cloud that separated us from the city above, it couldn't be from the sun.

As if sensing me watching him, he looked up. His dark eyes burned into mine, his lips curling into a hard smile.

"What's a leccy?" Daria asked. She looked at the man with interest. He returned her smile, and I felt an unexpected twinge of jealousy.

Don't be an idiot. It's his fault you're in here, isn't it?

"She can manipulate electricity," the man said, glancing over at Marissa. "This cage wouldn't be a prison for her. It would be a weapon."

I tore my eyes from him to stare at Marissa. "You can do what?"

Hesitantly, Marissa opened her hand. A tiny, purple spark cracked in the air above her palm.

The director's words came back to me. *The test activated new abilities in you.* Was this what she had referred to? But Marissa wasn't old enough to have taken the test, and she'd been arrested at home, not at the Academy.

Marissa curled her hand into a fist and the spark disappeared.

"So what's your ability? And how long have you been down here?" Daria asked, still staring at the dark-haired man. Even Shui had stopped shaking and looked curiously at him.

"Who says I have an ability?"

"Why else would you be down here in one of these cages?" I retorted.

The man's eyes shifted from Daria to me. "Good point." He shrugged. "I've always lived down here."

Silence followed his revelation.

"Always? Like, your whole life?" Aidan gaped at him.

"That's generally what 'always' means, fuzz-head," the man snapped.

Aidan opened his mouth to reply, but Daria shot him a glance and he subsided. "So there are people who live here?" she asked. "It's not just a wasteland?"

I tried to remember what little I'd seen of the city floor before the slavers had grabbed me. Towering buildings, dirt, and rubbish. And rats. I shivered. It had definitely felt like a wasteland.

"Course people live here. It's a city, right? You think people just disappear in a puff of smoke when they get chucked down from heaven? Not likely. Some people even *choose* to come down here."

Daria gave him a disbelieving look.

"If people got down here, that must mean there's some way of getting back up." My pulse quickened.

He smirked and opened his mouth, but at that moment, there was a groan from the cage next to me.

"Ah, it looks like His Highness is waking." The man looked at Cayden curiously. "Is he really a prince?"

"Yes," I replied, feeling Daria's glare burn into the back of my head. "But it seems the king doesn't care much for family."

Cayden pushed himself into a sitting position, clutching his head. "What the hell happened?"

"The slavers drugged you," the man told him. "It affects some people more than others, depending on your powers."

Cayden's head jerked up. At the same moment, the light bulb in the center of the room twitched. "Powers?"

The man rolled his dark eyes. "Yeah. There must be some reason they chucked you down here." He glanced at the swinging light. "Telky?"

"Pardon?" Cayden stared at him.

The man sighed impatiently. "A telky. Mind-mover." Getting no response, he chuckled. "Geez, you're not gonna survive very long in the arena if you don't even know what you can do."

"The arena?"

Before I could question the man further, his eyes flicked to the door and his gaze became distant. A faint crease of concentration puckered the skin between his thick eyebrows.

The sound of faint footsteps from outside the room grew louder. They stopped and there was the click of a key turning in a lock. Slowly, one of the doors opened.

A short, stocky man entered. He wore a thin jacket over a ragged vest that looked like it hadn't seen the inside of a washing machine for years. Dirt ingrained into his face made it hard to determine the color of his skin, and his hair hung in thick dreadlocks to his shoulders. His eyes seemed kind of vacant. He didn't even glance around as he walked over to a small box on the wall next to Marissa's cage. He flipped up the cover and flicked a switch. The purple lightning flickering around the bars of the man's cage disappeared.

Marissa gasped, but neither man turned to look at her. Turning away from the box, the slaver—I presumed this must be one of our captors—walked over to stand in front of the door to the dark-haired man's cage. Removing a key from his belt, he inserted it into the lock.

The dark-haired man still wore an intense look of concentration. Sweat began to bead on his brow, tension radiating from his body. I remembered how the Peacekeeper had stopped Daria when she tried to argue with Saskia. It had seemed like there was a barrier Daria couldn't break through, but this was different. It was like the man was controlling the slaver's mind.

An icy chill began to seep through my veins. The thought of someone being in my head, taking control of my body, was abhorrent. But that seemed to be this man's "power", as he called it.

If that's what people do with their abilities, no wonder society throws them out. It's wrong.

The door to the cage opened. Then, like a sleepwalker, the slaver turned and plodded out of the room. When the door closed behind him, the man fell to his knees, as if overcome by exhaustion.

Cayden stared through the bars of his cage. "What just happened?"

His question hung in the air. Then the dark-haired man got to his feet and stepped out of his cage. "Nice to meet you all. Good luck in the arena, and if you want my advice, try not to get picked by Caesar. Not that any of the others are much better."

"Wait!"

The man stopped and turned. Again, his eyes burned into me. Close up, I could see a thin scar tracing his forehead, almost covered by a lock of his thick, dark hair. More scars patterned his arm—some thin, pale lines, others more recent. His clothes looked old, though they were better kept than those the slaver had worn. He wore a faded t-shirt with a fanged snake and the words "Las Vegas Snake Eyes" underneath. It was tight across his chest, showing the outline of muscles underneath. I wondered if the effect was deliberate or if he just didn't own clothes the right size.

"Yes?" He raised one eyebrow.

"What's your name?"

The man didn't reply immediately. I sensed him appraising me, perhaps considering if I was worthy of this information.

"Elan," he said finally. "You?"

"Vesper," I replied.

His lips curled into a smile. "Good luck surviving, Vesper." He turned and strode over to the double doors. I got the impression he was trying to disguise his limp.

"Let us out!" I reached out to grasp the bars of my cage before remembering the electricity and stopping. A spark jumped between the bar and my finger, making my arm spasm.

Elan paused and turned to look at me. "Now, why would I do that?"

"Because it's the right thing to do. Because you're a good person."

I hope.

A sad smile tugged at the corner of his mouth. "Ah, but you see, I'm *not* a good person. Good people don't survive in this city. You'll learn that soon enough." His gaze lingered on me before he turned and pulled open the door. "Goodbye, Vesper. Perhaps we'll meet again."

7

Powers

I STARED AT THE double doors as they closed behind him.

"That went well," Daria said. She narrowed her eyes at me. "You should have let me talk to him, Vesper."

"I doubt that would have made a difference."

Daria snorted.

"We'll just have to figure our own way out. Surely if we all have . . . abilities, it can't be that hard to break free."

I turned to look at Cayden, who paced around his cage thoughtfully.

"Mind-mover," he muttered. He stopped suddenly and stared at the lightbulb hanging from the center of the ceiling. After a moment, it began to swing from side to side. Cayden's shoulders sagged. "Did you see that?"

"Wow, you moved that bulb all of an inch." Aidan folded his arms. "That's really going to help us get out of here."

Cayden scowled at him. "All right. What can you do?"

Aidan grinned wolfishly. "This." He turned his palm up, as Marissa had, but rather than a purple spark, a tiny ball of flame curled in the air above his hand.

"Is that *all*? Still, I guess that's to be expected from a lower-leveler." Daria twisted her own hand and a foot-tall flame leapt into the air.

Aidan clenched his jaw. The ball of flame in front of him grew until it was about four inches across. A vein on his forehead throbbed with effort. Then, without warning, his eyes rolled back in his head and he collapsed onto the floor.

"Aidan!" I scanned his body through the bars and let out a breath in relief when I caught the slight rise and fall of his chest.

"So you two can produce fire," Cayden said, ignoring Aidan. "And . . ." He looked at Marissa. "Marissa, was it?" She glanced up at him. "You can create electricity?"

She nodded, her cheeks flushing pink as the prince gazed at her.

He turned to look at Shui. "What about you?" he asked gently.

Shui's eyes darted around nervously. "I can do this." Her voice was barely audible. For a moment, nothing happened. Daria opened her mouth, but Cayden held his hand up to quiet her.

The air above Shui began to shimmer. I squinted, just able to make out droplets of water coalescing into a swirling mass. With a sigh, her shoulders sagged and the water plunged onto her head. She lifted a strand of now wet hair and smiled ruefully.

"Water," Cayden said appreciatively. "Nice work. I could do with a drink." He turned to me. "What about you, Vesper?"

I avoided his gaze and stretched out my hand experimentally, wondering if fire, sparks, or water would appear. But nothing happened. After a few seconds, I let my hand drop, feeling like a fool.

"Come on," Daria snapped.

Tears sprang to my eyes. The gnawing sensation I'd felt in my stomach when I realized I'd failed the test returned. "I-I think maybe they made a mistake. I can't do anything."

"Well, maybe you just need a bit more time to figure it out," Cayden suggested.

"Yeah," Aidan agreed. "Honestly, once you feel it, then it's like you've always known how to do it. Kind of like running. It takes effort, but you don't need to think about how to put one foot in front of the other."

Their words just made me feel worse. I stared at the floor, not wanting to see the pity on their faces.

The others' abilities seemed to come naturally, as if they'd always known how to do it. But if I didn't know what I could do, how was I supposed to know what to focus on?

I must be able to do something. Saskia said I passed the first test—the one that unlocked our abilities.

Unless there had been a mistake there, too. Perhaps my test results had been mixed up with someone else's. A queasy feeling developed in my stomach. I wasn't sure what was worse. That I'd somehow failed their second test, or that I'd not been good enough to join the Academy in the first place.

I was granted a reprieve from Daria's glacial stare by the sound of pounding footsteps. The double doors flew open and a huge man strode into the room, heading straight for the cage Elan had occupied. He wore an odd patchwork coat that hung to his knees and seemed to shimmer in the light. Beads hung from his long dreadlocks, pulled back from a face that was as black as the shadows coating the edges of the room. Teeth glistened, and a chill swept through me.

I remembered that crazed smile.

A slim woman with shifting eyes followed him into the room, along with the man who'd unwittingly freed Elan. They looked at the big man expectantly.

The beads in his hair clattered as his head whipped around, his teeth bared in an almost feral expression. He glared at each of us in turn.

"Where did he go?" His voice was rough.

When none of us answered, the man paced in front of our cages, twirling a wooden baton that was about three feet long. The stench of sweat and unwashed clothing rolled off him, but I couldn't take my eyes off his coat. It seemed to be made of mismatched pieces of animal fur.

Rats? Or some other creature?

My stomach clenched as a wave of nausea rose in my throat. No one killed animals, let alone wore their skin. At least, not in New Vegas.

"Where. Did. He. Go?" the man repeated, enunciating every word.

"We don't know."

In a flash, the man was in front of my cage, almost before I realized I'd spoken. His dark eyes bored into me. "You don't know?"

I shook my head, swallowing hard. "He got that man . . ." I nodded at the man standing behind him, "to unlock his cage and left through the doors."

He cocked his head. "And why didn't he take you with him?"

"He refused." I held my breath against the stink and forced myself to meet the man's gaze.

He let out a low, guttural curse and lifted his fist, as if to slam it into the bars of my cage, but the woman stepped forward. Placing a hand on his arm, she whispered something into his ear. The man's manic smile returned. He stepped back and, tucking the baton under his arm, raised his hands, pressing his fingers together.

"My name is Bobo. Welcome to the *other* city. Or, as we like to call it, the Shadow City. I'm afraid your life is going to be a bit different from now on."

"You have no right to keep us locked up." Daria did her best to sound haughty, but even she quailed under Bobo's frown.

"No right? I think you lost all rights when you fell down here from the heavens above, pretty one," he crooned. He whipped his baton out and jabbed Daria in the stomach through the bars of her cage. She stumbled back, her pale skin flushing as red as her hair.

When she rushed forward, Bobo waggled the baton at her. "Ah-ah-ah. I wouldn't get too close to the bars if I were you."

"Leave her alone!"

I glanced over at Cayden. His pale face was set in a determined expression.

"Why? Do you want to complain about your 'rights', too, boy?"

Bobo strode over, twirling the wooden baton. He jabbed it through the bars of Cayden's cage, but six inches from the prince, the baton stopped suddenly, as if it had hit an invisible wall. Then it slowly began to move up.

Bobo let out a low chuckle. "Ah, so we have ourselves a mind-mover then," he said softly.

Cayden's face was strained with the effort of keeping the baton at bay.

Bobo pulled it away. "Well, that's useful to know." He began to pace again. "So, we have two burners, a leccy, a water-weaver, a telky, and . . ." He stopped in front of my cage. "You. What are you, little bird?"

This time, I didn't meet his gaze.

"No matter. We will find out when you go into the arena. It's a shame the mind-talker escaped. Caesar would have paid a good price to get his hands on him."

"What's the arena?" Aidan's voice was weak.

Bobo slapped a hand against his forehead. "Of course. I haven't explained! Well, my precious ones, right now, you are underneath the Colosseum. Tomorrow, you will be sold to whichever of the factions bids the highest. But before that, you have to show them how much you're worth." He grinned, revealing pointed teeth. "Think of it as a test."

"We've had enough of tests," Cayden snapped. "Who are these factions you talk about?"

"And what do you mean by showing them what we're worth?" I added.

"The factions rule this city." Bobo strolled nonchalantly between the cages. "In a way, I'm actually doing you a favor. At least with a faction, you're more likely to get fed and less likely to get gored by a bison. Though, admittedly, there's a higher probability of you dying in a gang fight." He rocked his hands as if weighing the options. "But gang fights usually mean a cleaner death."

"Is there an option of *not* dying?" I asked.

Bobo pointed his baton at me and grinned. "Possibly, little bird. But that really depends on how quickly you adapt."

"And how much we're worth. I get it."

"You're a quick learner." He held his arms wide. "Once the faction leaders have had a chance to inspect you, you will each be taken up to the Colosseum. There, you will display whatever abilities you have. I suggest you put on a good show."

"Or what?" Daria retorted.

Bobo flashed her a cold smile. "Or else you die, pretty one. Or else you die."

8

The Inspection

W E TALKED LATE INTO the night, trying to figure out a way to escape. I'd hoped Marissa might be able to do something with the electrical fields around the cages, but she said they were too powerful for her to touch. The others practiced using their powers, but although Shui managed to conjure up enough water for each of us to wet our mouths—apparently, she drew it out of the air—no one else achieved anything remotely useful.

I couldn't contribute so much as a flicker of a flame. The more I thought about it, the more I was convinced that the Guardians had made a mistake. Perhaps they'd mixed up my record with someone else's, or the odd helmet device had malfunctioned. Not that this made me feel any better given Bobo's hints about what might happen to us in the Colosseum if we didn't prove our worth.

We had no way of knowing the time or whether it was day or night, but at some point, Cayden suggested we get some rest. Sleep did not come easily, and when the slim woman came in and delivered us each a bowl of watery gruel that I assumed was breakfast, we were all bleary-eyed. Even Daria looked exhausted.

"I don't think I slept a wink." Aidan yawned and stretched his arms out.

"You must have. You kept me awake for *hours* with your snoring," Daria snapped.

Aidan's eyes widened, and I had to bite back a smile. He *had* been pretty loud.

I sniffed the contents of the bowl cautiously. The beige gloop smelled warm and slightly fermented. "Anyone know what this is?"

Cayden sniffed his own bowl and wrinkled his nose. "No."

"Some kind of porridge maybe?" Marissa lifted the bowl to her mouth, taking a cautious sip. "It tastes pretty bland."

"I'm not drinking it," Daria declared. "It could be poisoned."

"More fool you." Aidan tilted his head back and gulped at the gruel. "Reckon we might need all the food we can get."

"He's right. Besides, why would they poison us if they want to sell us as slaves?" I took a sip. It didn't taste too bad. With a bit of sweetener and some fruit, it might even have been tasty.

In the end, everyone except Daria ate the gruel. When the woman returned to collect the bowls, she gave Daria a disparaging look. "You might want to rethink leaving food. Fussy eaters soon starve."

Her accent reminded me of my grandmother, who'd died two years ago. My grandfather had never been around, and my mother's parents died in a freak pod accident before she met my father, so our only remaining family was my father's sister, her husband, and children. They lived in a different tower, so we only got to see them a few times a year, but I always looked forward to our visits.

"What time is it?" Cayden asked as the woman reached through the bars of the cage for his bowl. The flickering electrical current didn't seem to bother her. In fact, as she pulled away, sparks danced around her arm and up her shoulder.

I sucked in a breath and glanced at Marissa, who stared at the woman, wide-eyed.

She's a leccy. Is she the one keeping us here?

The woman walked to the door, then turned to look back at us. "The faction leaders will come around soon. Be ready to show them what you've got."

Silence followed her departure. The thin gruel felt like concrete in my stomach. For the hundredth time, I looked around the sparse room, searching for anything that could help us escape. My gaze fell on Cayden, who paced his cage.

"If you've got some secret link to your grandfather or a platoon of commandos ready to break us out, now would be a good time to get things moving."

His face tightened. "I already told you, I don't even know why I'm here. And you know we don't have an army."

He had a point. New Vegas prided itself on being able to solve any political issues with diplomacy rather than violence. Not that we had much interaction with the outside world. No one ever left New Vegas, and as far as I was aware, no one from other cities came visiting.

I bit my lip, feeling bad about my outburst. Though not *that* bad. He was a prince, after all, and he'd had eighteen years in the lap of luxury. Despite what Saskia had said, I couldn't imagine the king abandoning his grandson down here to die. Then again, until yesterday, I hadn't imagined I'd be down here, either.

I wondered what Layla had told my parents—if she'd been able to tell them anything other than the Academy's lies. In my mind, Sol's little face crumpled as Father told him I'd never be coming home, never be there to play with his dragons again. I blinked away tears, turning my back so the others wouldn't see my weakness.

How could my own sister have let this happen?

"Someone is coming," Shui said.

As the footsteps neared, we all turned toward the door. Aidan cast me a nervous glance, his hands fisted at his side. Marissa looked about ready to cry, and Shui trembled in a ball at the back of her cage. I did my best to straighten my shoulders and look calm, but inside, my nerves crumbled.

In the end, the inspection wasn't as bad as I had feared. Groups of men and women traipsed through the small room, pausing in front of each of our cages to look us over. I felt like a fish in one of the aquariums at the posh upper-level restaurants, being sized up to see how tasty I'd be for dinner. Bobo announced each group, then escorted them around, though whether that was to keep an eye on them or to stop us misbehaving, I wasn't sure.

First up was a group Bobo introduced as the Players. They were led by a middle-aged Japanese man wearing a tailored suit that, to my untutored eye, looked very expensive. He would have blended in with the patrons at the New Vegas Opera House, but here, in a bare underground room where dust clung to the concrete and the smell of Bobo's fur coat mingled with sweat and fear, he seemed comically out of place. But Bobo treated the man with almost exaggerated respect, bowing and shuffling backward as he led him around.

The man spent the most time with Shui, who shyly lifted water from the bowl Bobo had placed near her cage and shaped it into the outline of a fat, thick-lipped fish. That earned her a smile from Bobo, which sent Shui scurrying to the back of her cage.

A group of women dressed in bizarre, warrior-like attire, whom Bobo announced as the Sirens, completely ignored the boys and Bobo—much to his evident displeasure. They looked impressed with Shui's water display, then lingered in front of Daria, who glowered at them with her arms folded. With a look from Bobo, his leccy woman sent a spark of electricity shooting from the cage bars across to Daria's arm. Cheeks flushed with anger, Daria shot a flame toward the visitors.

One of the women met it with a jet of water. There was a crackle and billowing steam as fire and water collided with the purple sparks on the cage bars.

When the steam cleared, Daria was soaking wet and furious, though not as mad as Bobo, who jabbed her with his stick and muttered something under his breath.

Oddly, the Sirens didn't seem at all perturbed. Their leader, a tall woman with olive skin and long, black braids, actually smiled before turning her back on Bobo and stalking over to me. I wondered if I, too, was going to be prodded and poked until I produced something dramatic, but Bobo murmured to the woman, who nodded and glanced at a slight woman with green eyes and dark hair that was coiled like twisting snakes on top of her head.

I avoided eye contact, the weight of their stares making my heart pound. An odd, itching sensation started in my head, but after a moment, it disappeared as the women moved on. The green-eyed woman hung back, appraising me. As she turned to leave, I noticed a strange mark, almost like a brand, on her upper left arm. It looked like a downward pointing dagger.

Two more groups filed through. The Venetians, led by a beautiful woman with golden curls, with whom Bobo flirted outrageously, and the Ragazzi, led by a man who bore such a striking resemblance to the blonde woman that I wondered if they were related. Both groups were casual in their inspection, seemingly disinterested.

"We'll see what they can do in the Colosseum," the woman said in a bored drawl when Bobo asked if she wanted to see our abilities.

The final group was the most interesting. We heard their voices as they approached the door, but when it opened, it was not human feet that padded into the room.

"What is that?" I breathed, backing away from the bars of the cage.

"Some kind of lion?" Cayden sounded more curious than scared. Perhaps he hadn't noticed the creature's fangs which curved three inches below its jaw.

The beast prowled in front of us, muscles rippling under its golden fur. I'd seen historical documentaries on big cats on the holonet and it didn't look quite like a lion. More like a tiger, but without the distinctive stripes. Whatever it was, it looked powerful, fast and hungry. Its barbed tail twitched as the door opened again and Bobo entered, followed by three people.

"Come, Nimra," a tall man with short, curly blond hair and a pale face ordered. He was dressed casually in dark clothes and heavy boots. The cat slunk over to him and rubbed its head against his waist. When the man scratched behind its ears, it let out a rumbling purr.

The man's companions couldn't have been more different. One was a short, elderly man with scraggly gray hair. His green robe was faded and tattered, but his eyes were sharp and clear as they rested on each of us in turn. When his gaze met mine, his eyes widened momentarily before moving on. The woman's close-fitting metal-and-leather armor was similar to the outfits the Sirens had worn, though less ornate. Although the room was cooler than the city streets, it was still hot enough to be unpleasant, and she must have been sweltering in her long sleeves.

As if she could read my thoughts, the woman's gaze flicked to me. Her long, golden hair was tied in tight braids gathered at the nape of her neck, and she carried a carved wooden staff that was as tall as her shoulder. She was neither tall nor stocky, but everything from her stance to her icy gaze screamed "protector".

"The Gladiators," Bobo announced. He treated the group with a wary kind of respect. There was none of the bowing or protestations he'd shown with the Japanese man, but neither did he laugh or joke. In fact, for the first time, I sensed something approaching fear in his manner.

The group went to Marissa first, then Cayden, then me. I eyed the prowling creature warily, but it ignored me and walked over to slurp from Shui's bowl of water.

"What can this one do?" the blond man asked in a bored voice.

"We don't know. Either she's not telling or she doesn't know herself."

"Really?" There was a disappointing lack of surprise in the man's voice. "Look at me, girl."

Reluctantly, I dragged my gaze up to meet his and sucked in a breath. His eyes were as black as the night.

Surely that's not natural.

A smile tugged at the corner of the man's mouth.

Bobo glanced at him anxiously. "Can *you* tell what she can do, Caesar?"

I stared at the blond man. So this was the one Elan had warned us about. *Try not to get picked by Caesar.*

"I'm not sure I can do anything," I said quickly. "At least, nothing as impressive as the others."

"What's your name, girl?" Caesar asked.

"Vesper."

"The evening star," the elderly man said softly.

"Indeed." Caesar folded his arms. "Would you like to come work for me, Vesper?"

I forced myself to meet his gaze. "Not really. Unless you've got a supply of headache pills you're willing to share."

This seemed to amuse him. "Well, that may be something we can help with. Good luck in the arena, Vesper."

When he moved to Aidan's cage, my shoulders sagged in relief. *Whatever happens, I am not getting sold to him.*

After Caesar's group left, we were left alone for perhaps an hour. Plenty of time to mull over what the Colosseum might hold.

My family already believed I was dead. By the end of the day, they might be right.

When Bobo returned, he was accompanied by the slight woman with long, dark hair. His sharp teeth flashed as he held up a ring of keys. "It's playtime, boys and girls."

Marissa was the first to be taken away, dragging her feet as Bobo pulled her toward the double doors. An anxious wait followed as I wondered if I'd ever see the frail, blonde girl from Level 135 again. But half an hour later, she staggered back into the room, leaning heavily on the slaver woman, who helped her back into her cage. Blood trickled from a deep slash on her arm. As soon as the woman let go of her, Marissa collapsed into a heap and clutched her head, moaning.

Cayden was next. He shook off Bobo's hand and walked to the door with as much dignity as he could muster. I wondered if that was part of his royal training.

"Marissa?" I asked when the door shut behind them. "Are . . . Are you okay?"

It was a stupid question. I could tell she was far from all right. But when she didn't reply, I asked again. Marissa lifted her head, staring at me with bleary eyes, her pale face blotchy.

"I'm alive, so I guess that's something." She managed a weak smile. "My head feels like it's about to explode, though. I had no idea I could do that." She gazed at her hands, as if seeing them for the first time.

"What happened?" Daria asked impatiently. "What did they make you do?"

Marissa paused for a moment before speaking. "There was a beast," she whispered. "I've never seen anything like it. Not even on the holonet. It was like a giant bison, but with three eyes. Its tail was a bladed whip." She inspected her bleeding arm. "I managed to dodge the beast, but not its tail."

A three-eyed beast with a razor-sharp blade for a tail.

I had thought the rumors about monsters had been kids' tales. Then again, I'd also thought that nothing could survive beneath the smog and I'd been proven wrong on that count. The list of secrets the society kept from us was growing longer.

"What did they give you to fight with?" I asked.

"Nothing." Marissa looked up at me, her eyes empty. "Nothing at all."

"It was a test of your powers," Shui whispered in her musical voice.

Marissa nodded. "I don't know where I got the strength. I've never had that much power before. It was like . . . like a lightning bolt hit the beast right between the eyes. It fell to the ground. I don't think I killed it, but I'm not sure because I passed out and when I came to, they were dragging me back down here."

My legs suddenly felt weak. I sat down heavily and hugged my knees to my chest.

What would have happened had Marissa not been able to stun the beast? Would they have let it kill her?

An icy chill trickled down my spine and radiated outward, sucking the warmth from my body. What chance did I have against such a beast?

We were silent, each lost in our own fear, until the doors slammed open and Cayden was carried into the room. It took the combined efforts of Bobo and a stocky man I hadn't seen before to carry his limp body into the cage.

Daria gasped and sprang to her feet. "What have you done to him?"

"Don't worry, pretty one. He's alive." Bobo dropped Cayden's shoulders to the floor with a grunt. "Just overexerted himself a bit." He dusted off his hands and nodded approvingly. "I do like a trier."

Bobo locked Cayden's cage and walked to the box on the wall, reactivating the electrical field. He flicked another switch and the crackling purple electricity around the bars of my cage vanished.

Slowly, I forced myself to stand, though my legs felt as if they could collapse under me at any minute. The room seemed to be closing in on me, crushing my lungs until I could barely breathe. I slapped my hand over my mouth and bent over as I retched. Acid burned my throat.

"It's time, little bird."

I looked up into Bobo's dark eyes. Did I imagine the flash of sympathy? But his grip was firm on my arm as he pulled me out of the cage.

It took all my focus to put one foot in front of the other as he led me through the double doors and down a corridor to a staircase. The pressure on my lungs eased as we got farther from the underground room and I was able to breathe again.

I needed a plan for what I was about to face. Being prepared made me feel in control. It was how I'd aced my exams, how I tackled every challenge life had dealt me. But how could I prepare for a strange beast that I had to defeat with no weapons, save whatever weird power I had gained in the past twenty-four hours?

If I even have a power.

Bobo paused in front of a pair of double doors. "The rules are simple, little bird. Defeat whatever you find in the arena." His pointed teeth flashed in the gloom. "Good luck."

He pushed me through the doors. Bright lights blinded my vision. I barely had time to make out a high fence before a shove on my back sent me stumbling forward.

I fell to my knees, wincing as pain shot through my kneecaps, and looked around. So *this* was the Colosseum.

9

The Colosseum

THE CLANG OF A metal gate slamming shut echoed behind me. I got to my feet, blinking furiously as my eyes adapted to the bright spotlights after the darkness of the underground room. A warm breeze ruffled the hair that hung loosely down my back. Glancing up, I saw the faint outline of a huge, jagged-edged hole in the building's roof. Air rushed in from the opening, tasting of dust, chemicals, and iron.

I stood in a circular arena bounded by a towering metal fence. Dust from the dirt floor coated my hands. Concrete blocks of various shapes and sizes were scattered around, all of them too big for me to lift and useless as any kind of weapon. A small pond was sunk into the ground to the right of me, and to my left, a few sad-looking vines weaved their way up a trellis. The only thing that looked remotely useful was a pair of iron bars propped up against the wire fence, but when I tried to pick one up, I found it was so heavy that I could barely lift it, let alone wield it with any effectiveness.

The bright spotlights made it hard to make out what was on the other side of the fence, but I had a vague impression of tiered seats rising up. I pressed my face up against the wire and peered through the gaps. Caesar stared down at me from a seat halfway up the first tier. He was flanked on either side by the man and woman who'd been with him earlier. Behind them, other people nudged each other and whispered among themselves.

I let my gaze wander, not wanting to look into those black eyes. In the next block of seats, I could just make out a group of women. The Sirens, perhaps. The hairs on the back of my neck prickled as I realized they must *all* be here, all the different faction leaders, waiting to see what I could do.

A drum roll sounded, followed by another clang of metal. I whirled around just in time to see a second gate on the far side of the arena swing back against the fence.

Move!

I managed to unfreeze my feet from the floor and ran to the largest of the concrete blocks, quickly scaling it. The surface was rough and crumbling, and as I perched on the tiny platform that formed the top of the block, I wondered if I'd made a deadly mistake. But without weapons, I couldn't think of another option. At least up here, I'd be higher than the beast. If I were lucky, it wouldn't be able to reach me.

Of course, luck hadn't exactly shone on me the past few days.

Smoke billowed from the gap in the fence. I crouched, my body tensed like a spring.

But what eventually emerged through the smoke was not the beast Marissa had described, but a man. He strode into the arena, a spear in one hand and a flat-bladed sword in the other. With a jolt, I recognized the slaver Elan had manipulated. He'd removed his jacket to reveal a thin vest that might once have been white. Underneath it, his chest bulged. The man swaggered into the center of the arena and raised his arms, getting a cheer from the crowd, but his gaze flicked around nervously as tiny droplets of sweat beaded on his forehead.

He's afraid? Of me?

The thought was almost enough to make me laugh. Though he wasn't tall, the man must have weighed at least two hundred pounds, whereas I clocked in at a hundred and twenty in boots and a heavy coat. Plus, he was armed. Though where he'd gotten the ancient-looking weapons, I had no idea.

I didn't stand a chance.

His gaze alighted on me and the muscles in his face relaxed ever so slightly. "Come down and fight!"

"Or what?" I called back.

He didn't reply as he hefted the spear in his hand.

I eyed it warily. "Don't you need to save that thing for the beast?"

The man sneered. "Did no one tell you, girl? I *am* the beast."

A flash of movement was all the warning I had. I ducked, the spear whistling through the air inches above my back. The sudden movement knocked me off balance, and for a split second, I teetered precariously, arms flailing. Then gravity won out and I fell back off the block.

I hit the floor and rolled, the impact knocking the breath from my body and sending stars dancing in front of my eyes.

That was definitely a mistake.

Footsteps came toward me as I lay there, winded, trying to figure out if the pain racking my body was just a general pain or if I'd broken something.

Feeling something prod my ribs, I cracked open an eye. The slaver stared down at me and poked me again with the butt of his spear.

"You goin' to lie there all day?"

He moved to prod me again, but I grabbed the wooden shaft and yanked. The man's eyes widened as the spear began to slip from his grasp, but he quickly tightened his grip and pulled it back. Then he stepped back and gestured for me to stand.

Cautiously, I got to my feet, eying him warily. I didn't think anything was broken, but I suspected I'd wake up tomorrow with enough aches and pains to confine me to bed.

If there was a tomorrow. A bed was probably a bit too much to hope for given my current situation.

The man was quick to launch his next attack. I stumbled back as the flat side of his blade came down on my arm. My back slammed into the concrete block I'd fallen from moments earlier.

I ducked to the side and ran around the block. The man followed, almost lazily. I put as much distance between us as I could and tried to figure out my next move. I still wasn't sure what his orders were. He'd had plenty of opportunities to kill me if he'd wanted, but perhaps that wasn't the purpose of the exercise.

The spear flew through the air again, but this time, it missed me by a few feet and struck the metal fence. I darted over and picked it up. It was lighter than I'd thought, though the blade weighed one end down. I hefted it, trying to get the feel of its balance. I'd never been in a fight before, and the only thing I'd held that could remotely be considered a weapon was the kitchen knife we used for chopping vegetables from the garden-yard. I couldn't help feeling it was a bit convenient that the spear had landed right next to me. Still, I wasn't about to give it back, even if I had no clue how to use it.

Stab with the sharp end. How hard can it be?

We circled each other. I waved the spear in what I hoped was a threatening manner, but the man didn't respond. Just as I wondered how to break this deadlock, he lunged forward.

Instinctively, I brought up my spear, somehow managing to deflect his sword. To my surprise, he let the sword drop and wrestled the spear from my grasp, throwing it to one side before pushing me backward until I felt the bite of the wire fence against my back.

The slaver's fingers closed around my neck. I tasted his sour breath and could see the flecks of dirt and dead skin on the side of his pudgy nose.

"Ready to die, girl?"

I clawed at his chest, but it was like trying to fight off a brick wall. He didn't even seem to notice. The pressure on my windpipe increased and I felt an overwhelming urge to swallow. Saliva dribbled from the corner of my mouth as I fought for breath.

"Stop," I croaked.

The man glanced up suddenly as if something had startled him. I used the opportunity to kick out. My boot connected with his shin. He grunted in pain but didn't release his grip. His gaze returned to me, and I stared into his eyes—brown with flecks of green—hoping to find some shred of mercy in them. But there was none.

Spots danced in front of my vision as I clenched my hands, too weak to even strike out. Anger built inside me. Anger at this man, at Bobo, at this place. Anger that I was going to die without even having a chance to say goodbye to my family. It grew into a raging inferno that rushed up my throat and out through my mouth in one desperate, final scream.

STOP!

The word bounced around inside my skull.

Stop, stop, stop. . .

The pressure on my throat suddenly eased. I was vaguely aware of the man stumbling backward and falling to the floor, but the pain in my head was so intense, I could think of nothing else. I collapsed to my knees beside him.

The slaver stared up at me with unseeing eyes. Eyes that would never close again.

"What have I done?" I whispered, throat raw.

Blackness tugged at me, pulling me down into a void so deep and dark that I could see no escape from it. For a moment, I resisted, my body swaying as I fought to stay upright, but the throbbing in my skull overwhelmed me. Breath trickled from my lips. I felt myself falling, then everything went dark.

10

Sold

"**I**S SHE AWAKE YET?"

"I don't think so."

"Still got a pulse?"

Delicate fingers pressed into the side of my neck, making me wince.

"Yes. I think . . . I think she's coming around."

I opened my eyes. Shui's face swam into view, her blue eyes wide with concern.

"What . . ." I croaked, unable to force any more words out of my swollen throat. I reached one hand up to my head, which felt as if a hundred drums beat a rhythm inside my skull.

"Here. See if she can swallow this." Bobo's voice sounded far away.

Shui left. A minute later, she returned holding a cup of water and something else. "Can you sit up, Vesper?"

With Shui's help, I managed to sit and swallow the pill she gave me. It scratched my throat on the way down, but after a few minutes, the intense pain in my head had receded to a slightly more manageable ache and I was able to look up.

Outside the cage, I saw Bobo grinning. "That was quite a performance, little bird. Even if it did cost me a good man."

Memories rushed back and I felt the blood drain from my face. When I closed my eyes, the slaver's sightless eyes stared back at me. Nausea churned in my gut.

I killed him.

"Hey now, no fainting on me," Bobo said in alarm. "I've got an auction to run, and the leaders are already getting pissed at the delay. Not to mention the headaches you've given them all."

I looked down at my hands. They didn't look any different, other than a few scratches I must have picked up in the fight.

What have I done?

"What . . . What am I?" My words were barely audible, but Bobo must have had sharp hearing as he gave a low chuckle.

"You're a mind-talker, little bird, and a powerful one at that. Reckon you're stronger than the one who escaped. You should fetch me a good price once the bargaining starts."

I stared at him in confusion. He had called Elan a mind-talker. I guessed that was how he managed to convince the slaver to release him from the cage. But what I'd done was different. I hadn't persuaded the man to do anything. I'd just killed him.

Was this what Saskia had meant when she'd said we were dangerous? She was right. Even if I could find a way to get back to New Vegas, as soon as the Guardians found me and read my thoughts, they would know that I had murdered a man. My hands began to tremble as the reality of my situation sunk in.

Bobo clapped his hands. "That's enough moping. We need to get you up to join the others."

It was only then that I realized the cages around Shui and me were empty. I looked at her, trying to convey my question with my eyes as I still wasn't sure I could talk.

She nodded, seeming to understand. "Everyone is alive. You were unconscious the longest." Her gaze flicked to Bobo. "He took the others up ten minutes ago."

"Am I going to have to carry you up?" Bobo stomped into the cage impatiently, his fur coat billowing around him. Shui shrank back at his approach, but he ignored her and grasped my arm, yanking me to my feet.

He ended up having to carry me up the stairs, but by the time we reached the metal fence of the Colosseum, I was strong enough to walk. A set of six smaller cages were evenly spaced in the center of the arena. Four were already occupied by Marissa, Cayden, Aidan, and Daria. Shui and I were shoved into the final two. Two men stood slightly to one side. One I didn't recognize, but the other was the elderly man who'd accompanied Caesar on his inspection. I didn't have time to wonder what they were doing here because as soon as Shui and I were in position, Bobo began to speak.

He started with some long, rambling speech about the lengths he'd gone to in order to capture and contain us. With my headache receding, I used the opportunity to look around. The spotlights had been dimmed, allowing me to see beyond them to the groups of people sitting in the tiered seats surrounding the arena. In the most prominent spots sat the faction leaders, but many more people filled the lower blocks and some of the seats farther away. I wondered who they all were and why they'd come to see this spectacle.

Once the speech was over, Bobo began the bidding, dragging each of us out in turn to be paraded in front of the spectators. I had to hand it to him. He was a natural, getting the audience on his side and playing the faction leaders against one another to try and push the bids higher. The audience participated fully, booing and cheering in response to Bobo's flamboyant hand gestures.

I wasn't sure what currency they were bidding with—it wasn't New Vegas credits for sure—but I hadn't seen much in the way of technology down here, so perhaps they had some old-style paper money rather than digital currency.

Aidan was the first to be sold, to the handsome blond-haired leader of the Ragazzi. The man's companions cheered and slapped his back. Their clothing was dark with flashes of bright red. Some wore pieces of red cloth tied around their heads. They, too, had some kind of symbol on their upper arms, though from this distance, I couldn't make out what it was. Their leader flicked his fingers. A man broke off from the group and sauntered down into the arena. Bobo gave Aidan a shove and he stumbled after the man, his face stricken with terror.

The bidding for Daria went on longer. The tall woman with black braids who was the leader of the Sirens stood against the beautiful blonde from the Venetians. In the end, the golden-haired woman waved her hand to indicate she was no longer interested, and Daria was taken off to join the Sirens.

Cayden was next, then Marissa, both of whom were bought by Caesar. There were some murmurs from the audience. Even Bobo seemed slightly surprised, but he rallied and carried on.

All the faction leaders bid on Shui, though they were gradually whittled down until only the Venetian's leader and the Japanese man remained. Shui's eyes skipped nervously between them. I managed to catch her eye and smile, but she couldn't return the gesture.

Eventually, the blonde woman relented. A pale, slim woman descended to take Shui to the group of men and women seated quietly around the leader of the Players.

There was only me left.

When Bobo opened the cage, I walked out, trying to keep my fear contained. The bids had gone up as the auction progressed, indicating the faction leaders valued Marissa and Shui more than Aidan and Daria. I wondered if that was due to the type of ability they had or the strength of their abilities.

"Finally, we have Vesper, the mind-talker," Bobo announced, waving his arm in my direction. "You all saw—and felt—the extent of her power." Scattered laughter rippled through the audience.

I felt their eyes on me, appraising me, and it took all my strength not to quiver. Some glared at me in hatred, others in something approaching fear. The sick feeling returned to my stomach. These people were afraid of me.

They have good reason to be.

I stood quietly as the bidding went on, the price going beyond Cayden's, Marissa's, and Shui's until only two leaders were left. The woman who'd bought Daria . . . and Caesar.

The tall woman stood and tossed her black braids over her shoulder. "Caesar can't possibly afford three slaves, not at this price," she snapped in a strange accent that I'd never heard before. "Don't be a fool, Bobo. You know I can pay."

"As can I," drawled Caesar. He lounged in his chair, tapping his fingers on the arm. "Don't talk about what you don't know, Apollina."

The bidding went on a little longer, until Apollina, with a stiff nod and a look that promised vengeance if she ever got close enough to Caesar to enact it, relented.

Breath rushed from my body. When a hand touched my arm, I turned to look into the blue eyes of the elderly man in the green robe. He gave me a kind smile.

"Follow me, Vesper."

Not knowing what else to do, I trailed after him, up the steps, toward the man with the blond curls and piercing black eyes.

The man Elan had warned me about.

The man who was now my master.

11

Enslaved

I'D HOPED WE WOULD at least be able to see a bit more of this underworld city when we were taken to what Caesar called "our new home", but we never even stepped outside. It turned out that Caesar owned the Colosseum, along with a whole host of adjoining buildings. I wasn't sure of the legality of his ownership, but from the little I had grasped of this strange place, the laws of New Vegas didn't apply.

"Welcome to Caesar's Palace, home of the Gladiators," Caesar said, sitting regally on a huge chair shaped like a man's head. His fanged pet padded over and curled up at his feet. I wondered if he expected us to bow.

He called it a palace, but that wasn't how I would describe the endless series of corridors and streets that we'd been led down. Palaces were symbols of wealth and elegance. I had only ever seen pictures of the Royal Palace on the holonet, but it was all sparkling white marble and gold-rimmed oil paintings, with vast windows and fabrics so rich and soft, one throw probably cost more than our whole apartment.

Caesar's Palace couldn't have been more different. The gloomy streets were lit only by candles and intermittent flickering bulbs, the wires trailing like spiderwebs from the ceiling. There were no windows. The people staring at us from the shadows wore tattered garments in murky shades of green and gray, which seemed to have been stitched together from pieces of fabric that might once have been clothes, curtains, or part of some small mammal. The combined odor of sweat, excrement, and roasting meat lingered in my nostrils long after we'd left the streets behind and passed through more doors and corridors to the room we now stood in.

"Tomorrow, your training will begin," Caesar continued. "Marcus will help you focus and control your powers, and Diana will deal with your physical education." He gestured to the older man and the warrior-like woman standing to one side. "You had better learn quickly. I paid a lot of money for you and expect you to earn your keep. We have seven weeks until you'll have a chance to prove yourselves in the Games."

As he spoke, I glanced around the room. There were no chairs or seating, just several large, white marble statues. The top half of a winged horse seemed to spring from the floor, and in the opposite corner, an eagle, wings spread, perched on top of a pedestal. Near the door, a brazier glowed, and mismatched tables were scattered around the room, holding candles that bathed the room in a warm glow.

Cayden stepped forward. Whereas Marissa jumped at every movement the guards made, Cayden had been a ball of burning fury since the moment we left the Colosseum. "You realize that this is all highly illegal? Slavery has been outlawed for hundreds of years. When I get back to New Vegas—"

Caesar laughed, a high-pitched giggle that set my teeth on edge. "When you get back?" He leaned forward in his chair. "There *is* no going back, boy. New Vegas threw you out. They didn't *want* you. The Shadow City is your home now, so you had better get used to it."

"I don't think you realize who I am." Cayden's hands clenched at his sides. "My father—"

"Your father could be the king himself for all I care," Caesar snapped. "*I* am your father now." His black eyes turned from Cayden to Marissa to me. "Inside my palace, you will be safe. The city outside is *not* safe. Not for people who have lived here their whole lives, and certainly not for you. It is perfectly clear that none of you know how to defend yourselves. As you will soon realize, there are a lot of dangers in this city, not all of them human. Besides, once you bear my mark, everyone will know you are my property. If you try to run, you will be brought back."

Sensing her master's anger, the fanged cat raised its head and growled. Caesar reached a hand down to pet it. "Hush, Nimra." He rose and walked toward us. "The Shadow City is your home now. Your *only* home."

Caesar stopped as Cayden blocked his path. The two men stared at each other until Nimra barred her teeth. Cayden's eyes flicked to the beast. Reluctantly, he stepped aside.

Nimra padded after her master like a faithful puppy. At the double doors, Caesar turned and nodded to Diana. "Brand them."

Brand them?

Marissa shot me a puzzled look, but I was just as confused.

We didn't have long to wonder. One of the guards grasped Cayden's arms and forced them behind his back, shoving him toward the brazier where Diana waited. My eyes widened as I saw the metal rod extending out from the glowing center of the white-hot fire.

Surely she can't mean to—

Diana whipped out the rod and, before I could shout a warning, pressed the red-hot end against Cayden's upper arm. He let out a scream of pain and tried to yank his arm away, but the guard held firm. A horrific stench filled the room. Beside me, Marissa fainted.

They grabbed her next, and the pain of the brand was enough to wake her, screaming. When it was my turn, I closed my eyes and prayed to any god who might be listening for strength.

Agony seared through my arm, spreading across my skin until it felt as if my whole body were on fire. Only the hands holding me stopped me falling to the floor, and I tasted blood in my mouth as I bit my lip against the pain.

"There. It's done. You will find painkillers and salve in your room." Diana's voice sounded far away. "Now, you are Caesar's."

Her words rang in my head long after I was half dragged, half carried from the room and taken up more flights of stairs to a plain room holding three beds. We were thrown inside, the door locked behind us.

On a small table beside each bed was a cup of water, two pills, a chunk of bread and some kind of meat, and a small tub, which I presumed contained the salve Diana had mentioned.

I swallowed the pills eagerly, though my stomach churned at the thought of food, even if I could have gotten it down my raw throat. My hand shook as I reached for the pot of salve. It took me a good ten seconds before my fumbling fingers managed to open it.

Touching the raw flesh sent another wave of agony washing over me, but I gritted my teeth and turned my face away. The salve was cool on my skin, and relief rushed through me as the painkillers kicked in.

"What is it?" Marissa asked. "The mark?"

I steeled myself and turned to look at the mark on her arm. It was roughly circular in shape and consisted of two sets of leaves curving like wings from the bottom of the brand.

"It's a laurel wreath," Cayden said. The anger was still in his voice but had started to fade. "Senators used to wear them in Ancient Rome." He gave a harsh laugh. "I guess that's who Caesar named himself for. The great Julius Caesar."

I had no idea what he was talking about. From Marissa's expression, she didn't either. I lifted the lid of a small box on one of the tables and pulled out a roll of thin plastic and some scraps of gray cloth. I lifted one to my nose and sniffed. At least it smelled clean.

"Plastic . . . and bandages. I guess they're to dress our wounds."

Marissa wrapped plastic around my arm, followed by one of the bandages, then moved to Cayden. Her hands shook slightly as she wrapped the cloth around the muscle of his arm. Then I told Marissa to sit down on her bed while I dressed her wound.

"So what did you do to get thrown down here?" I asked. "You're not old enough to go to the Academy, are you?"

Marissa shook her head. "No, I . . ." She opened her hand and tiny sparks danced in the air above her palm. "Two weeks ago, I was attacked on my way back from the market." She glanced at Cayden, then at me. "The *other* market."

I nodded. The black market was a network of people you could get things from. Extra food, toys, luxury items that were too expensive to buy legally. Apparently, it operated out of the lowest levels of the towers, but my parents had always said it didn't exist. It was only a rumor. Still, they had never permitted me to go below Level 140.

"The man beat me and tried to . . ." She swallowed. "Tried to . . ." Her fingers began to tremble, and she shoved her hand between her legs. Her pale cheeks flushed pink.

Gently, I wrapped my arm around her shoulders, my chest tightening at her distress. "He tried to rape you?"

Marissa gave a slight nod. "The power just shot from my hands. One minute, he was trying to pull my top up. The next, he was gibbering on the ground. I—" Her voice broke. "I ran. For the next week, I expected the Peacekeepers to come knocking, but they didn't. Then I realized I could power our lights and hydroponic pod. We'd never been able to afford the electricity to get it to work properly."

I squeezed her shoulders, then pulled my arm back and finished tying off the bandage. "But they eventually found you?"

Marissa nodded. "Yes. They said I was a criminal, but I didn't do anything wrong. I only defended myself. I didn't even know what I was doing!"

Cayden looked like he was about to say something, but when I glared at him, he shut his mouth. "Of course not," I said, rubbing Marissa's back. "It wasn't your fault.

I wondered what had happened to Marissa's attacker and if he'd ended up in the Shadow City, too. My heart went out to her. The thought of being mugged, let alone raped, had rarely crossed my mind. New Vegas was safe. That was why we had all the cameras and the Peacekeepers to protect us.

And where were the Peacekeepers when Marissa was attacked?

Perhaps the society wasn't as safe as we'd been led to believe.

Marissa yawned and hurriedly covered her mouth, casting a half-frightened, half-awestruck glance in Cayden's direction.

"Sorry. I just feel so tired." She curled up on her bed, facing the wall, and after a minute, her breathing deepened.

How could she fall asleep so fast?

As I glanced at her empty tray, the answer hit me. The pills. One blue, one pink. I'd assumed they were both painkillers, but perhaps one was a sleeping pill.

I sat down on the bed opposite Cayden's, the candles on the tables between us the only light in the room. Cayden glanced at Marissa's sleeping form, then back at me. "You want to get back home, right?" he asked in a low voice.

I nodded, fighting the tiredness that threatened to overcome me.

Cayden bent closer. "I made a bargain with your sister."

Instantly, I was more alert. I straightened my spine. "With Layla?"

He nodded. "When they dropped me on the city floor, she fell out after me. We had a few seconds before they picked her up. She asked me to look out for you."

Warmth blossomed my chest. Not that the prince could do much down here, but just the fact that Layla had tried to do something for me made me feel better.

"What else did she say?"

"We didn't have time to talk much. I gave her a message to give to my father." Cayden frowned. "I don't know how I could have failed that test, and I *know* Grandfather wouldn't have sent me down here. This must be a ploy by one of his rivals. Someone must have manipulated the test results." He hesitated and glanced at me. "Perhaps they were wrong about all of us."

A surge of hope rushed through me. I wanted to believe he was right, that all of this was just a mistake and that if I could get back to New Vegas, the Academy would welcome me with open arms.

"So what do we do now?" I whispered.

"Learn as much as we can about this place. If your sister can get the message to my father, he'll find a way to get us out of here. Don't you worry."

I wished I had his confidence, but as I lay back on the bed, the sleep-inducing powers of the pill overwhelming me, I couldn't stop thinking that even if help did come, it may be too late.

12

The Shadow Academy

I AWOKE TO A loud banging and pushed myself up on one elbow, wincing as every muscle in my body protested. The door flew open, a bright light flooding in.

"Come on, sleeping beauties," Diana said, striding into the room. "Time to get up."

I blinked at her through bleary eyes. "What time is it?"

"Morning."

"I don't know how you can tell. It's so bloody dark in this place," Cayden grumbled, swinging his feet over the edge of his bed. Marissa sat up and stretched her arms over her head.

Diana favored him with a small smile. "You get used to it."

I wasn't sure I could ever get used to permanent darkness. I already craved the sense of day and night the dome over our garden-yard gave us, not to mention the thin crack of sunlight I could see if I craned my neck to the sky.

"There's food waiting for you downstairs," Diana said, "*if* you get a move on."

My stomach took that moment to gurgle, reminding me that I hadn't had a proper meal in . . . What? Two days?

Diana shot me a glance. "After yesterday, you're sure to be hungry. Using your *powers*"—she sneered the word

—"apparently takes a lot of energy. You need to replace calories."

I scrambled to pull on my boots, then grabbed the chunk of bread I'd left on the table last night, stuffing it into my mouth as we followed her out of the room. Although the pain in my head was almost gone, my throat was still sore and I found it hard to swallow. I caught Marissa glancing at my neck, eyes wide, making me wonder what marks the slaver had left on my neck. But the ache in my throat was nothing compared to the pain from the brand on my arm. My skin felt as if it were on fire.

Breakfast was some kind of meat stew. Ravenous, we ate quickly, Diana watching over us. Just as we finished, the door opened and Marcus walked in. He smiled at us and nodded to Diana.

"I hope you all slept well," he said, clasping his hands in front of him. "I'm sure you're feeling a bit battered and bruised, but Caesar is keen to get your training under way as soon as possible."

Training?

Memories of what happened the day before came flooding back. The spoon dropped from my hand and clattered in the bowl. I had killed a man. Struck him dead with the power of my mind. His eyes stared back at me from the depths of the empty bowl. Brown with flecks of green.

I shoved the bowl away and stumbled from the table, reaching out blindly until my hand touched a cool wall. I bent over and pressed my forehead against it. My stomach heaved as I fought the urge to vomit.

Had it only been two days ago that I'd stood in our garden-yard staring at the Royal Tower, imagining what it would be like to live there? I was so confident I would win a place at the

Academy. Too confident. I wanted to make my family proud. Instead, they thought I was dead, and I was a slave in a city I hadn't even known existed.

A single tear leaked from the corner of my eye. It burned my skin, more painful than the brand that now scarred my arm.

"Is everything all right, Vesper?"

Marcus's voice broke through my thoughts. I sensed him standing close and sucked air into my lungs to control my emotions. I would not cry in front of *them*.

I raised my hand to my mouth and feigned a cough in order to wipe the tear from my face. When I turned to face Marcus, his expression was sympathetic. Somehow, that just made me angrier.

"No, everything is *not* all right. Right now, we should be up there!" I jerked my finger at the ceiling. "In the Royal Academy, learning how to use our powers for good. We've been torn from our families, imprisoned in cages, and are now slaves of some crazed, deluded tyrant who wants us to use our powers to kill. And you have the *gall* to ask if everything is all right?"

As the words left my lips, I vowed that I would not use my powers. I couldn't, *wouldn't*, kill again. Whatever it took, I'd find some way of escaping this city.

Marcus seemed strangely nonplussed by my outburst. "It is rather a lot to come to terms with, but given it was the Royal Academy who threw you down here in the first place, are you sure they are the paragons of virtue you believe them to be?" His accent was smooth. If we were in New Vegas, I'd have assumed he was an upper-leveler.

"At least the Academy doesn't enslave people," I retorted.

No, they just throw them down here to die.

I quashed the thought and scowled at Marcus.

"We will teach you how to control your powers so you don't end up killing yourself and other people," Diana said. "Each of you will have a session with Marcus today. You'll spend the rest of the time with me." Her lips curled into a cold smile. "We have a lot of work to do to get you into shape."

"What is this? The Shadow Academy?" Cayden asked, scowling. Clearly, the prince wasn't used to being ordered around.

The corner of Marcus's mouth twitched. "In a sense. If you don't learn to control your powers, they will control you, and that rarely ends well." He turned to me. "Vesper, I'd like to work with you first. Follow me, please."

I trailed him down corridors and through doors. As we walked, my anger and grief subsided, leaving me feeling numb.

"How big is this place?" I muttered under my breath.

Marcus had sharper hearing than I thought. "It was once a huge entertainment and hotel complex, back before New Vegas was built on top of the old city. Millions of people from all over the world visited every year. Now it houses the people who align themselves with Caesar and look to him for protection."

"Protection from who? The other factions?"

"Yes, as well as other people and creatures in the city. Most feel life is safer under the protection of one of the faction leaders."

He set a surprisingly brisk pace, and I hurried to keep up. "But there are people who live outside? In the city itself?"

"Yes, but I wouldn't recommend trying it. Most people don't survive very long. It's not just criminals who are thrown down here to die." He stopped so suddenly, I nearly ran into the back of him. "Here we are."

He pushed open a nondescript door. I followed him into a room that was dimly lit by a single flickering light. "I believe this was once some kind of bathing area. Give me a minute to light some candles. You may have noticed that electricity is limited down here. Unfortunately, we lost one of our leccies last year. That was one reason Caesar was so keen to buy your friend."

"Marissa?"

Marcus nodded. "Leccies are one of the most sought-after talents, along with water-weavers and growers. Water is always in short supply, and growers are essential for food production."

"So we're not just going to be used as weapons?" I asked, more sharply than I'd intended.

Marcus's hand paused above the wick of one of the candles. "Is that what you thought?"

When I didn't reply, he glanced over at me. "Jules's first priority is to keep his people alive. Yes, that sometimes means fighting, but it's also about making sure we have the basics we need to live. Leccies help power machines and lighting, burners create furnaces for us to mold metal and glass, growers help our crops grow, and water-weavers can draw clean water from the most unlikely of places."

"And me?" I swallowed. "Why did they want me?"

Marcus moved between the thick candles, lighting each one in turn. They gave off a strange, unpleasant odor, but the flickering light was kind of comforting. The room was split into two, with two sets of stairs leading up to the higher level that was mostly taken up by a deep hole cut into the floor. At the back of the room was another sunken area, shallower than the first. The floor and walls seemed to be made of some kind of stone or marble, but they were chipped and cracked.

"Mind-talkers are rare, Vesper. Particularly ones with your strength." Marcus hesitated, then added, "Jules also thinks you have a second talent—empathy. It's not unheard of for people to have more than one talent, but it's unusual."

"Jules? You mean Caesar?"

Marcus nodded. "Caesar is more of a title. His father was Caesar before he passed away, and Jules took over from him."

It was hard not to like Marcus. His manner was open and honest, and he was the first person we'd met down here who seemed to treat us like human beings rather than an object to be bought or sold. Back in New Vegas, I wouldn't have hesitated to trust him.

The brand on my arm burned.

We were not in New Vegas now. Trust was something I was going to have to learn to live without. Still, Marcus seemed to be the only one willing to answer questions, and the more information I had, the better armed I'd be to escape.

But first, I needed to understand who—or what—I was.

"You called them talents, Diana called them powers, and at the Academy, Sas—" I cleared my throat. "The Guardians called them abilities. But no one's told me what they are or why we suddenly got them."

"Sit down." Marcus waved me over to a long stone lounger next to the sunken area in the floor. "I don't know when the talents first emerged. Perhaps there are historians at the Royal Academy who may know, but I was never privy to that information. As for how you got them . . . Well, your power was always there, dormant inside you. For a talent to manifest, something must happen to trigger your brain into activating it. The most common method is to put the subject in a terrifying situation where they believe they are fighting for their life."

"Which activates the fight or flight response," I murmured, remembering my biology classes at school.

Marcus nodded. "That's right."

"So that's why we were put in the Colosseum? The slaver *was* trying to kill me?"

"Bobo probably gave him orders to make it look that way, though he would have been ordered to avoid killing you if at all possible."

I looked down at my hands. "So he wouldn't have strangled me to death?"

"No."

I remembered how the spear had missed me, even though the slaver had been close. How he'd thrown away the spear and the sword—the two weapons that could have seriously injured me—and used his hands, so he could control the pressure.

I shivered. "But I killed him."

Marcus placed his hand over mine. His skin was worn and lined, like a piece of paper that had been crumpled, then pressed flat again. "It wasn't your fault, Vesper. Sometimes it happens, particularly when a person has a very strong talent."

I threw his hand off me and stood. "Don't call it that! Like it's something . . . something good. It's horrible. I—" I snapped my mouth shut.

"A talent is like anything," Marcus said quietly. "It can be used for good or evil. But until you learn to control it, you do not have a choice over what it does."

I closed my eyes and sucked in air, trying to calm the anger raging inside me.

I don't want this power. All I want is to go home.

When I opened my eyes, Marcus was wincing and rubbing his head. "The first thing you need to learn is how to stop projecting your thoughts."

My jaw dropped. "You *heard* what I just thought?"

"That you don't want your power? Yes. You practically shouted it."

My knees felt weak and I sank back onto the seat. *Does that mean everyone can hear what I'm thinking? All the time?*

"No," he said, then smiled at the scowl on my face. "And that was just a guess at what you were thinking. Your expression gave it away. I can only hear what you're thinking if you actively project it. I'm receptive to that kind of thing. Most people wouldn't be able to hear it at all, unless they were mind-talkers. But you need to understand when you're doing it and how to use it effectively."

I bent over and massaged my temples. It was hard to focus through the pain in my arm and the aches from my bruised and battered body. To cap it off, my headache seemed to be returning.

"Let's back up a minute," I said. "So my experience in the Colosseum activated this mind-talking ability I have?"

Marcus shook his head. "No. The tests they did at the Royal Academy activated your talent. You just didn't realize it then. What happened in the Colosseum forced you to use it. Do they still use a virtual reality simulation?"

I nodded.

"The simulation is designed to induce fear. A scanning device then picks up whether the part of your brain where your power resides has been activated."

I glanced at him suspiciously. "How come you know so much about the Academy and its tests?"

He smiled sadly. "Because I used to conduct them myself, a long time ago."

My jaw dropped. "You were a Guardian?"

"Yes, for a time."

"But how did you end up here?"

"That is a long story, and we have limited time. We need to get on with assessing your ability and seeing how I can help you control it."

"Wait!" I held my hand up as he stood. "One more question."

He sighed patiently. "Fine. One more."

"Marissa didn't take the Academy tests—she's a year or two younger than the rest of us—but her ability was already active. That was why they threw her down here."

Marcus's eyes widened a fraction. "Ah, that's interesting. She likely experienced some traumatic event. Abilities can be activated at any time during childhood, though they usually come to light during the teenage years. New Vegas is such a safe place to live that most young people would never have an experience strong enough to activate their talent. That was why they introduced the testing system."

"But why didn't they take her to the Academy to train her?"

Marcus shrugged. "Why did they throw you down here? They see you as a threat."

I opened my mouth, but Marcus shook his head. "No more questions. Now, we're going to start with shielding, for my sake as much as yours, then we'll move on to look at how you can use your talent."

He calls it a talent. But it's not a talent. It is a curse. A curse that made me a murderer and could make me kill again.

A dreadful thought struck me. Even if Cayden was right and our test results had been mixed up, would the Academy even want someone with my power? What use would I be to New Vegas society?

"Everyone has a natural mental shield," Marcus continued, oblivious to my blank expression. "Your shield stops your power from leaking out and inadvertently affecting others, as well as protecting you from those who might use their powers against you. For example, it would stop a fellow telepath from getting inside your head."

"Telepath?"

Marcus smiled. "That's the scientific name for it. You'll find most people down here refer to you as a mind-talker. I mentioned that we also think you may have a touch of empathy, which means you can sense people's feelings and emotions and may be able to influence them."

I opened my mouth to dismiss the suggestion, then closed it again when I remembered the waves of fear that had washed over me when we were caged in the room under the Colosseum. Had I been sensing my companions' fear as well as my own?

"When you feel a strong emotion, your feelings and thoughts can leak through your shield," Marcus continued. "That's why it's so important you learn to control your talent. Only then can we move on to using it proactively."

That sounded sensible. "Okay, where do we start?"

"First, I'd like your permission to run a little test. I will attempt to block your talent. This will tell me how strong your natural shield is and how much work we have to do to improve it."

"You want to get inside my head?"

"In a sense. Not in the same way you would—I wouldn't be able to read your thoughts, for example—but for the test to work, it's really important you don't make an effort to push me away."

"Surely you don't have to ask my permission," I snapped. "I'm Caesar's slave, after all. I'm surprised you haven't jumped in already."

Marcus grimaced. "I would much rather do this with your cooperation."

"What if I refuse?"

He sighed. "I beg you not to. This is for your safety, as well as everyone else's. If you can't properly shield your power, there's a risk you could project too strongly if you become emotional."

He seemed about to say something else, then stopped himself. But I could put the pieces together myself. "Was that what happened in the Colosseum? How I killed him?"

"When you screamed at him to stop, almost everyone in the Colosseum heard you, even those of us who have strong shields. But that was just the scatter effect. Think of your thought projection as a beam of light. The focus of your fear was the man attacking you. What we got was just the faint glow around it." Uncertainty clouded Marcus's expression. "I've never seen it happen before, so I don't know for sure, but my theory is it overwhelmed his senses so completely that it disrupted the synapses in his brain."

I frowned. "I zapped him?"

Marcus winced. "That's a rather crude way of putting it, but yes."

"And if I can't figure out this shielding thing, there's a risk I could do it again?"

"I'm afraid so. I can teach you the techniques, but without probing, I won't be able to tell if the lessons have any effect."

I stood and walked to the back of the room, needing a moment to think without his kindly "trust me" expression in front of me.

You can't trust him. You can't trust any of them.

But I didn't want to accidentally hurt, let alone kill, anyone else. And learning how to shield my "talents" wasn't the same as actually *using* my power on someone. Besides, I wouldn't be able to escape if I projected my thoughts every time someone made me jump.

"You definitely can't read my memories or thoughts?" I asked, staring at the cracked stonework in front of me.

"No. I don't have that ability, Vesper."

I turned to look back at him. "What ability *do* you have?"

"Stop changing the subject." Marcus gave me a warning look. "We only have ten minutes left. Let's at least attempt to *start* trying to improve your shielding."

"Fine." I returned to take the seat opposite him.

"Close your eyes and relax," Marcus instructed. "You may feel an odd sensation inside your head, but it shouldn't be painful. Whatever you do, don't push back at it and *don't* shout."

I did as he asked, trying not to think about anything important, just in case he was lying about reading my thoughts. Instead, I focused on my breathing and the pain in my arm. After a moment, I sensed a slight pressure inside my head. It was uncomfortable, but not painful. Then the pressure spread, as if a thousand fingers encircled my skull.

Just as it became unbearable, the pressure disappeared.

"You can open your eyes now," Marcus said. He looked at me with a thoughtful expression. "That's not as bad as I feared. You do have a decent natural shield . . ."

"Why am I sensing there's a 'but'?"

"It's not really a 'but'. You're just stronger than I thought." Marcus flicked his eyes to a strap on his wrist and frowned. "Five minutes. Right. I want you to try a simple strengthening exercise. Close your eyes."

I obeyed, stifling a groan. *If I am that strong and important, surely he can spend longer than an hour training me.*

"Empty your mind and search for the source of your power."

My eyes flew open. "What?"

"Search for the source of your power," Marcus repeated. "You'll know what I mean when you find it."

I closed my eyes again and tried to empty my mind, which was next to impossible given all the questions I had spinning around my head.

"Focus on your breathing," Marcus advised.

I sucked air in and out. In and out.

This isn't working. What kind of stupid exercise is this?

I gritted my teeth and tried to push the negative thoughts from my mind. And then I felt it.

A faint pulsing that was so much a part of me, I hadn't even known it was there. Noticing it was like trying to remember how to breathe, yet once I knew it was there, I became hyperaware of how the energy swirled around my head.

"Have you found it yet?"

Marcus's voice seemed to come from a distance, as if I were underwater.

"Yes."

"Good. You should be able to sense a barrier around it. Something that stops it from spreading out of your head."

Now that he mentioned it, the power swirling around my head *was* contained by something. Not a hard, rigid barrier, but something flexible . . . like water swirling around inside a plastic bag.

"You need to strengthen that barrier. Imagine you're inside a sphere and you need to defend yourself from attackers. Build layer upon layer of armor around the whole surface."

"How?" I already felt drained trying to hold onto the energy pulsing in my mind. I squeezed my eyes shut as my concentration began to slip.

"Let it go, Vesper, and open your eyes."

But I didn't want to let it go. The power swirled inside me. If I let it go, would I ever find it again?

"Vesper, let it go!"

Marcus's voice broke the gossamer thread that connected me to the energy source and my eyes snapped open.

I was back in my body, suddenly aware that my heart raced. Sweat trickled down my forehead.

Marcus smiled reassuringly. "You need to build up your strength gradually. *Never* get to the point where you're too tired or afraid to let go of it."

"I thought . . ."

"That you would lose it?" Marcus shook his head. "It's part of you, Vesper. But it takes a lot of energy to build a shield and control a talent, particularly a powerful one. That's enough for today. I want you to practice finding your power and see if you can start to strengthen your shield. Only try it for a few minutes at a time and only two or three times a day. You'll make progress faster than you think."

He rose and began to walk stiffly toward the door. "Come. I will take you back to Diana."

"What kind of talent does Diana have?"

Marcus paused, his hand on the door handle. "Diana is the greatest hunter ever to have lived in this city," he said quietly. "You would do well to heed what she says. You are fortunate to have her as a teacher."

We'd gotten halfway down the corridor before I realized he hadn't answered my question.

13

The Shadow City

"**F**ASTER!" DIANA SHOUTED AS I ran around the outside of the arena.

Her whip cracked and a puff of dust rose from the ground a couple of feet in front of me. I gritted my teeth and tried to force my aching legs to move faster. It was no use. I just couldn't suck enough air into my lungs to get rid of the lactic acid in my muscles. Spots danced at the edges of my vision, and the pain in my lungs almost equaled that of the lash from Diana's whip that I'd received five minutes earlier.

"Enough!"

I collapsed to the ground, my whole body shaking with fatigue and adrenaline. An iron grip on my arm yanked me up.

"Stand," Diana ordered. "Hands on your knees, suck in deep breaths."

I did as she said, though my calf muscles burned.

"Now walk, slowly, to get rid of the acid. *Never* just stop after exercise, do you hear?"

I nodded, wishing I had the breath to snap a retort.

When Marcus had brought me to the Colosseum and asked Cayden to follow him, the look of relief in the prince's eyes should have been warning enough. I hadn't even had a chance to speak with Marissa before Diana started barking orders, saying I needed to catch up. I glanced over at Marissa now. She risked a slight smile behind Diana's back. I guess me turning up had been something of a reprieve for her.

"Marcus's job is to keep you from killing other people," Diana said, striding over to the concrete block on which Marissa sat. The girl flinched as the blonde woman approached, but Diana ignored her as she picked up two wooden staffs. One of them was the thick staff with strange carvings that she seemed to carry everywhere. The other was shorter and undecorated. "My job is to stop you from getting yourselves killed."

She threw the plain staff toward me. Instinctively, I reached out to catch it. The wooden pole slammed into my palm so hard, I nearly dropped the damn thing.

I barely had time to raise the staff in defense before Diana brought her own down, aimed directly at my head. Wood cracked on wood, the impact ringing through my teeth. I staggered back, barely able to block her strikes as Diana casually sauntered forward, seemingly putting little effort into her blows.

"And just how is this stopping me from getting killed?" I panted, ducking as the carved wooden pole whistled through the air above my head.

Time to run for it.

I got three paces before I tripped on something I could have sworn hadn't been there a split second earlier and sprawled forward to land with a thud onto the floor.

I twisted onto my back. Diana's staff pressed into my chest. I glared up at her, but her expression remained impassive.

"I'm teaching you to respect danger and not underestimate your opponent."

I shoved the staff off my chest. "Don't worry. I'm not."

Diana waited for me to get my feet. "Take two minutes and get a drink."

She followed me over to the concrete block where Marissa waited.

I downed the cup of water Marissa handed me in one gulp, then held it out for more.

"One cup only." Diana frowned. "Water is precious. Treat it as such."

Marissa's hands shook as she refilled the cup and handed it to Diana, who sipped at the lukewarm water. The leather jacket I'd seen her wearing before lay on one of the concrete slabs. Underneath it, she wore a vest of the same supple leather tucked into a tight belt. She was slim, yet muscular, and I was pretty sure she didn't carry an ounce of fat. Just looking at her made me feel lazy.

My eyes were drawn to two sets of marks on her arms, inked in black on her golden skin. On her left arm, a series of arrow-shaped bars ran from her wrist to her shoulder. There must have been more than fifty. On her right arm were tiny skulls—thirteen in total.

"With the state you're in, neither of you would last five minutes out in the city. And once you've learned to control your talents, you will be required to do whatever Caesar orders. That may involve killing beasts or fighting members of the other factions." Diana scowled as she caught me staring at her arms. "Yes, Vesper?"

"What do the marks represent?" I asked.

I wasn't expecting an answer, but Diana raised her left arm in a fist in front of her. "One arrow for every monster I've killed." She switched the staff to her left hand and raised her right fist. "One skull for every death of a person with powers." She lowered her arm, something flickering in her eyes. "The scars remind me of the evil we must defeat and the price of ensuring our safety." Her voice held a trace of sadness that contrasted with her usual brusque manner. I was still trying to place her accent. It sounded slightly foreign.

She turned sharply and strode back to the center of the arena. "Come on, both of you. We don't have all day."

With a groan, Marissa jumped down off the block. "And here I was, thinking we were done for the day."

Diana had us practice sparring with the wooden staffs, interspersed with sets of push-ups and sprints around the outside of the arena. Marissa was faster than me, but she struggled with the push-ups and staff work. Not that I was much better. The weekly gym sessions we were forced to do at school were the only exercise I got, and comparing them to this workout was like correlating a ten-minute spelling test to a three-hour timed essay.

I let out an audible sigh of relief when the door opened and Marcus walked in, followed by Cayden. If the prince had looked tired before, he looked haggard now, stumbling after the elderly man as if he'd just run a marathon.

"Do I look as bad as you two?" he mumbled as he came over to join us.

I eyed his swaying figure. "Worse."

"Yeah, well, this powers stuff is intense."

"You're not kidding," I muttered.

"Marissa, come with me!" Marcus called.

Reluctantly, Marissa walked over to him, her shoulders hunched as if going to her execution.

"Good luck, Marissa!" I called after her.

That earned me another glare from Diana, but the small smile from Marissa was worth it.

"They're working us pretty hard." Cayden blew out a breath. "Do you think she's going to give us a break until Marissa comes back?"

I looked over at Diana, who twirled the staff in her hand as if it were a twig. A small smile played at the corner of her lips.

"No chance. She's enjoying this far too much."

I was right. Diana spent the next hour running us around in circles until I was so exhausted that I could barely stand. But when Marissa returned, it seemed we had a bit of a reprieve.

"Lunchtime," Marcus announced with a smile.

We followed him out of the Colosseum. "What delights do you think they've got in store for us this afternoon?" I murmured to Marissa.

"More of the same, I bet," Cayden said into my ear, making me jump.

I shot him a glare. "I wasn't asking you."

He looked affronted. "I thought we were allies?"

I stopped and turned to face him. "Perhaps. But let's not pretend that if you saw either of us back home, you'd stoop so low as to acknowledge our presence."

Cayden raised an eyebrow in an expression that made me want to punch his perfectly straight nose into something more crooked. "Oh, I think I'd have certainly noticed you both." His gaze slid to Marissa, who blushed.

I rolled my eyes and stalked off, leaving the two of them to follow. *Boys.*

Lunch was a similar kind of stew as breakfast, though there were greens and a chunk of bread to go with it. I almost inhaled the food, immediately feeling better with something solid in my belly.

"We have a number of food production levels in the basement and first floor of the palace," Marcus explained. "We supplement the vegetables and grains with meat from the creatures that live in the city. Those with talents get more generous rations. You'll find that using your power takes a lot out of you, physically and mentally. You won't be putting on weight down here, that's for sure."

"Don't other people resent that?" Marissa asked in a small voice.

"Some do," Marcus admitted. "But most realize the value the talented provide. Without us, everyone would have less food to eat, less electricity, and we'd be at greater risk of attack."

"So when do we get to go outside?" Cayden asked, scraping the last remnants of stew from his bowl.

"This afternoon." Diana's voice came from behind us. I hadn't even heard her approach.

Marcus frowned. "Are you sure that's wise?"

She shrugged. "Caesar's orders. He wants them to see what the city's like. I'll be taking Cato with me."

"Well, I guess they can't get into too much trouble with the two of you guarding them," Marcus replied, though concern flickered in his eyes.

I used the last of my bread to wipe out the bowl and shoved it into my mouth, chewing quickly. I pushed my chair back and stood. "Let's go."

Cayden also stood, excitement burning in his eyes. Marissa was more reluctant, but at a glance from Diana, she finished her food and the three of us followed the warrior out of the room. Her wooden staff was strapped to her back, along with a tube of arrows, and she carried a curved bow. As we walked down the corridor, we were joined by a tall, well-built man with scruffy brown hair and kind brown eyes. He grinned and introduced himself as Cato.

We walked through the streets filled with makeshift shops, which Diana called the Forum, and down a long, twisted staircase that deposited us in front of a pair of huge double doors. Some complex, mechanical rigging system was set up around them, and four guards stood at attention.

Nervously, I eyed the weapons slung around their necks. *Were they guns?* I'd never seen a gun, only heard about them in history class. They'd been outlawed since New Vegas was created.

"We're taking the newbies out," Diana said. "We'll be two hours, at most."

One of the guards nodded respectfully. "Yes, ma'am. Call if you need backup." He flushed as Diana gave him a disparaging look.

I'm guessing she doesn't usually have to call for backup.

Anticipation tingled in my veins as another of the guards pulled a lever on the wall. Slowly, the double doors began to open.

"When we're out in the city, you stay with me at all times," Diana said, her gaze not leaving the widening gap between the doors. "If we run into any problems, Cato and I will defend you. Just drop to the ground and stay out of trouble, and whatever you do, *don't* try to help." When we didn't reply, she snapped, "Got that?"

We each mumbled our assent.

As soon as the doors had opened wide enough for us to slip through, Diana set off at a brisk walk. I squeezed in front of Cayden, to his obvious annoyance, and followed her out into the open air.

I'd presumed the city would be as dark as the day I'd been dropped down here, but it was more like the dusky gloom between evening and night. It wasn't the bright daylight I craved, but at least I wouldn't have to worry about tripping over my own feet. We stood on the edge of a wide road lined by tall buildings. Glancing back, I saw the palace doors close. Green paint scrawled above them proclaimed the building to be Caesar's Palace.

"What is that?" Marissa whispered, pointing to a gigantic plinth stretching up into the thick layer of clouds.

"It must be part of the foundations of the towers," Cayden replied. "New Vegas was built on top of the old city, but I guess rather than demolishing what was here before, they just left it to deteriorate."

It was almost impossible to believe that somewhere, far above, were the towers of New Vegas. The construction looked featureless but there must be some way of getting up to the city above.

"Shush," Diana hissed.

Since stepping out of the safety of the palace, her posture had changed. She moved like Caesar's cat, her gaze constantly flicking around. Her bow was held at the ready, an arrow already nocked.

I wondered what she expected to encounter.

We set off up the street, keeping to the shadows of the buildings until Diana held up a hand. "We'll cross the road here. Just keep moving, calmly and slowly, to the other side."

I followed her into the street, my nerves getting more on edge with every minute that passed. The air felt thick and oppressive, and the farther we got from the shelter of the buildings, the more exposed I felt. Tension radiated off my companions, and I had to clench my jaw to prevent it from overwhelming me.

Just another ten paces and we'll be on the other side of the street.

Then the rat ran out.

It scurried toward us, its red eyes flashing, making a beeline right for my legs. A squeak escaped my lips. I clamped my hand over my mouth as Diana whirled around and glared at me. Behind me, Marissa let out a screech of terror, which was suddenly cut off. Glancing back, I saw Cato's arm wrapped around her neck, his large hand covering her mouth. When he whispered something into her ear, she nodded, and he released his grip.

The rat detoured away from us and scurried across the street. I shuddered. Those eyes freaked me out. Diana touched my arm and motioned for us to continue.

I hadn't gone two paces before a high-pitched keening cut through the silence like a saw screeching through metal. Instinctively, I pressed my hands to my ears, trying to drown out the horrific noise.

"*Camazotz,*" Cato muttered.

Diana whipped her bow up, aiming at the sky. "Move!"

A shove from behind made me stumble forward. As Diana stood guard, Cato herded us toward the side of the street, his face pale in the dim light.

Then the creatures descended.

Their movements were a blur. It was only once Diana had loosed two arrows, forcing them to retreat and hover above us, that I could get any sense of what they were. One thing was certain. They were unlike anything I'd ever seen before.

Taut, leather wings spread from elongated, furry bodies. Oversized eyes, almost comically set on top of a small head, seemed to glow in the dark. Two short, clawed arms were tucked up under their bodies in front of a pair of long, powerful legs that ended in fearsome-looking claws. Their wingspan was perhaps fifteen feet, and I dreaded to think what damage their claws could do.

"Vesper, come on," Cato whispered urgently.

I backed away, but at that moment, one of the creatures let out a screech and all three dove straight for Diana.

Cato cursed and shoved me behind him. Diana loosed another arrow. One of the winged creatures tumbled from the sky, landing with a thump onto the street. A second was thrown back against a building on the other side of the street, as if an invisible fist had punched it in mid-air. It keened again and flew off, disappearing into the darkness.

I guess that makes Cato a telky, like Cayden.

The third beast tightened its wings against its body and plummeted toward Diana, who made no move to run. My heart jumped into my throat as it slammed into her, then lay motionless.

A few seconds later, one wing lifted and Diana crawled out, a bloody blade in her hand. She wiped her knife on the creature's fur and stalked over to the second beast to retrieve her arrow.

"Nice work," Cato murmured as she returned to us. "You'll be needing to visit the tattooist again."

Diana ignored him. "Let's go. And stay close to me."

I fell in behind her, Caesar's warning about the city outside the palace suddenly feeling very real indeed.

And you thought you could survive out here by yourself.

Home suddenly felt a very long way away.

14

An Unexpected Discovery

I F I'D THOUGHT CAESAR'S Palace was weird, out here in the city, things were downright bizarre. After the attack by the strange winged beasts, Diana ushered us through a battered metal door set into a single-story building. Judging from the cracks in the crumbling concrete and the way Cato had to kick the door three times to get it to sit back in the crooked frame, I wasn't convinced we were much safer in here.

"What were those things?" Marissa asked Cato.

"*Camazotz*," he replied in a low voice. "They feed on anything they can get, but they like human best."

Marissa made a choked noise. When I glanced at her, her face was white.

At first, I'd thought the building was empty, but as we ventured farther in, I heard the sounds of scurrying footsteps, the clatter of metal, and low voices.

"What is this place?" I asked Diana.

"Market Street," she replied, not turning to look at me. Her bow was now strapped to her back, her staff in one hand. "Kind of like the city equivalent of the Forum. We don't often come out here, but Caesar needs something from one of the traders. Don't let anyone talk to you and *don't* wander off."

She yanked open another door. I gasped.

It was like something out of a history book. Candles wedged in sconces on the walls illuminated a winding, dirty street lined with grubby storefronts. Makeshift stalls and carts were scattered about, laden with animal skins, bubbling stew pots, and a cornucopia of battered weaponry. I felt as if I'd walked through a time portal to some medieval European city.

I scrunched up my nose. It smelled pretty medieval, too.

Hunched figures in ragged clothing stopped their conversations to stare as Diana led us down the center of the street. The flickering candlelight reflected off beady eyes and the glint of metal. The hairs on my neck prickled, and I was so on edge, I nearly jumped out of my skin when Cayden tripped and bumped into me.

"Did they not teach you to walk properly in the Royal Palace?" I hissed.

"Shut up," Cayden muttered in a low voice.

Diana shot us a look over her shoulder that clearly stated if we didn't shut our mouths, we'd be in a world of trouble when we got back to Caesar's.

I wondered how much farther we had to go. I already looked forward to getting back to the relative safety of Caesar's Palace. Then something caught my eye. Momentarily illuminated in an electric light hanging over a store entrance, a pair of dark eyes stared at me from underneath a tuft of scruffy, dark hair.

Elan.

My heart skipped a beat, though I wasn't sure if it was from anger or something else.

"Vesper, where are you going?" Cayden's hand on my arm jerked me to a halt. I looked around and saw Diana and Cato both glaring at me.

No wandering off, I reminded myself.

I fell back in line and glanced over at the store entrance again. Empty.

Dammit. My one chance to collar the sneaky jerk and he'd disappeared. Not that I was exactly sure what I was going to do if I did get hold of him, other than chew him out for leaving us at the mercy of Bobo and his slavers. Caesar's brand burned on my arm as a reminder of what Elan could have prevented.

Noooo!

A deafening scream rang in my ears, making me wince. It was followed by a heart-wrenching moan of pain and despair, as if the person were slowly having their toenails extracted, one at a time.

My feet moved before I had time to think. I sprinted down the street, dimly aware of Diana cursing behind me. I turned into a dark alleyway, barreling through a group of men who seemed as surprised by my presence as I was by theirs.

Why isn't anyone else responding?

From the shrieks of terror bouncing around my skull, someone was being tortured. Surely even Diana couldn't ignore this.

I rounded another corner and slowed as realization dawned. The shrieks, which had reduced to a whimper, *were* in my head. Literally. That was why no one else had responded to them. They couldn't hear them.

I let out a curse and stopped, looking around at the small courtyard I found myself in. It was lit by a single candle on either side of an arched doorway. A sign above the arch read *Antiques and Curiosities.* A second door on the opposite wall had a padlock around the handle and looked disused. Above me, sheets hung from a pair of washing lines strung between windows.

A heavy curtain hung down across the arched doorway, but a small, curved window on the wall next to it indicated there was a light inside. Somehow, I knew the person wailing in my head was inside this shop. The voice had silenced since I'd gotten here. I wasn't sure if that were a good thing, but it made it easier to think.

Stepping closer to the curtain, I listened for any sign of torturers, injured people, or weird monsters. It only struck me then that perhaps the reason the voice was no longer in my head was because the person had died. Was I going to walk into the shop to be faced with a dead body and a killer?

I bit my lip and closed my eyes. In my first, unsuccessful lesson with Marcus, we hadn't even talked about trying to communicate with someone else's mind. But I guessed it was theoretically possible. I was a mind-talker, after all.

It was hard to calm my mind but after a minute, my breathing steadied, and I reached for the well of power inside me. Then, I felt someone else inside my head.

You came!

What the . . .

My power burst to life and I pushed against the voice—the person—in my head. Tendrils of energy burst through the thin membrane of the shield Marcus had wanted me to strengthen. My knees went weak and a wave of dizziness washed over me as I remembered his warning about getting too drawn into my power.

I yanked myself away and snapped open my eyes, leaning back against the doorway so I wouldn't collapse to the ground. My heart raced, as if Diana had just made me do three laps of the arena. A copper taste filled my mouth.

What the hell was that? the voice asked. *What kind of crazy idiot are you? Trying to get every 'path in the city down on us?*

I groaned inwardly. It was a guy. Of course it was. Only a man would be pissed at a woman coming to rescue him.

My worries about finding a body disappeared. He sounded very much alive and not at all in pain.

Are you the person who was screaming? I thought.

Silence greeted my question. I wondered if I was supposed to push the question out using my power, but before I could try it, the voice spoke. *Yes.* There was a pause. *Sorry. I just sensed you out there and thought that maybe if you thought I was in pain, you'd come find me.* I felt a flash of jubilation. *And it worked!*

You mean you weren't being tortured? I asked. What sort of con was this?

Not today. The voice sounded affronted. *But I have been tortured many times over the years.*

I got the feeling the man wasn't being quite truthful with me. *Who are you?*

Another hesitation. *Why don't you come inside? The master's out back at the moment.*

Cautiously, I pulled back the curtain and stepped into the shop. It was a chaotic jumble of ancient objects, most of which looked as if they'd seen better days. Or better centuries. Shelves were stacked high with books. I ran my finger over one, marveling at the feel of the paper. Paper books in New Vegas were typically confined to museums or kept as antiquities by rich upper-levelers. I'd only ever seen them in glass cabinets and had never touched one before. They smelled musty but oddly comforting. Along the far wall was a set of what seemed to be some kind of gaming machines, the screens dark and cracked. Dust covered everything, and an electric light hanging from the ceiling near the window cast the back part of the store into shadow.

Back here, the voice in my head hissed.

I felt a slight pull from one of the dark aisles. Carefully, I walked down it, stepping over a pile of books, which seemed to have taken a nosedive from one of the upper shelves, and squeezing around what appeared to be a metal bathtub. I wondered if the shopkeeper ever sold any of this stuff or if he'd just been hoarding it for decades.

At the end of the aisle, I peered into the inky blackness. Against the wall was a large birdcage perched on top of a low table, a chest of drawers, and two huge mirrors in gilded frames. There was no sign of a person.

Hello? I thought cautiously.

Over here.

The tugging seemed to come from the birdcage. I frowned and took a step closer, then jumped back when something moved inside.

A flash of bright light cut through the darkness, landing on the cage. I gasped.

"Can I help you with something, miss?"

I turned and squinted at the man holding the light. "Um, I . . ." I looked back at the cage. "Is that a . . ." My voice trailed off. It felt stupid to even voice the thought.

Inside the cage, a pale creature with a long neck and wings cocked its head to one side.

"A dragon? Yes, miss."

The dragon ducked its head. *Nice to meet you, Vesper.*

I stared at it. *You're the one talking to me? The one that screamed?*

The pale head bobbed again. I took a step toward it.

"I'd stay back, miss." The shopkeeper sounded alarmed. "He's a nasty bugger. Get too close and he bites." He held up a bandaged hand as evidence, fresh blood leaking through the dirty cloth.

I'd thought dragons were supposed to be big creatures, but this one was no bigger than a small monkey. It looked pathetic, curled up in the cage.

I may be small, but that doesn't mean I'm helpless, the dragon said haughtily.

I ground my teeth together. *Stop reading my mind.*

Stop projecting your thoughts.

I closed my eyes, counted to five, then opened them again. Nope, nothing had changed. I was still in a dark back-alley shop with what appeared to be a tiny dragon with an attitude problem and a grumpy shopkeeper who made me increasingly uncomfortable.

"Are you wanting to buy him?" The shopkeeper sounded eager. Too eager.

Yes!

"No," I said quickly. "I don't have any money."

The dragon groaned. *Come on. You must have something. Please. I can help you. I'm the last surviving dragon. That's got to count for something?*

How do you know you're the last dragon?

The pale creature made a jerky movement that looked very much like a shrug. *I've never heard of any others. I've always been alone.* There was so much self-pity in the words that a wave of empathy washed over me.

I wondered what Sol would think of the situation and couldn't help but smile. He'd beg me to buy the dragon. Even the sight of it would send him into raptures. I couldn't wait to see his face when I told him.

My face fell. Except I'd never be able to tell him, would I? He thought I was dead.

My eyes welled with tears as memories of my family and my life as it could have been threatened to overwhelm me. I turned my head away and stared down the aisle of books, blinking rapidly.

Vesper? What's wrong?

The dragon's words were laced with concern. My body suddenly flooded with warmth, as if my mother had wrapped her arms around me and pulled me into a tight, comforting hug. I eyed the creature warily. His faceted eyes twinkled at me in the gloom.

"How long have you had him?" I asked the shopkeeper.

"Forty years. Maybe a few more." The man shrugged. "He was one of the first things I bought, back when I was a dumb kid. Thought I'd gotten myself a bargain. Little did I know."

Forty years? You've been in that cage forty years?

The dragon snorted. *Feels like longer.*

That did it. No creature deserved to be locked up in a cramped cage for decades. Besides, I'd heard stories about dragons, and having one on my side could only improve my situation. Though, admittedly, I had pictured them as giant fire-breathing monsters, not a skinny lizard the size of a small cat.

I told you, size isn't everything, the dragon huffed.

I turned to the shopkeeper. "Do you take credit?"

He scowled, his thick eyebrows meeting in the middle. "Cash only."

I unwrapped the bandage from my arm to show him the swollen brand on my skin. "Not even Caesar's credit?"

The shopkeeper's eyebrows shot up. "Well now, that's a different story. I'm sure if you're on Caesar's business, we can come to an agreement." He looked me up and down. "Thirty thousand."

"Thirty thousand what?"

"Dollars, of course."

Too much! Not that I'm not worth it, of course, but he wants to get rid of me. Offer him a thousand.

"A thousand," I said tentatively.

The shopkeeper threw back his head and laughed. "Now you're just wasting my time. If you're not going to make me a decent offer, you can get out."

"You said yourself you've had him forty years. Seems to me you haven't got a queue of buyers waiting to hand over their cash." I folded my arms. "Two thousand."

"Well, given you're a pretty girl and one of Caesar's, I'm willing to compromise." The man held out his hand. "Twenty thousand, and that's a bargain."

He'll go lower than that.

"Five."

The shopkeeper scowled again. "Fifteen."

"Six." I had no idea what six thousand dollars was worth around here. I tried to remember how much we'd been sold for in the Colosseum, but my mind was blank.

"Thirteen thousand. That is my final offer," the shopkeeper said. "Take it or leave it."

What do you think? I asked.

There was a momentary pause. *Try and get him down to ten. He hasn't had a sale in months, and ten thousand dollars is worth more than half the shop's stock.*

I appeared to consider the man's offer, then shrugged. "I'm only authorized to pay up to eight thousand," I said. "Sorry, but if you're not prepared to settle for that, I'll have to go back to Caesar and tell him you weren't willing to be reasonable." I got halfway up the aisle before the man's voice called me back.

"Fine. Eight thousand."

He spat on his hand and held it out expectantly. Grimacing, I spat on my own and shook it. The man pulled out a battered tablet and tapped the screen. I pressed my thumb where he told me to, then he scanned the brand on my arm. Finally, he unlocked the birdcage and stepped back.

"Vicious beast is all yours," he said with a grin and scurried into the back room.

I'm freeeeee!

There was a rush of air and something caught in my hair, yanking it painfully. "Ow!"

Sorry. Just getting used to the wings again.

A weight landed on my shoulder and sharp claws dug through my thin t-shirt. I clenched my jaw. *Yeah, and you can stop that, too. I'm not some kind of clawing post.*

The claws retracted, though the grip was still uncomfortable. *That better?*

Kind of. Can't you just fly?

Not for long. I haven't had a chance to fly in years.

A pair of hard studs rubbed against my neck, followed by what felt like cold scales and hot breath. The dragon let out a slight grumbling noise.

Was that supposed to be a purr? I sighed. *What's your name anyway?*

I don't have one, the dragon admitted. *It's . . . complicated.* He shifted his weight from one foot to the other, making me wince. *What's the name of the most badass dragon you know?*

Well, up until ten minutes ago, I thought all dragons were extinct. Typhon was the last.

He must have been pretty badass then.

I chuckled, thinking of my brother's toy dragon. *I guess so.*

Great! I'll be Typhon then. But you can call me Ty.

I squeezed around the metal bathtub and slowly made my way back up the aisle toward the door of the shop, Ty bouncing excitedly on my shoulder.

We are going to have so much fun, Vesper!

His enthusiasm was infectious, and a bubble of hope grew inside me. Perhaps something would go right for a change. But as I pulled aside the curtain and walked out, I couldn't help wondering just how Caesar was going to react to the loss of eight thousand dollars.

15

Unintended Consequences

"**Y**OU MANAGED TO FREE him then?"

I froze as Elan stepped out from the shadows of the courtyard. Ty chirruped and glided over to his broad shoulder.

"Hey there, bud. Feeling better out of that cage?" Elan scratched behind a pair of small, rounded protrusions on the dragon's head.

Ty gave a low rumble of pleasure before returning to my shoulder.

"You know him?"

Elan wore the same faded t-shirt with the snake on it that he'd worn the day we'd been captured. It was just as tight as I remembered. I tried not to stare, while reminded myself that he was the jerk who'd left me locked up at the Colosseum.

Elan nodded. "Poor thing's been tortured by Eben for years. He doesn't like me in his shop, because he knows I don't have money, but I sneak in every now and then to bring that little one a piece of rat."

"He's decided his name is Ty," I told him.

"I know." His face softened into a smile that made my stomach wobble. "Thanks, Vesper. I guess you're not the wimpy, upper-city snob I thought."

And with that, he turned and limped from the courtyard.

Upper-city snob?

I ran after him, ignoring the flash of pain as Ty hung on, digging his claws into my shoulder. I grasped Elan's arm, stopping him. "Firstly, I'm a lower-leveler, not an upper-city snob."

Elan looked confused. "What's a lower-leveler?"

"It's— Never mind. What do you know about the foundations of the towers? Is there a way to get up to New Vegas?"

He pulled his arm from my grasp. "Why would you want to go? They'll only throw you back down here."

I bit my lip, wondering if he was right.

"I'm sorry, Vesper, but interfering with one of Caesar's slaves is more than my life's worth."

Anger flashed inside me, and my hands balled into fists. "I'm only a slave because *you* left me at Bobo's mercy. You could at least have let us out before you ran off. Do you know what they did to us in the Colosseum?"

He avoided my gaze. "I saw."

I blinked at him. He saw? That meant he turned up to watch. Presumably at some risk to himself, given how pissed off Bobo was to lose him. Why would he do that?

Elan sighed. "Look, I can't help any of you. This is just the way things are down here. If I get caught by Caesar, I won't be able to—" He broke off and whipped his head around. "I have to go."

Before I could stop him, he limped off into the dark at a surprising speed, leaving me alone again.

Not quite alone. Ty nuzzled my neck. *You'll never be alone with me.*

I wasn't convinced that was a good thing.

My thoughts were interrupted by the sound of running footsteps. A moment later, Diana rounded the corner and skidded to a halt in front of me. There was a long scratch on her cheek and a dark stain across the front of her jacket. In one hand, she wielded her staff. In the other, the dagger she'd used to stab the winged creature that had attacked us in the street.

Her eyes widened when she saw the dragon on my shoulder. "Where in ten hells did you get that?"

"Um, his name is Ty. He's a dragon."

"Really." She gave Ty a disparaging look. "Looks a bit weedy for a dragon. But I asked where you got him."

"Um, well, he was being tortured by a shopkeeper back there . . ." I jerked my thumb over my shoulder. "So I, um, released him."

Diana's eyes narrowed. "Released him or bought him?"

I quailed under her glare. "Bought him. The shopkeeper took credit . . ."

"I bet he did," Diana muttered. She glanced around. "How much?"

"Eight thousand dollars," I whispered.

Diana's eyes bulged. "*Eight thousand*?"

"Is that a lot?"

She grabbed my arm and pulled me forward. "That is a stupid question. You'd better have a good explanation for Caesar."

Is this a friend of yours? Want me to gouge her eyes out? Ty extended his wings and hissed.

Diana raised the tip of her knife, which was wet with blood, and pointed it at him. "Don't even think about it, runt," she said menacingly. "I've killed monsters that would swallow you for breakfast."

Ty shuffled closer to my neck. *Maybe I'll leave her for another day.*

I stifled a smile. *Probably best,* I told him as Diana dragged me down the street. *We'll only get ourselves in more trouble.*

It seemed as if we were in plenty already.

⚜

"You did *what*?" Caesar roared.

I glanced over at Cayden and Marissa, but both studiously ignored my gaze as they nursed their own, albeit minor, injuries. No one had spoken to me on the walk back to the Forum. When I'd heard Diana report to Caesar that, while trying to chase after me, they'd been attacked by a group of renegades with a *chupacabra*, whatever that was, I felt more than a little guilty. Cato was in the infirmary, and Diana said he'd be out of action for the next week.

It'll be worth it, Ty said, still sounding jubilant.

Give me one good reason why I shouldn't just take you back to the shopkeeper? I snapped.

He fell silent. I sensed a mixture of chagrin and fear oozing off him.

Caesar pushed himself out of his chair. "Do you know how much I paid to keep you out of Apollina's clutches? To give you the best training this city has to offer?"

I swallowed and looked down at the floor. A faint smell of antiseptic wafted from him.

"Ten thousand dollars. The highest price that has *ever* been paid for a slave." He stood in front of me, close enough to invade my personal space.

Behind him, Nimra growled, picking up on her master's anger.

I gritted my teeth but stood my ground.

"And now you have the audacity to spend another eight thousand dollars of my money on a reptilian runt you found in a back-alley curiosity shop?" His hand shot out. Before I could react, Ty dangled in mid-air.

Help! Ty's faceted eyes spun, his wings flapping feebly as he tried to pull away from Caesar's iron grip.

"H-He can be useful," I managed.

"Really? How?" Caesar gave the small dragon a shake. "Damn thing doesn't even look like he can breathe fire."

I can take away pain, Ty said quickly. *And heal a bit.*

Can you?

Despite having Caesar's fingers clamped around his neck, he managed to give me a disparaging look. *You can't feel that mark on your arm anymore, can you?*

To my surprise, he was right. The burning pain from the brand on my arm had faded to a dull ache.

"He's taken away the pain in my arm," I told Caesar. "That's got to be useful, right? Plus, he can fly."

"That's what I'm worried about," Caesar snapped. "What's to stop him from flying out of here? Not much of an investment if it disappears in five minutes. Though I guess we could come up with some kind of collar and chain to keep him tied up."

"No," I said quickly before Ty's enraged roar filled my head. I winced. *Can you keep it down a bit?* "He doesn't need to be tied up. He'll follow my orders."

I got a soft *harrumph* from Ty for that but ignored him.

"Why doesn't that entirely reassure me?" Caesar's black eyes bored into me.

I racked my brain, trying to think of something that would stop Caesar from throttling the dragon. Mind you, I wasn't exactly impressed that Ty had manipulated me into helping him.

While it was nice that my arm wasn't hurting, I wasn't convinced he wouldn't turn out to be more trouble than he was worth.

Marcus hurried forward. "Can you communicate with him telepathically, Vesper?"

I nodded.

Marcus turned excitedly to Caesar. "Think about what tactical advantage that could give us. An eye in the sky able to communicate with someone on the ground. No one else has that. It could win the Games for us."

Games? What Games?

Caesar flashed Marcus a hard look.

"Come on, Jules," Marcus wheedled. "It's not every day a dragon lands in your lap. I thought they'd died out decades ago."

"He says he's the last one," I said, hoping it would help. Ty's face was gradually turning a darker shade of gray, and though I knew nothing about dragon biology, it didn't look healthy.

I forced myself to look into Caesar's eyes. Two black pits to his even darker soul.

"Marcus tells me that you're reluctant to use your powers, Vesper."

I opened my mouth to speak, but his look silenced me.

"You can keep your runt on two conditions. One, you follow every instruction Marcus gives you down to the letter. You take part in any training exercise or fight Diana or I deem necessary. Secondly, you do not, *ever*, try to escape."

My blood ran cold. It was as if the man could read my mind.

Perhaps he can.

I tried to push that thought away.

"Do you agree?"

Ty gazed at me mournfully. I owed him nothing, yet I couldn't just let Caesar kill him.

Reluctantly, I nodded.

"If you do not keep your side of the bargain," Caesar continued, "I will feed the dragon to Nimra." His gaze flicked to Cayden and Marissa, then he lowered his voice so only I could hear. "And your friends will also suffer. That is a promise."

He let go of Ty's neck and the dragon plummeted down, barely managing to extend his wings in time to avoid slamming into the floor. Caesar turned and strode back to his sculpted chair.

"Dismissed!"

Ty feebly fluttered up to perch on my shoulder and wrapped his tail around my neck. His small body trembled.

Thank you, Vesper.

I reached up and tentatively patted his back. I expected to feel sharp scales, but it was more like running my fingers over a rippling metal coat. Cool to the touch, but with a hidden warmth underneath. I pulled my hand away as the reality of Caesar's bargain sank in.

You owe me. And don't think I'll forget how you manipulated me into helping you. Do that again and I'll feed you to Nimra myself.

For once, Ty had no reply.

That night, I lay in my narrow bed staring at the wall, unable to sleep, as Marissa's soft snores and Cayden's heavy breathing filled the room. Ty was curled up at my feet like a faithful puppy, though I sensed he wasn't asleep.

I had no doubt Caesar would keep his word if I broke my side of the bargain, and I cursed myself for being so stupid, so soft, as to give up everything for some pitiful creature just because he begged. Even when I was captured, when I fought in the Colosseum, when I was sold to Caesar and been branded with his mark, I still clung to the hope that somehow, I would find a way to escape this place and get home.

A tear trickled from the corner of my eye. It was quickly followed by another, then another. Loneliness clawed at my chest as the despair I'd tried so hard to keep at bay tore a ragged wound inside of me that was so deep and wide, I knew it could never be healed.

Vesper, what's wrong? Ty's voice was tentative. *Do you hurt again? I can help you heal.* When he rested his head on my foot, a wave of reassurance washed over me. But it wasn't enough. It would never be enough.

Don't you realize what you've done? I said, anger bursting through my tears. *You forced me to help you. Now any hope I had of escaping, of going home, has disappeared. In freeing you from your cage, I've only tightened the locks on my own.*

I pulled my feet away from him, embracing the despair that flooded over me at the loss of his touch and reassurance.

I'm sorry. I didn't realize what this would mean for you . . .

Ty sounded pained, and some dark part of me deep inside felt glad.

No, you didn't.

He fell silent. I stared blankly at the wall, unable to see anything in the pitch black of the room. My life as I'd known it was over. I would never see my family again and had just agreed to be a weapon in a tyrant's hand.

Things couldn't get much worse.

Yet, despite my words to Ty, I still held an ember of hope that somehow, I would find a way home. That tiny, glowing ball of hope was all I had to cling to, and I knew the day that ember finally died would be the day my life was truly no longer worth living.

16

Marcus

T HE DAYS OF MY new life dragged by monotonously. I spent the mornings training with Marcus, the afternoons trying to avoid Diana's whip, and the evenings learning about the other factions and the city from Cato. Although we were fed three bland but filling meals a day, my weight still dropped. When I ran my fingers down my chest, I felt my ribs poking through my skin.

Since the day Caesar had given his ultimatum, I'd sunk into a dark depression. I gave everything during my training sessions—Marcus and Diana couldn't fault me for trying—but the little free time I had was mostly spent curled up on my bed. At first, I whiled away the time daydreaming about my family and picturing myself back with them. Laughing at my father's stories about the latest mix-up at the farm or helping Sol with his reading. But after a few days, it became too painful to think about them. Instead, my thoughts turned to this new world I inhabited, and then, eventually, to nothing at all.

Cayden tried to engage me in conversation. He was still obsessed with the idea of escaping and had scoffed at Caesar's threat, saying I shouldn't let him wear me down. After I'd refused to talk to him about it for the third time, he gave up.

Hope could give you strength to keep going, but false hope would break you down, day after day, until you had shattered into such small pieces, you could never be remade.

I'd joined Cayden and Marissa on one of their trips around the Forum shops, but that was my one and only exploration of the palace. It wasn't just my lethargy and depression. It was the way people looked at me. When I walked through a crowd, people parted in front of me, avoiding eye contact and shrinking back so they didn't risk my arm brushing against theirs. They were afraid of me. Afraid of what I might do.

Ty did his best to cheer me up, but I pushed him away, too. Unlike Cayden, though, he didn't have anywhere else to go. Caesar hadn't followed through on his threat of chaining him up, but he'd made it clear that Ty was supposed to stick near me at all times. So he just curled up on my bed and gazed dolefully at me, his sadness magnifying my own. When I let him close enough, he'd soothe the pain from the bruises and muscle strains I'd picked up during my sessions with Diana, but though he could mask my physical pain, he wasn't able to touch the deeper hurt inside.

The Games lingered at the back of my mind, a distant gnawing threat that grew closer every day. All we knew was that it was some kind of contest between the factions and I was part of Caesar's plan to win. When I tried to ask Marcus and Diana about it, all they said was we'd learn more soon.

Three weeks into my training, Marcus announced that I'd made sufficient progress in building my mental shield and could move on to the next stage. "You'll still need to work on your shield," he told me. "Whenever you have a bit of spare time and energy, try to add another layer to it. You need your shield to be as strong as possible to protect you."

Protect me from what? I wanted to ask, but didn't.

At the start of our next session, Marcus asked me to sit on one of the long, stone loungers flanking what had once been the bathing pool in the underground room we used for training. To my surprise, he called Ty over from the corner where the dragon usually spent my lessons. Ty settled on my lap and let out a low, rumbling sound that was his equivalent of a purr. His concern and reassurance seeped into me.

"I know you aren't happy, Vesper," said Marcus quietly. "Would you like to talk about it?" He reached out for my hand, but I pulled back.

"What's there to talk about? Unless you can send me home, back to my family, there's nothing you can do to help."

Marcus sighed. "You know I can't do that."

"Then leave me alone," I snapped.

Silence fell between us. I wondered if I'd gone too far. *Would he report me to Caesar?* My hand strayed to Ty's back, and he twisted his neck to rub his head on my arm.

"In our first session together," Marcus said eventually, "you asked me what abilities I have. Do you still want to know?"

I glanced up at him in surprise. Curiosity battled with my gloomy reluctance to show an interest in anything. Curiosity won. "Yes."

"Like you, I actually have two abilities, though one is stronger than the other. That is usually the case. When I was tested at the Royal Academy, they only picked up on my strongest ability—blocking other people's powers."

I stared at him. "What do you mean?"

"They call us blockers. It's not quite as rare as telepathy, but I am the only person I know of with the talent who isn't part of the

Royal Academy." He gave a wry smile. "The Academy likes to keep control of blockers, more so than any other talent."

My chest tightened. "Why?"

"Blockers maintain the barrier between the city above and the city below." He frowned at my puzzled look. "Has Cato not taught you about the barrier yet?"

I shook my head. "The Peacekeepers who escorted me down here mentioned something about a barrier."

Marcus nodded. "It's difficult to describe. It's not a physical barrier in the way you'd think. More a layer of null power that separates the two cities. Its main purpose is to prevent the powers of any talented people down here from affecting New Vegas. Think of it like a blanket. You could be right up close to it, yet you wouldn't be able to influence anything on the other side."

"So it prevents anyone down here from attacking the city above?"

"That is correct. I think they presume that most of the people they throw down here die quickly, but they're not taking any chances. Any blocker they find during the testing process is immediately trained to help power the barrier. They are also used on the rare occasion a talented person is found in the city and has to be brought in for questioning, as blockers can both sense power in others and dampen or even prevent a person from using their talent."

I remembered the morning Marissa had been arrested and the puzzled look on her face when she'd thrown out her hands and nothing happened.

"Because of the nature of their power, the Academy fears rogue blockers most of all. That's why—"

"Wait. Why would the Academy fear them? They have control of all the talented people."

Marcus smiled at my impatience. Even Ty had straightened on my lap, his full attention focused on the gray-haired man in front of us. "Academy *members* are talented, Vesper, but the leadership is not. As for fearing them, well . . . That is just my hypothesis. But why else would they throw anyone who shows the slightest hint of questioning their harsh rules down here to die?" He leaned forward. "They keep the talented hidden from the general population because they're scared that if people found out what Academy members could really do, there'd be widespread rebellion. Equally, they're terrified of Academy members. Think about what could happen if all the talented rebelled against the government and the king. Who could stop them? No one. So, instead, they're given all the luxuries and money they could want in exchange for handing their lives over to the society."

It took a moment for his words to sink in. I'd never thought about the Academy like that. I'd longed for the luxuries and status of being an Academy trainee, but from what Marcus said, it sounded like some kind of underhand bribe. "Do they know?"

"I'm sure some Academy members have thought about it. But when you have everything you want, why would you choose to give that up? Besides, there's so much brainwashing that goes on up there, they probably believe the trumped-up lies they're told about being the saviors of society." Marcus's voice carried a bitter note.

"And Layla is one of them," I whispered.

"Layla?"

"My sister. She's a Guardian. I don't know what . . . power she has, though."

And Fergus, kind, cheerful Fergus, who was so surprised to have qualified for the Academy. Is he now wielding fire or throwing people around?

"If she's a Guardian, most likely she's a blocker or mind-talker. Telkies and leccies are the most common talents. Depending on their aptitude, they may join the Peacekeepers or become Technicians. The majority of talents who go through the Academy become Technicians. They keep New Vegas running. Wind weavers make sure the turbines don't stop, leccies support the electricity grid, burners provide heat for forges and other manufacturing. We end up with quite a few burners down here. Perhaps their fiery nature makes them more likely to rebel." Marcus allowed himself a small chuckle.

"So Layla would be responsible for this barrier?"

"If she's a blocker. If she's a mind-talker, like you, then most likely, she's involved with the justice department."

Finding and sentencing criminals. I couldn't imagine my kind, gentle sister being responsible for banishing people to the Shadow City. But she had been in the transporter pod with Cayden. She had let Marissa get arrested, had stood by while I was dragged to my own pod. Perhaps I didn't really know my sister at all.

"The propensity to have powers is thought to have a genetic link, but there seems to be no correlation between the type of power displayed in different members of the family," Marcus said. "In case you were wondering."

I wriggled on my seat, feeling my butt going numb on the hard surface. "So why did you get chucked out?"

"I didn't. I passed the entrance tests with flying colors. Even if I hadn't, the Academy never releases blockers down here. If I had failed the test, I would have been locked away in a dark cell somewhere to live out the rest of my days or rethink my allegiance." Marcus clasped his hands in front of him. "No. I became an Academy member, went through my training, and was assigned a job powering the barrier. I had a good life and was happy, until my secondary talent changed things."

His face darkened momentarily. "In addition to being a blocker, I also have limited seeing powers. At first, I didn't know it was a talent. I just thought I was having strange dreams. But as some of the dreams began to come true, I realized there was something different about me." He shook his head. "No one else I knew had more than one power. Perhaps if it had been picked up at the start, I would have been trained on how to properly make sense of the visions, but I was scared at what my dreams showed me, so I didn't confide in anyone."

Marcus paused and fingered a plain, metal ring on his right hand. "The thing about visions is that they only tell you one possible future. The real talent in being a seer is to be able to determine where your vision lies along the spectrum of probability and how it evolves from the millions of actions people choose every day. I didn't realize that at the time."

He took the ring from his finger and handed it to me. I held it up to the dim candlelight and caught sight of an inscription inside.

Love you always. Cleo.

"Was Cleo your wife?"

"Husband. Or, rather, fiancé." He smiled at my embarrassment. "I met him on my first day at the Academy, and we were inseparable. We had just gotten engaged when I had the vision. I remember waking up, sweating, and staring down at him, scarcely able to believe he was still there. I . . . I dreamed he was killed in a raid by the Academy. It terrified me so much, I tried to put safeguards in place so that what I'd seen could never come to pass." He smiled sadly. "But in doing so, I triggered the very chain of events that led to his death."

He held out his hand. I handed him back the ring. "I'm sorry."

Marcus pushed the ring back onto his finger. "Thank you. In the confusion, I managed to steal a pod." His tone turned bitter. "Perhaps I should have stayed and fought them, tried to avenge his death, but I was too much of a coward. So I came down here to die. After all, without Cleo, what did I have to live for?"

"But you survived."

"Yes. And I am happy, in a different way." He reached out and squeezed my hand. "And you will be, too, Vesper, even if it doesn't feel like it right now."

I knew he was trying to be kind, but his words didn't make me feel any better. I didn't think I could ever be happy as a slave. "I don't know how you can stand to be at his beck and call all the time."

"I wouldn't exactly call it that. I am not Jules's slave, and though I carry the Caesar brand, it was my choice to take it." He paused. "Many slaves earn their freedom, and although some leave the factions, others continue working for their leader on different terms. It's a strange kind of family, true, but it is a family."

My hand froze on Ty's back. "You can earn your freedom?" The ember of hope flared in my belly.

"It's possible, yes." Marcus smiled. "Now, shall we get on with the training session? I'd like to move on from shielding to projection. We know you can communicate with Ty telepathically when you're close to each other, but I want to see what your range is."

He stood and walked over to the door, beckoning me to follow. Ty jumped up to my shoulder and settled himself on the leather vest Marcus had found for me. Another thing to add to my tally of debt.

At the door, Marcus turned. "Ty, I'd like you to stay here. We'll walk away from the room and see how far we get before Vesper loses touch with you."

Ty looked disgruntled as he flew off my shoulder and perched on one of the steps. He began washing himself like a cat, his rough tongue grating on his scaled body as he studiously ignored us.

A smile tugged at the corner of my lips as we stepped out of the room. Marcus extracted a key from his pocket and locked the door. "For his safety," he said quickly.

We walked through the palace, stopping at various intervals to test if I was still able to communicate with Ty. It felt like we walked miles. Up and down stairs, through vast, empty rooms and long, dingy corridors. Eventually, Marcus threw up his hands in defeat.

"Well, you don't seem to have any limits. Within these boundaries anyway." His expression turned thoughtful. "I wonder if it's different if you're communicating with a person."

We returned to the training room, where Ty made a great show of sniffing my pockets for any sign of meat.

Huh. So much for rewarding me for my help, he said grumpily.

You can wait until lunch like the rest of us.

He huffed and curled up in my lap.

"I'm not an expert on mind-talkers," Marcus admitted, "but I've done what research I can into how your ability works based on what I know of the other mind-talkers in the city."

"How many are there?"

"The Sirens have three, we believe Bellagio has one, and there's at least one who is factionless."

"The guy who escaped from the slavers?"

Marcus nodded. "Yes."

I hesitated, then added, "He warned us about Caesar."

Marcus raised an eyebrow. "Really? Well, that's not really surprising." He smiled as I opened my mouth to ask why. "Let's get started, shall we? Now, as a mind-talker, you should have the ability to implant thoughts into the heads of non-telepaths and influence their actions. The ability to control other people's thoughts and actions depends on the strength of the mind-talker, how strong the other person's shield is, and whether they have any talent themselves. Compared to other talents, I believe it takes a lot of power to influence another person's mind enough to get them to do even a small action."

I remember how the veins on Elan's neck had stood out as he'd forced the slaver to unlock his cage and how the man had seemed to be in a trance, his eyes glazed over . . .

My stomach flipped, and I squeezed my eyes shut. But his eyes, brown with flecks of green, stared lifelessly back at me.

I killed him. Me.

A sharp pain pulled me back to the present. I stared down at the trickle of blood on my hand.

Sorry. Ty shifted uneasily on my lap. His pale snout had a red dot on the end. *You went all weird.*

"Are you all right, Vesper?" Frown lines creased Marcus's weathered skin.

"Y-Yes," I managed. "Sorry."

No wonder mind-talkers were feared. That explained why people looked at me warily and gave me space as I passed. It wasn't just what I did in the Colosseum. They were worried I'd control them. A shiver ran down my spine.

"Do I have to?"

Marcus gave me a sympathetic smile. "I'm afraid so. It could give us a key advantage in the Games."

"What *are* these Games?"

Marcus ignored me and placed his ring on the seat next to him. "I want you to try to get me to pick up the ring. I'll lower my shield gradually to let you in."

I chewed on my lip.

Marcus sighed. "What is it?

"What if I hurt you?"

He smiled reassuringly. "You won't. I wouldn't allow you to try this unless I was confident you had control."

"Okay." I took a deep breath. "Should I close my eyes?"

"It might help you focus."

As Marcus had taught me, I focused on my breathing until I was calm, then reached for the source of my power. Cracking open my shield, I let a tendril drift out. At that point, I got stuck.

I opened my eyes. "It's no good. I'm not sure what to do."

Marcus looked thoughtful. "Hmm. Maybe start by bringing the thought of what you want me to do together in your mind, then push it out toward me."

After half an hour, Marcus's ring still sat on the seat. I rubbed my temples, feeling the beginning of a headache. "I'm sorry. I was trying."

But were you trying hard enough? Really?

I pushed the thought away.

Marcus stood and stretched. "Well, it's about time we finished. We're due in Caesar's room in five minutes. I want you to practice reaching out to other people's minds. Not to intrude on their thoughts, but just to practice pushing your power out away from your body. I'll think about how we can best approach this."

I woke a sleepy Ty, who perched grumpily on my shoulder, then followed Marcus to the door.

"Marcus, what would happen if I did lose control of my power?"

My trainer paused, his hand on the door handle. "It would depend. At the moment, you are strong enough to kill. The more you use and develop your power, the stronger you will become." He turned to look at me. "The most dangerous thing that can happen with any talent is to hold too much power, then lose control when using it. Normally, a person blacks out before this happens—your body intervenes to save itself—but occasionally, an exceptionally strong talent takes on too much."

"What happens then?" I asked, part of me not wanting to know the answer.

"Their power consumes them and anyone in the immediate vicinity. That is not something you ever want to see happen."

Marcus opened the door and gestured for me to precede him.

I stopped in the doorway. "Have you seen it happen?"

"Only once," Marcus said. He suddenly looked old and fragile. "A long time ago. And I will never forget the sight."

17

The Games

C AESAR LOUNGED IN HIS chair, Nimra prowling around him, tail twitching. The creature seemed nervous around people, and I wasn't surprised that the crowd gathered in the room stayed well back. When I spotted Cayden and Marissa, I hurried over to join them as Marcus made his way to the front of the room. Diana had already taken her customary position behind Caesar's right shoulder, and I spotted Cato talking to a man and woman in the far corner. He nodded in acknowledgment and gave me a small smile. His companions eyed me curiously. Heat rose to my cheeks as I looked away.

"Do you know what this is about?" I asked.

"Diana wouldn't tell me anything," Marissa replied. "But you know what she's like."

"It must be something big," Cayden said. "I think this is pretty much all the talented people in the faction."

"Do you know anyone else?" I asked in surprise. I'd seen a few of the faces around the Forum, but I couldn't remember having spoken to anyone. There were about thirty people in total, pretty much an even mix of men and women. Some seemed not much older than us, but most were in their late twenties or thirties. Marcus was by far the oldest.

"Not all of us lock ourselves in our room every night." Cayden lowered his voice. "I've had drinks with a few of them to try and find out a bit more about this place and how we might be able to get out."

"What did you find out?"

He shot me a sour look. "I thought you weren't interested?"

I was about to reply when Caesar clapped his hands to draw everyone's attention. "Those who have been here a while will know what this is about." His eyes strayed to us. "For those of you who are new, I'll start with an explanation. As you know, food and water are in short supply down here. You get the best of what there is, but you have to earn your keep. Every year, the factions compete for control of the water wells. This year's Games will take place in exactly twenty-eight days."

I hadn't even thought about where our water came from. In New Vegas, water was endlessly recycled, but from what I'd seen, there was little technology on the city floor. A low murmur rippled around the room. Ty's tail swished across my neck, the sharp point scratching my skin.

Caesar frowned. "Bellagio has controlled the supply for the past three years, but he's getting cocky. He doesn't believe he can lose. With our new assets, we have the strength to win."

All eyes in the room turned to us. I pushed my shoulders back and stared defiantly at Caesar.

Assets, my ass. We're people.

On my shoulder, Ty let out a rumbling growl, but even I had to admit he didn't sound very threatening.

Maybe you need to grow some fangs, I suggested, eying Nimra. *Then you'd scare people.*

I already have pointy things, thank you very much. Ty's talons bit gently through my vest as a reminder.

"Based on last year's experiences, we'll be experimenting with some changes and the abilities Vesper, Marissa, and Cayden bring to the team." Caesar reached up behind him and languidly stroked Diana's arm. "As usual, my hunter will be in charge."

"First session is in the Colosseum at ten tomorrow morning," Diana announced, seemingly oblivious to Caesar's touch. "I expect to see all of you there."

Caesar swiveled his chair around, which I took as a sign that the briefing was at an end. We joined the line of people filing out of the room.

"But what *are* the Games?" Marissa asked as we headed for the dining room.

"I want to know what happened last year," I added darkly. Something about Caesar's tone of voice implied it hadn't gone well.

A tall, blonde woman walking in front of me turned, and I recognized her as the woman who'd been talking to Cato. She looked to be in her thirties and had a sharp, angular face. Her smile was bright, but fear lingered in her eyes.

"Would you like to come to lunch with us? We can fill you in on some of the details Caesar didn't bother to mention."

I glanced back at Diana, who was talking to Caesar.

"Oh, don't worry," the woman said, as if reading my mind. "You won't have any other training sessions today. Diana and Marcus will be meeting with Caesar all day."

"Are you sure?" I asked. It was the first time anyone other than Cayden, Marissa, and my tutors had voluntarily spoken to me.

"Positive." She grinned. "You might want to make the most of your time off. They may have treated you gently up until now, but tomorrow, the real training starts."

My heart sank. I'd just gotten to the point where I felt like I could almost complete one of Diana's sessions without thinking I would drop dead from exhaustion. If that was considered treating us gently, what would the real training entail?

We followed the blonde woman into the dining hall, grabbed bowls of stew from the servers, and headed over to a table where Cato and a red-headed man sat. The blonde woman sat next to the man and gave him an affectionate nudge.

"Move along. We got company."

Cato grinned at us as both he and the man shifted along the bench to make room. He introduced the woman as Thora and the man as Bren. From the way their hands casually brushed each other's on the table, I guessed they were a couple.

"What powers do you guys have?" Cayden asked.

Thora opened her hands and a spark of electricity danced between them. "I'm a leccy, like you, Marissa. Bren is a burner."

"One of the strongest in the city," Cato said.

"What do you mean *one* of the strongest?" Bren asked indignantly.

Thora gave him a light punch in the shoulder. "Come on, Cato. You know his ego is big enough as it is."

Their banter helped lighten the atmosphere. Cayden continued asking questions about how long they'd been here and what other powers people in the faction had. I guessed being a prince meant he was good at small talk.

Ty jumped onto the table and eyed my stew greedily. He preferred raw meat to cooked, but years of being half-starved and locked in a cage meant he wasn't fussy. I let him nab a floating chunk, then batted him away with my spoon.

I have to eat, too, you know.

He made a noise of disgust and sidled over to Marissa. She eyed him warily, but her lips twitched as he rested his snout on his front legs and gazed up at her forlornly.

I took a gulp of the tepid liquid. Tasted like rat again. "So what happens in the Games? And what happened last year?"

Immediately, the atmosphere soured. The smile dropped from Cato's face and he carefully placed his spoon onto the table. "We lost someone," he said shortly.

"A leccy?" I asked, remembering Marcus's comment about the lack of electricity in the palace.

"Yes."

Thora reached out and took Cato's hand. "She was very dear to us."

From the grief that ravaged Cato's face, the woman had been more than a friend to him. A sister perhaps? Or a lover? I looked down at my stew.

"What's the deal with these wells?" Cayden broke the awkward silence.

"They're the only reliable source of water down here," Bren said. "One is located in front of Bellagio's headquarters, the other out behind the Palazzo. Whoever has control of the wells can charge the other factions and the factionless for water. Water is, hands down, the most precious resource down here. We do our best to reuse it, but we don't have the technology New Vegas has."

"So whoever wins the Games controls the city?" Cayden asked.

Bren held up two fingers. "There are two winners. The top faction gets to pick which well they want, and whoever comes in second gets the other one. Theoretically, having two rival groups in charge of the water supply means they can't hold everyone else hostage and it helps to keep the price down."

I finished my stew and let the spoon clatter into the bowl. "So if Bellagio controls one well, who controls the other?"

"At last year's Games, the Ragazzi and the Venetians joined forces." Thora glanced at Cato. "Even so, they didn't win, but they agreed to jointly take on the second water supply at Wynn."

"But the truce didn't last. They've been fighting among themselves all year." Cato picked up the story. "It's been so dangerous to go near their well that most people have bought from Bellagio."

I tried to remember what Cato had taught me about the different factions in the city. "The Ragazzi and Venetians are run by a brother and sister, right?"

Thora nodded. "Venilia is in charge of the Venetians. She's a wind- and water-weaver. Nero rules the Ragazzi. He's a telky. Their headquarters used to be linked, but they fight like cats and dogs."

"And bring the rest of the city into their squabbles," Cato muttered darkly.

I thought back to the auction in the Colosseum and remembered the beautiful blonde-haired woman and man who'd born a remarkable resemblance to each other. "Nero must've been the man who bought Aidan."

Marissa nodded. "Shui went to Bellagio, and Daria to Apollina, head of the Sirens."

Out of the corner of my eye, I saw Ty grab a chunk of meat out of Marissa's bowl while she was distracted. He retreated back to me and swallowed it down in one gulp.

You shouldn't steal other people's food, I told him.

She wasn't watching, he replied smugly, licking one of his sharp talons.

"Do all factions compete at the Games?" Marissa asked.

Bren shook his head. "Most of the minor factions don't bother. They know they don't have the power or skill to win and just accept they'll have to pay for their water. It's usually only the five largest who compete: Sirens, Ragazzi, Venetians, Players, and us."

"Caesar's Gladiators," Cayden finished.

I gripped my bowl a little tighter. "So what do the Games actually consist of?"

"There's a tower in the middle of the arena with two flagpoles on top," Cato explained. "First team to raise their flag is the winner. Second place goes to the team that claims the second flagpole—if the winners let them."

Cayden frowned. "Why wouldn't they if they've already won?"

Cato and Thora exchanged a look. "People don't always play fair," Cato said. "The winner might try to negotiate extra benefits in exchange for allowing the team up. The Games is about strategy. That's why Bellagio does so well. He's a trickster. You wouldn't think he has the strongest team, but somehow, they always win."

"Why don't people just cheat?" I asked.

"They sometimes try," Cato admitted. "But if the Gamesmasters catch you, your team forfeits the contest."

"Years ago, the Games were agreed upon to settle the fight over water," Thora said quietly. "Before that, the factions constantly fought and many people, talented and non-talented, were killed."

"Is that why there aren't many talented people over the age of forty?" I asked.

Thora gave me a sharp glance. "Partly. Though the number of young people abandoned down here has increased over the years."

Interesting. So either the society are classing more people with powers as criminals, or there are more children emerging with powers.

"Diana thinks Apollina's going all out this year," Cato said, looking at Bren. "That's why she was trying to buy all the slaves at the auction."

Bren snorted. "She handicaps herself by focusing on the mind-talkers. Her Furies are a force to be reckoned with, but she doesn't have strength across the talents."

Thora looked thoughtful. "True. And I don't think she makes best use of the Furies. Bellagio only has one mind-talker to her three, but I'm sure Damon is part of the reason the Players have won the last three Games. Apollina's too impetuous. She needs to learn patience."

"She's always been impatient. Not like Diana," Bren muttered.

"Does Diana compete in the Games?" Marissa asked, looking from Bren to Thora. "She doesn't have powers, does she?"

Thora shook her head. "No, but she's the best damn fighter in the city, and even the Furies can't get into her mind. She's the only non-talented person who competes."

"So what's Diana's plan?" Cayden asked.

Cato blew out a breath. "We'll find out tomorrow." He smiled. "You've been training individually up until now, but the Games are all about teamwork. It's time to show us what you've got."

I looked down at the table, thinking of my training session with Marcus. I'd only just gotten my shield up to strength. I couldn't *do* anything useful yet. *They're going to realize soon enough that I'm a waste of space. Then what?*

Ty looked up at me, eyes whirring. *There are two of us, remember? I can fight, too!*

I stifled a smile. Ty's claws *were* pretty sharp, but despite his confidence, I couldn't see him lasting a minute against a telky with Cato's strength. The only way we would survive the Games would be if I could figure out how to use my powers. But the last time I used them against someone, that person died.

And I nearly died, too.

A shiver ran down my spine. I couldn't let that happen again.

⚘

I lay in bed that night listening to the grumbling noises Ty made while sleeping. I'd tossed and turned for hours, but there were too many thoughts spinning around my mind to allow me to sleep. Caesar had made it clear that my friends' safety was dependent on me learning to use my powers. But what if they'd overestimated my abilities and I wasn't able to do what they wanted? Even if I could figure it out, did they really expect me to hurt or kill other people for them? Caesar's soul seemed as cold and dark as his eyes, but Marcus . . . Marcus had only been nice.

You can't trust anyone down here.

Elan had been right. Trust was a luxury I couldn't afford anymore.

I sighed and closed my eyes, letting tendrils of sleep wrap around me. But just as I felt myself falling, in that dim moment between consciousness and unconsciousness, a thought hit me. My eyes flew open.

"Elan," I whispered.

Elan was a mind-talker. And he wasn't associated with any of the factions, which meant that, technically, he wasn't the enemy. Marcus had admitted he wasn't sure how to help me use my power, but Elan would know.

Whether he'd teach me was another matter. But perhaps if there was something in it for him . . .

Sleep fled my body. I rolled onto my back and closed my eyes, going through the breathing exercises Marcus had taught me to calm my mind and focus. Then I reached out.

After our first week sharing a room, Cayden, Marissa and I had each been granted the privacy of a small room in a corridor with some of the other talented members of the faction. I immediately sensed Cayden's and Marissa's minds in the rooms on either side of me. Their minds felt uniquely *them*. It was like recognizing somebody standing behind you from their scent or the way they moved. More intimate than seeing the person or even hearing them speak.

I let my mind wander and picked up traces of other people sleeping in the rooms around us. At one point, I sensed a familiar warmth, which I instantly knew to be Marcus. The farther I pushed outward, the more overwhelming the sheer number of people became. It was like being lost in a crowd. Part of me wanted to pull back so I could be alone again, but I knew I had to persevere.

As I explored further, I realized I could easily tell the difference between the mind of a talented person and that of someone without powers. They felt richer, more complex. Knowing this helped me focus on a much smaller subsection of people and the sense of being overwhelmed lessened.

With no concept of distance, I had no idea if the minds I sensed were still those of Caesar's people or if I had left the palace. The farther my mind roamed, the more my power felt stretched, like pulling an elastic thread. If I pushed too far, would it snap?

I gritted my teeth against the exhaustion that made my body tremble. If I could just hold out a little longer . . .

And then, just as I was about to give up, I sensed him.

A burst of excitement surged through me, and my power throbbed with new strength.

Elan? I pushed the thought along the thread connecting me to his mind. I felt a flash of surprise.

Vesper?

Relief flooded through me. *Yes. I—*

A wave of anger radiated out as Elan slammed his shields up. My eyes flew open and I tasted blood on my lip. Tiny claws dug into my chest.

Vesper? What happened?

I blinked. Ty's face swam into focus in front of me. For a moment, all I could concentrate on was my heart thumping in my chest.

Vesper?

When Ty dug his claws in deeper, I let out a moan.

That hurts!

That was my intention. Are you okay?

I looked pointedly at his feet. *I will be as soon as you stop impaling me.*

He relaxed his grip and came to curl up on my shoulder, his tail snaking around my neck. *What happened?*

I yawned, feeling exhaustion dragging me down. Marcus was right. Diana's workouts left my muscles aching, but using my power made my whole body weak.

Tell you tomorrow. Need to sleep.

As I fell into a deep sleep, a flood of disappointment washed over me. I may have found Elan, but he'd made it perfectly clear he didn't wish to talk to me.

18

Strategy and Skulls

AT FIVE TO TEN the next morning, I sat between Cayden and Marissa on the lowest tier of seating surrounding the Colosseum arena, waiting for the final few people to arrive. Diana stood in the center of the arena, staff in hand, clearly impatient to get started. From a few blocks down, Thora caught my eye and raised a hand in greeting. I waved back, forcing a smile onto my face.

I'd slept until nine, but despite the extra rest, I still felt completely exhausted. A dull ache filled my head, and even the double helping of breakfast the cook had given me hadn't flushed the nausea from my stomach. The last thing I felt like doing was training with Diana, particularly in front of all these people.

Curious, I reached out with my mind toward Diana. She didn't have the feel of a talented person, but neither did she have the emptiness of a person without powers. Instead, her mind was like a polished sphere—smooth and completely impenetrable.

Odd.

Diana's gaze turned to me, her lips tightened into a thin line of displeasure. I pulled back, wondering if she could sense my probing. Just then, a door slammed and a young, gangly man ran in to take his seat.

"About time," Diana snapped, causing the man to flush and mumble an apology. She slammed her staff onto the ground three times, and the chatter around us quieted.

My eyes strayed to the marks on her arms. I'd already seen her prowess at killing the monsters that seemed to inhabit the city, so the black arrows on her left arm didn't come as a surprise. But it was the skulls on her right arm that sent a chill tingling down my spine. She had said the skulls represented those she'd killed who had powers. Did the rest not matter? Or did she only kill those who were talented?

"You all heard what Caesar said yesterday," Diana said. "This year, we must win the Games. Bellagio cannot be allowed to rule the city for another year. He has too much power already."

"So now we give Caesar all the power?" Cayden muttered next to me.

Diana's sharp gaze landed on him. "Do you have something to contribute, *slave*?"

Cayden's body tensed, but I caught the warning look Marissa shot him as her hand brushed against his leg.

"No," Cayden mumbled, almost inaudibly.

"However, given that he *has* won for the past three years," Diana continued, "at least we have some information about his strategy. His tactics may have varied every year, but his approach is always the same. Cause confusion and chaos, separate the members of other factions and get them to fight each other while his team pushes for the tower." Diana began to pace the arena. "So our first job will be to try and corral the members of his team and surround them. Once we have dealt with the Players, we can go after the tower."

Bren stuck up his hand. "What about the other factions? Won't we just be giving them a chance to get to the tower first?"

Diana shook her head. "Not all of us will be dealing with the Players. A small team will take the flag to the tower, staying hidden as much as possible. Nero's and Venilia's teams will head straight for the tower. They always do. And it doesn't do them any favors."

"Seemed to work for them last year if they won," Marissa murmured.

"Quiet!" Diana whirled around to face us. Marissa cowered in her seat, her face red. "Apollina is likely to do the same, though she may wait for the Ragazzi and Venetians to finish fighting before moving in. If there is an opportunity to sneak into the tower, the team carrying the flag will take it. If not, they'll stay out of the fighting and let the other three factions battle among themselves. Then, once the main part of the team has dealt with the Players, they will descend on what's left of the other factions and help create an opportunity for the flag team to get up into the tower."

She made it sound so simple, but the thought of having so many people fighting each other with fire, electricity, water, and wind, not to mention the influence of the other mind-talkers, had my stomach in knots.

"As usual, we are only permitted to have twenty people in the Games. There are twenty-five of you here now, and I will make the final selection the week before the Games. For those of you who are slaves, competing in the Games advances your prospects of freedom. For those of you who are free men and women, Caesar will reward you for your part in helping safeguard the Gladiators' future."

Diana slammed her staff onto the ground. "*Coniuncti stamus.*"

"*Coniuncti stamus*," came the murmured reply.

Some looked almost bored by the speech, as if they'd heard it a hundred times and just wanted to get started. Others leaned forward in their seats, their eyes alight with pride. Everyone was marked by Caesar's brand. Everyone apart from Diana.

Why hadn't I noticed that before?

"Thora, Bren, Cayden and Vesper, you will be with me. Our job is to get the flag to the tower." Diana beckoned to us. Reluctantly, I pushed myself up out of my seat and stumbled down into the arena. Ty chittered anxiously on my shoulder. "Cato will lead the rest of you, who will be responsible for putting Bellagio's Players out of action."

Diana turned to me. "Vesper, your dragon will go with Cato."

"What?" Ty's claws almost pierced the leather patches on my shoulder, causing me to wince. I placed a reassuring hand on his back. "He stays with me."

"You two are the only way we can communicate between the groups," Diana said coldly. "The plan hinges on you being able to liaise telepathically. I presume the lizard is able to speak to people other than you?"

Ty hissed in response.

Diana seemed to take this as an affirmative. "Let's get started. You lot, come with me. Everyone else, stay here with Cato."

Cato walked over to join us, an apologetic smile on his face as I transferred a reluctant Ty onto his shoulder. "Sorry about this, Vesper. I'll look after him." He winced as Ty dug his claws into his unprotected shoulder.

Behave. I know you're not happy about this, but Cato is a good guy. Don't take it out on him.

But I'm supposed to protect you, Ty replied sulkily.

You are *helping to protect me by keeping the Players away. Didn't you hear what Diana said? You're the key to our plan working.*

Ty huffed in response, but I could tell his ego was soothed.

"You might want to get some leather shoulder patches," I told Cato. "His claws are pretty sharp."

Cato arched his eyebrow. "I noticed."

Once Diana had established that I could speak to Ty from anywhere in Caesar's Palace and that Ty could make himself heard to whomever he chose, we spent the rest of the training session sparring, one power against another. It was an impressive sight. Lumps of concrete exploded in mid-air as fireballs tore the ancient material apart. Electricity crackled and steam hissed as fire met water. A woman I hadn't seen before seemed to have vines wrapped around her arms. She threw them out, binding her opponent's arms and legs. Diana stalked between the combatants, barking orders. Whenever a person seemed to be winning their bout, she would jump in and attack them with her staff, so they'd have to fend off two assailants.

As I watched, I began to see the reasoning behind her interference. It wasn't just to even the odds, but to bring into play both physical and mental power. After all, just because we were fighting with our minds didn't mean we couldn't use our bodies, as well. If we ever got to the point where our powers were exhausted, we'd still have our hands and feet.

Cayden, Marissa and I were pitted against each other. Cayden and Marissa threw flames and sparks in a hesitant manner, each one obviously afraid of hurting the other. Diana had made it clear that my role was to shield the flag-carrying team by making our enemies believe they hadn't seen us, but although I was able to push against Cayden's and Marissa's shields, I couldn't seem to *do* anything.

"Oww!" Marissa squeaked as one of Cayden's fireballs caught her on the back of the hand. She scowled at me. "I can't do this with you in my head, Vesper."

Cayden sighed. "It's the same with me. It's hard to keep my shield up while also trying to fight."

"That's the point." Diana's voice came from behind us, and I flinched reflexively. "If you don't keep your shield up, you'll be vulnerable. If the Furies get into your head, they'll do more damage than Vesper."

Marissa paled. Her gaze flicked to me, then she exchanged a look with Cayden.

"It's not as if I can even get into your head," I mumbled, slumping down onto a chair and cradling my head in my hands.

Diana sighed. "Take a break, all of you. We'll reconvene here after lunch. Vesper, I suggest you find Marcus and continue training. Either you need to make a breakthrough soon or we have to hope Marcus was wrong about you." She spun around and stalked off.

Cayden squeezed my shoulder. "I'm sure you'll get there, Vesper. Marcus said that everyone progresses at different rates. Perhaps you just haven't found the key to using your power yet." He gave me a sympathetic smile that was almost unbearable.

"You coming to lunch?" Marissa asked. "Bet you could do with some food after that."

"You guys go ahead. I'll follow in a bit."

Was it my imagination, or did Marissa look just a tiny bit relieved? And the look they had exchanged . . . I knew the people in the Forum feared me, but my own friends?

A pang of loneliness shot through me. For everyone else, their shared abilities seemed to create a bond. But I was different. My power was a curse.

The chattering voices faded as people headed to lunch. Just when I thought I was alone, light footsteps approached.

Thora sat down beside me and placed a comforting hand on my arm. "Things not going to plan?"

The sympathy in her voice caused tears to spring to my eyes. I shook my head, not trusting myself to speak.

"You know, not everyone has an easy time learning to use their powers. Everyone's abilities are different, and it can sometimes take a while to figure out where your real strength lies. I remember when Bren first arrived. Marcus tried to get him to throw fireballs, but Bren just couldn't do it. Eventually, he realized his ability was to create sheets of flame, not small fireballs. Once he figured that out, nothing held him back."

I heard the smile in her voice.

She gave my arm a squeeze, then withdrew her hand. "We all saw what you did in the Colosseum. You have the power. You just have to figure out how to use it."

I balled my hands. "But I don't *want* to use it that way. Not to . . . to kill people."

"That was an extreme situation. You didn't know what you could do then. Training will help you learn to harness and control your power."

Guilt coated my tongue with iron. The only good thing about training myself into exhaustion was that sometimes when I went to bed, I could fall asleep without the slaver's eyes staring accusingly at me from behind my eyelids.

"No one wants to kill people, you know."

"Apart from Diana," I said bitterly.

Thora shot me a sideways glance. "Is that what you think?"

"Why else does she get every kill tattooed on her arm?"

Silence stretched between us.

"When Indra—Cato's girlfriend—died, no one took it harder than Diana," Thora said finally. "She disappeared for three days, and when she returned, she refused to talk to anyone about it. There was nothing she could have done, but she still blamed herself."

I looked at her in surprise.

"The skulls on her arm . . . Did you ask her about them?"

"Yes," I said. "She said they were for all the people with powers she'd killed."

Thora shook her head. "Not killed, Vesper. They're for all the people who've died on her watch. Thirteen in total. That's why she trains us so hard. She is the best fighter in the city, but she prides herself on winning without killing. Monsters are a different story, of course, but people . . . Well, it damn near kills her to lose someone."

I glanced down at my hands. I thought Diana had a heart of stone, that she took sadistic pleasure in running us into the ground. Perhaps I had misjudged her.

The scars remind me of the evil we must defeat and the price of ensuring our safety.

I'd assumed Diana had meant the people she had to kill. Not the people she'd failed to save.

"I killed someone once, you know," Thora said quietly. "In the Games."

She stared out across the Colosseum, her face as expressionless as the carved marble busts in Caesar's room.

"What happened?"

"It was my first Games. He was one of Venilia's pretty boys." She snorted. "She always picks the attractive ones, you know. He attacked me, so I fought back." Her gaze flicked to me. "A little too hard."

"But that was the Games. He attacked you. You didn't have a choice."

"Yes, I did. I . . . I lost control." A tear trickled from the corner of her eye, leaving a track through the shimmer of dust coating her pale cheek. "He was only a boy."

We sat in silence for a moment. "Does the guilt ever go away?" I whispered.

Thora straightened and wiped the tear from her cheek. "No, but you can learn to look at it differently. As a mistake to be learned from. After it happened, I worked night and day until I could control my power precisely. I made sure I would never be in a situation where I lost control again." She gave me a wan smile. "I don't know if that helps at all."

"A little." I returned the smile. Her words may not have eased the guilt that still lingered in my belly, but at least I didn't feel quite so alone. And if Thora had learned to control her power, I could, too.

Thora stood and held out her hand. "Come on. Let's go get some food before those scavengers eat it all."

I took her hand and stood, feeling stronger than I had all morning. "Thanks, Thora."

"You're part of the family now, Vesper. We're an odd, dysfunctional kind of family, to be sure, but family all the same."

I couldn't tell her what else was troubling me. Marcus's comments about what happened when a talented person lost control of their powers had kept me awake half the night.

Thora thought I was only afraid of what my power could do to others.

But I was also afraid of what it could do to me.

19

Training

I SPENT THE AFTERNOON with Marcus, trying, and failing, to make him pick up a stone off the floor. He was patient and kind, but I could tell he was getting frustrated with my lack of progress.

"You have the strength, Vesper. I can feel it inside you." He ran his fingers through his thinning hair and sighed. "I just wish I knew how to help you."

I hesitated, unsure whether to confide in him about my idea of trying to get Elan to help. But Thora's words had inspired a new hope within me. If I needed to learn to do what Elan could do, perhaps he was the only person who could teach me.

To my surprise, Marcus's eyes lit up. "I hadn't even considered that," he mused. "Do you think you'll be able to persuade him to help you?"

"I don't know," I admitted. "I'm not sure I'm his favorite person right now."

Understatement of the century.

Marcus pursed his lips. "I don't know much about the boy, other than he's very good at keeping away from the factions. But if he's factionless, he must struggle to afford food and water."

"Unless he persuades people to give them to him?"

"That might work on the factionless, but not on the talented, and it's the talented who control the water supply."

"Perhaps I could offer to pay him. But I don't want Caesar to know. Elan . . ." I hesitated.

Marcus raised a brow. "Yes?"

"I don't want to get Elan in trouble." I bit my lip.

Marcus's face softened. "I understand. Well, I have some money of my own and am happy for you to use it if you think it will help. But you can't leave the palace on your own. It's not safe. You'll have to communicate with him telepathically."

Now, as I lay on my back in bed, I couldn't help feeling that the confidence I had about Elan helping was misplaced. If he wouldn't even talk to me, what hope did I have of persuading him to teach me?

Can I help? Ty asked.

I don't think so. I just have to hope he lets me in.

Ty's eyes glowed brightly in the dark. *Elan is a good person.*

I didn't reply, but I had my doubts. A good person wouldn't have left us caged up at the slaver's mercy when he could have released us.

I closed my eyes and reached out with my mind. I found I remembered how far away he'd been the last time I'd made contact. It wasn't a physical distance I could measure. More a sensation of knowing how much power I needed to reach him.

When I sensed Elan's mind, I hung back for a moment, trying to figure out how to approach him.

Elan? I sent the thought spinning along a thread of power, trying to put as much warmth and openness into it as I could. *Can we talk?*

Immediately, I felt his shield slam up. Despair washed over me, leaking down the line connecting us.

Please?

What do you want? He sounded cautious and more than a little grumpy.

I need your help. I . . . I don't know how to use my power. No one here can teach me, and I don't know . . . I hesitated, knowing my desperation must be clear to him, yet not wanting to beg. Talking in this way made me feel open and vulnerable, as if he could see right inside me. *I don't know what will happen if I can't control it.*

And you think I can help you?

There are no other mind-talkers here. You know how to control your power. I thought maybe you could teach me.

Amusement rippled out from him. *And why would I give away my secrets to one of Caesar's slaves?*

I'm not a slave. At least I don't want to be. I want to get out of here eventually, but unless I can control my power, I've got no hope of winning my freedom. Please, Elan. I can pay you . . .

You're a slave. What are you planning to pay me with? Your body?

Heat and anger coursed through me. *I have money,* I said tightly. *It doesn't matter how I got it. I can pay. I'm pretty sure you could do with some extra cash.*

Another pause. I held my breath, wondering if I'd gone too far.

You have yourself a deal. But I want partial payment upfront. Once I get that, we can figure out how your mind works.

He gave me a convoluted description about where to stash the money, then abruptly cut the connection between us. I withdrew back into my body and opened my eyes, staring up at the ceiling.

Finally, something was going right.

Are you going to speak to him? Ty hopped from one leg to the other like an overexcited puppy.

I slumped on my bed. *Maybe.*

I'd planted the money in the place Elan had described yesterday but had heard nothing since. Perhaps he was waiting for me to reach out to him, but I felt strangely reluctant to do so. I had still made no progress with Marcus and knew he was worried about how close we were to the Games. Plus, he'd given me a sizeable chunk of cash to bribe Elan into helping me.

I hoped I wasn't wrong trusting Elan to keep his word. What if he just took the money and disappeared?

He's not as bad as you think he is, Ty said, curling up in the crook of my arm as I settled myself in a comfortable position. *He's just a survivor. It makes him suspicious.*

Well, he'd better be able to help. We're paying him enough.

I caught a flash of surprise from the dragon, a split second before I felt the touch of another person on my mind. I froze, then relaxed as I realized it was Elan.

Vesper? Is now a good time to talk?

I sank back into my pillow, a thrill of excitement, or perhaps nerves, fluttering in my stomach. *Elan? Did you get your money?*

Yes. Thank you, he added, almost as an afterthought.

Well, I hope you buy something nice with it.

Immediately, I sensed a surge of irritation pulse down the connection between us. I cursed inwardly. Why had I said that? As if I didn't *want* him to like me. As if I wanted to push away that sense of warmth and reassurance I got when his mind and mine connected.

Sorry. I didn't—

Shall we get started? His mental voice was clipped and professional. He had the same accent as the kids I'd heard calling to each other as they ran through the Forum shops. The kids who, like Elan, were born and raised down here.

Yes, let's. I explained what Marcus had been trying to get me to do and our lack of success. *Everyone else can use their powers. I don't know why I can't!*

My final words were almost a wail as frustration and shame at my inability to use my supposed talent welled up inside me. I tried to push my emotions down, aware that they might be leaking out.

Hey, calm down, Elan soothed. *We'll find a solution. I know it's . . . it's hard being different.*

How did you learn to use your ability?

There was a slight pause, like a mental shrug. *Mostly by trial and error. My parents helped with the basics, but my power was different to theirs. I've been practicing since I was eight, though, so I've had time to get used to it.*

Eight? So young. I thought about what I was doing when I was eight. Running around with my friends and playing with dolls, I guessed. Not learning how to manage a terrifying, dangerous ability.

Dad said that kids in the Shadow City tend to get their powers earlier than you lot. Something to do with it being more dangerous down here, Elan said, answering my unspoken question.

That made sense. A shiver ran through me. Ty shifted against my arm, and I sensed him projecting calmness.

I'm sorry.

About what?

That you had to grow up down here.

Again, that mental shrug. *I've not known anything different.*

He was holding back something. Curiosity perhaps? Was that why he had agreed to help me?

Okay. So, from the sound of it, you've been trying to get inside someone's mind and influence their thoughts directly, like you did in the Colosseum.

The reminder of that day made me feel sick. But he was right. I had blasted my way into the slaver's mind to get him to stop choking me.

I nodded, then realized Elan couldn't see me. *Yes.*

That's what you're doing wrong. For it to work, they must not be able to sense you in their mind. It's like if you tell someone you're going to punch them. You've lost the element of surprise, so they can just dodge the blow.

That makes sense. But how do I get into their mind without them knowing?

Well, firstly, it'd help if they didn't know you were trying. So practice outside training time, when they're not expecting it.

I pursed my lips, remembering the fear on Cayden's and Marissa's faces. That didn't sound very ethical, and it definitely wouldn't help people trust me.

Then, when you're trying to get inside their mind, don't push against their shield. If you do that, they'll sense your intrusion and immediately become defensive. You have to find a weakness and ease your way in. Elan paused. *The stronger their shield is, the harder it'll be, but very few people can keep their shield strong all the time. With non-talented people, it's much easier, as their natural shield tends to be weak and they're less likely to be able to sense you.*

Okay, so once I've gotten into their mind, what then?

I wondered if I should speak to Marcus about practicing on some of the non-talented faction members. But they would have no defenses against my power, and the thought of hurting them if something went wrong made my whole body tense.

Then you plant the idea of what you want them to do. It's best to stay at the very edge of their mind, so you don't get drawn into their thoughts.

I gulped. *What happens if I get drawn in?*

You might panic and lose control, which would be very bad. You need them to think the idea you're planting is their own. That's the hard part. Elan paused. I sensed a mixture of pride and caution emanate from him. *It takes a lot of effort. You saw how exhausted I was when I got the slaver to free me. But you . . .*

Yes? I asked when he didn't continue.

You're powerful, Vesper. But power alone isn't enough. You need to develop the skill to be able to get into their thoughts without hurting the person—or yourself.

So I had to creep into a person's mind, not get drawn into their thoughts, then somehow persuade them to do something and make them think it was their idea. All while knowing that if I lost control of my power for even a second, I could scramble their brain.

How could it be so easy to kill?

I can't do this.

You just have to trust yourself, Elan said quietly. *You didn't know what you were doing in the Colosseum. Now, you do.*

I remembered when I first met Elan. He'd been just a voice in the dark. *That first day you found me, you said I'd screamed loud enough to wake the city. But no one else came. I screamed telepathically, didn't I?*

Yes. Gave me a bloody headache, too.

I smiled at the humor in his voice. *Sorry.*

It wasn't your fault. You don't need to apologize for everything, you know.

We fell silent, but it was a comfortable silence. The kind you get between friends who had known each other a long time. I didn't want to break it, but there was something itching at me that I had to ask.

Why are you helping me? Is it just the money?

Elan paused, and I could sense him weighing up how to answer. *Money always comes in useful out here. Especially when you're factionless. Food and water are expensive.*

I waited.

My mother is a seer. She told me I should help you. I've learned to listen to what she says.

I felt like he still wasn't quite telling me the whole truth, but I didn't push it. I yawned, feeling a wave of exhaustion wash over me.

You should go, Elan said. *It's hard keeping this link up. I'm pretty tired myself.*

I'll try doing what you said. I hesitated, then added, *Can we talk again tomorrow night?*

Sure. Goodnight, Vesper.

Goodnight.

Did I imagine it, or was there a note of tenderness in his voice?

I shook my head. I was definitely imagining it. Elan was doing this for the money, not because he cared about me.

Yet when his mind pulled back, I felt an almost overwhelming sense of loss, as if he had taken part of me with him. I turned onto my side, Ty curled up beside me. But even with the warmth of his small body, the room felt cold and empty, and I felt more alone than I believed possible.

20

The Arena

"TODAY'S TRAINING IS CANCELED," Diana announced as soon as I sat down in the arena. I'd slept in again, after another training session with Elan last night and had skipped breakfast, running to the Colosseum to make it on time.

"What's going on?" I whispered to Marissa while trying to catch my breath. Ty landed on my shoulder and nuzzled my neck.

She shrugged and opened her mouth to reply, but a look from Diana silenced her.

"The Gamesmasters are allowing us to scout out the arena today," Diana continued. "Leo, Nina, Tallulah, and Shant, you're to go with Cato to see what they've got in store for us. You know the drill. Thora, Bren, Cayden, Marissa, Vesper, you're with me. Everyone else, enjoy your day off."

There was a smattering of cheers and good-natured back slapping for those who were to go with Cato. I followed Marissa and Cayden across the arena to where Diana waited.

Diana nodded to us. "Meet you at the front exit in ten minutes. Make sure you've had enough to eat. It's a twenty-minute walk to the arena, and there's no guarantee we won't encounter beasts on the way."

I exchanged a nervous glance with Marissa as we left the Colosseum. "Apparently, there are bison out there—on the streets," she whispered. "Bren said they can smell fear."

If that was the case, Marissa would be the first to be taken down. But then again, she'd already faced a bison and won. Which was more than I had done. "I'm sure Diana wouldn't take us out if it wasn't safe," I replied, though despite my conversation with Thora, I wasn't totally convinced our welfare was at the forefront of our trainer's mind.

Ten minutes later, having seen the arsenal of weapons Diana was carrying, I began to reassess that opinion. Even Bren and Thora had long knives hanging from their belts, and Thora carried a thin, metal pole.

"It's to help amplify my electricity," she explained, catching me looking at it. "Just in case we meet anything."

Fortunately, the hike to the arena passed uneventfully, though my nerves were frayed to the breaking point by the time we entered a low building through an opening that may once have been a window. The city was the dull gray of a cloudy morning, the ever-present smog making it all too easy to forget about the city and the sun above.

Diana led us up four flights of stairs, then down a long corridor that ended in a large, empty room. "We can talk here but keep the noise down. We don't want to draw attention to ourselves." She beckoned us over to the window. "This is the arena."

I stared out of the window at a wasteland of dried earth, rubble, and burned metal husks, surrounded by a wire-topped concrete wall. The ground was contoured, as if someone had taken a giant spoon and carved out troughs and curves in a bid to make the landscape more interesting. A few gnarled, gray tree trunks perched like carrion crows atop one of the taller ridgelines, and I wondered if there had been grass and trees once, before the smog had sucked the life and color from this place.

In the center of the arena stood a stone tower, perhaps fifty feet tall. It looked out of place, like a medieval turret that had been transported through time and space to land in the derelict city. A pair of flagpoles rose from the flat roof, one slightly taller than the other.

"Each faction starts an equal distance from the tower," Diana said quietly. "As well as encouraging us to fight each other, the Gamesmasters like to throw in some surprises. Last year, they let a pack of *chupacabra* loose. The year before, they flooded the place with rats."

"And snakes before that." Thora shivered. "That was a bad year."

"Who are the Gamesmasters?" I asked.

"Slaves who left the factions," Diana said.

I eyed her inquiringly, waiting for her to continue.

"Slaves who were granted their freedom," Bren continued when Diana made no move to speak. "Now, even when granted their freedom, most slaves choose to remain affiliated with a faction." He shared a fond look with Thora. "We did. There are benefits to being part of a larger group. But back then, when the factions were constantly warring, nowhere was safe. Everyone knew the continual fighting over water had to end, but until Remo came along, no one did anything about it. He and a small group of other ex-slaves called together the faction leaders and proposed a solution. An annual contest, pitting faction against faction, that they—a neutral intermediary—would organize. The winners would gain control of water rights for the following year. Given the chaos the city was in, the faction leaders didn't have much choice, so the Games started."

"In return for hosting the Games, the Gamesmasters get free access to water and a small tithe from each faction," Thora said. She took in Marissa's pale face. "I know it must seem a cruel way of settling things, but honestly, if you'd seen what it was like before . . ."

Bren reached out and squeezed her hand. I felt a pang of envy at their companionship. It echoed the odd sense of loss I felt after each of my training sessions with Elan. I still hadn't figured that one out.

"The Gamesmasters provide resources for people with different powers." Diana pointed out the window. "Concrete and rubble for the telkies, metal for the leccies, water for the water-weavers . . ."

I gazed at the piles of sludge lining some of the deeper trenches. There didn't look to be much for the water-weavers to work with, but perhaps coating people in toxic slime was a more effective weapon than drowning them in water.

"The pools are usually topped up the night before the Games," Diana continued. "Burners create their own fire, but sometimes, the Gamesmasters will hide explosives or fuel sources around the arena."

"Can we take weapons in?" Cayden asked.

Diana shook her head. "Not unless you get an exemption from the Gamesmasters."

I glanced at her in surprise. "Not even you? But you don't have powers, do you?"

Diana's face tightened. "No. I am permitted to take my staff only." Her tone indicated that she would say nothing more on the matter. "One of the reasons I brought you up here is so you can see the other factions. When we're in the arena, we wear armbands in our faction's color. Ours are green, the Players wear purple, the Venetians gold, the Ragazzi red, and the Sirens blue. In practice, the bands often get ripped off or covered with dirt, so it's not always easy to tell who you're fighting."

"Over time, you get to know who's who, but it's hard your first time out." Thora smiled sympathetically.

"There's Aidan." Marissa pointed out of the window. "That must be the Ragazzi."

I followed her gaze to where a small group of men loitered outside a gate. Aidan stood a few paces apart from them, his shoulders hunched and hands shoved in his pockets. He looked as if he'd lost weight in the last few weeks, or perhaps he was just wearing oversized clothes. Lines of misery were etched into his skin.

"Is that your friend?" Bren asked.

I nodded, not bothering to explain that none of us had known Aidan before we were thrown down here.

"The Ragazzi can be brutal with their slaves. Their motto translates to 'Survival of the Fittest'."

I glanced over at him. "And what's ours?"

"*Coniuncti stamus,*" Diana said before Bren could reply. "Together We Stand."

We watched as the Ragazzi were let into the arena by a tall woman, who ignored their catcalls with a haughty indifference. I caught sight of Cato and the other Gladiators he'd taken with him into the arena, carrying out what looked like a methodical search. About ten minutes later, the beautiful blonde woman I recognized as Venilia, leader of the Venetians, turned up with a large group of followers. After a brief altercation with the woman at the gate, four of them were dismissed and the others let through.

"Venilia always tries to break the rules," Diana said, making a noise of disgust in her throat.

"Do the faction leaders compete in the Games?" I asked.

"Not usually. Except for Apollina, who always likes to show off her powers." Diana's voice soured at the mention of the Sirens' leader. "They usually come to check out the arena, though most, like us, will stay hidden." She waved at the towers and lower buildings surrounding the arena on two sides. "It's not unheard of for people to spring some of the traps the Gamesmasters have set when inspecting the arena."

"The only place you're not allowed to search is the tower," Bren said. "That's off limits until the day of the Games."

A loud bang made my heart jump. Marissa let out a squeak. I searched the arena, looking for the source of the noise, but nothing seemed to have changed. Then, a faint *put-put-put* sound came from farther up the street. It gradually got louder, and I leaned forward to see what it was.

"Here comes Apollina," Diana muttered, pulling me back with such force that Ty tumbled off my shoulder and fell through the window. He flapped once before returning to my shoulder and hissing at Diana.

Diana made a tsk of annoyance and glowered at me. "So much for keeping the dragon a secret."

She pushed me! Ty screeched in annoyance.

I opened my mouth to snap a retort to Diana, but the words fell from my mouth as the source of the odd noise appeared on the street below.

It looked like an oversized, elongated bicycle, but using a word that plain to describe such a machine was like calling the Royal Palace a house. Purple sparks crackled around the gleaming silver body, which seemed to fly down the street, skidding to a halt with a screech of brakes outside the arena gate. The front part was sculpted into a woman's head, her long hair flowing back to where the leader of the Sirens sat astride the machine, her long black braids swinging as she glanced impatiently down the street behind her.

"She does like to make an entrance," Thora muttered under her breath.

"What *is* that thing?" Cayden asked, more than a trace of admiration in his voice.

"A motorbike," Bren said. "It's some ancient relic Apollina found in her headquarters and somehow got working again. I don't know where she finds the fuel to power it, though."

"She uses her electricity most of the time," Diana said acidly. "The backfiring noises are just for show."

As we watched, four women appeared. With a jolt, I recognized Daria, her red hair making her stand out from her dark-haired companions. Like the others, she was dressed in the odd leather and metal fighting gear that seemed to be the uniform of the faction. It wasn't too dissimilar to what Diana wore, though Diana's clothes seemed more practical and less ornamental.

Unlike Aidan, Daria walked with her head held high, and though she deferred to the women around her, she didn't seem intimidated by them. She'd put on muscle and wore her uniform like a second skin.

"Vesper, look at the three women to the left of the redhead," Diana ordered. "Memorize their faces. They are your enemy."

"Apollina's Furies," Thora murmured.

Diana shot her an irritated look. "Mara, Lorelei, and Evalie. They are all mind-talkers and the strongest threat the Sirens can offer. If they get into your head, they'll have you bowing down before them or, worse, taking yourself out of the Games altogether."

A sick feeling settled in my stomach. "You mean, they make people hurt themselves?"

Diana nodded. "We lost someone to them last year. Harpies made the girl stab herself with an iron pole."

I glanced at Thora, whose lips had tightened. Was that how Indra, Cato's girlfriend, had died?

"The stronger your personal shield is, the harder it is for them to break through," Diana added.

So that's why Marcus is so insistent we work on our mental shields.

I stared down at the women. Apart from their getup, they didn't look alike. One was tall and muscular with brown hair, cropped short, and a strong jaw. The second had skin the color of the darkest shadows. She was lithe and moved like a cat stalking a mouse. The third woman was slightly built with copper skin and long, black hair coiled on top of her head. I recognized her as one of the women who'd accompanied Apollina when she'd inspected us before the auction.

Curious, I reached out with my power, trying to get a sense of how their minds felt. They were sharp and alert, having a similarity with Elan's that made me wonder if I was able to distinguish people's powers by their mental signature. I filed that thought away to talk to Marcus about later. I pulled back, unsure whether they could sense my probing.

As if reading my mind, the copper-skinned woman jerked her head around. She said something to her companions, who also glanced in our direction.

"They know we're here." Marissa's voice trembled.

"Of course they know," Diana snapped, though she gave me an odd look. "Don't try anything, Vesper."

We watched as the Sirens approached their leader and they all entered the arena, Apollina leaving her motorbike by the barrier.

"I could just throw a fireball at it, you know," Bren said impishly, giving Diana a sideways glance.

She rolled her eyes at him. "Not worth the hassle." Her fingers tightened on her staff. "Where has Bellagio got to?" she muttered under her breath.

We waited in silence. My back ached from standing still for so long, so I distracted myself by trying to sense the minds of those around me. I detected a similarity between Thora and Marissa, which supported my theory that the minds of people with the same powers had a similar feel. There was a subtle difference, but once I knew what to look for, it was easier to identify. I pushed out farther, trying to identify what powers the members of the different factions had, until something caught my attention.

There was another mind-talker coming.

I opened my mouth to say something. At the same time, Diana twisted her head to look out the window. "About time," she muttered.

Walking down the street was the final group of men and women. Compared to everyone else we'd seen, they were smartly dressed, walking with a purpose and focus that was the opposite of the relaxed, easy-going air the Ragazzi and Venetians had exhibited.

"Shui's not with them," Cayden commented, echoing my own surprise.

Diana shrugged. "She was a water-weaver, wasn't she? Bellagio probably won't risk her in the Games. Water-weavers often struggle to defend themselves and don't have the temperament needed to survive the Games. Same with growers. Plus, they're needed to draw the water up from the wells."

I noticed that the Japanese man who Bobo had treated with such respect was also not with the group. They were led by a tall, thin man with a long scar running down his left cheek. The man next to him caught my attention. I frowned, trying to place him. He was pale, slightly built, and appeared to have Asian blood, like Shui, though his face was rounder and his hair dark brown rather than black. His countenance was oddly serene, as if he were walking in a park, not about to put his life at risk.

I had seen him when the faction leaders had inspected us, though I hadn't realized who—or what—he was.

"That's him," I breathed.

Diana shot me a sharp glance. "Damon? You recognize him."

"He feels like a mind-talker."

My fingers tightened on the rough concrete wall. He looked up at us. No, not at us. At *me*. Our eyes met, and I felt a dark presence press against my mental shield, like a worm seeking out a weakness in a concrete slab.

Vesper? Ty's voice was anxious.

He's testing me.

And I felt the weaknesses in my armor. I drew on my power, throwing up layer after layer inside my shield, desperately trying to form a barrier strong and smooth enough to resist Damon's probing. His eyes, pale as ice, bored into me as my muscles strained, my heart racing.

Then the pressure eased. A cold smile twisted Damon's lips. He raised a hand in greeting before turning to follow the rest of his group.

My shoulders sagged as I wiped a trickle of sweat from my forehead. Everyone stared at me, their expressions ranging from concern to displeasure.

"Well, I guess Damon knows who you are now," Thora said shakily.

"He already knew who she was." Diana stared at me. "The question is, which of them is stronger?"

21

A New Approach

MARCUS PACED. AS OUR training room was only ten feet across, this necessitated a lot of turning, which began to make me dizzy.

"What are you thinking?" I asked.

Marcus scratched his head but didn't slow. "Damon was testing you. I think he sees you as a threat, but a minor one. It may be a good thing that you struggled to resist his probing. He will think you weak and untrained. His arrogance could be his downfall."

"I don't feel like much of a threat at the moment. I can't even get you to pick up a spoon." I scraped my fingernail along the stone chair, a shiver running down my spine at the scratching sound. I'd tried doing what Elan had told me, but it felt like being lectured on how to build a tower and then being faced with a pile of stone and a shovel.

"Hmm, maybe we need to try something different." Marcus paused and turned toward me. "I think we should forget everything we've tried and approach things from a different angle. Influencing people's thoughts and actions during the Games *would* be extremely useful, but it's not the only thing you could help with."

I jerked my head up. "You mean there's some other way I can use my power?"

Marcus nodded. "You could use it to disable the opposition, like you did in the Colosseum."

"No," I said flatly, nausea twisting my gut like a wrench. I dug my fingernails into my thighs, hoping the pain would distract me from the memories lurking in the dark corners of my mind. "I won't kill."

"I didn't say kill," Marcus replied. "I said *disable*." He sat down in front of me and reached for my hand.

I pulled back and stood, walking to the far side of the room and pressing my hands flat against the cool, marble wall. "I won't do it. It's too much of a risk."

Deep breaths. Deep breaths.

A movement disturbed the air around me. Ty landed on my shoulder and pressed his cool head into my cheek. At his touch, my nausea abated and I managed to open my eyes.

"When you lashed out at the man in the Colosseum, you didn't even know what your ability was, Vesper. Your control has improved significantly over the past few weeks." Marcus's heavy footsteps came to a halt behind me. "You don't have to be afraid of it."

Easy for him to say. He's not the one who accidentally killed a man and nearly died doing so.

Remember what Thora said? Ty nuzzled my neck, sending a ripple of warmth through my body.

That was different.

How?

I sighed. He had a point. If I wasn't able to control my power, there would always be a risk that what happened with the slaver would happen again. But learning to control my power and deliberately choosing to attack people with it were two entirely different things.

I wondered if I'd have had the same struggles with learning to control my power if I'd been accepted into the Academy. Marcus tried his best, but he couldn't be as effective as an experienced trainer who was also a mind-talker.

If only I hadn't failed that test.

With effort, I pushed the thought from my mind. It was no use dwelling on that now. Although Cayden was still convinced his father would find a way of rescuing him, I had given up on the idea of getting back to New Vegas weeks ago.

Mostly.

Marcus had been right when he'd said that Caesar's Palace would begin to feel more like home. The other faction members seemed less afraid of me since I hadn't actually hurt anyone since I'd been here, and since I'd started talking to Elan, it felt as if I had someone to confide in who understood my struggle with controlling my powers.

And you have me. Ty blew gently on my neck.

I smiled softly. *And you.*

What I had to focus on now was surviving the Games.

Marcus rested a hand on my shoulder. I stiffened but didn't push him away. "I believe with a bit of practice, you should have enough control that you can exert just a tiny bit of pressure on people's minds," he said quietly. "Just enough to put them to sleep or give a small jolt of pain. There would be no permanent damage. Being able to do that could save the lives of your friends."

"And win the Games," I said, more sharply than I'd intended. "That's what all this is about, isn't it? Winning?"

"I would rather come in last and have every one of our Gladiators come back unharmed than lose any of you in that arena."

I turned to face my mentor. "You may feel that, but you're not the one in charge, are you? Caesar is. And Diana."

"And whatever you may think, both of them feel the same." Marcus's face sagged, making him look even older than his gray hair and wrinkles suggested. "We have lost too many people in the past. Diana would give her life to protect any of you."

I felt a twinge of guilt, remembering my conversation with Thora.

"What's the deal with her anyway? Her shield is so strong . . ."

Marcus nodded. "Even I can't penetrate it," he admitted, smiling softly. "It is the strongest I've come across in any person, talented or not. Anyway, we're not talking about Diana. We're talking about you." He looked at me expectantly.

"Fine, I'll try it," I muttered. "But if it doesn't work . . ."

"It will." Marcus's smile lit up his face. "I know you can do this, Vesper."

I spent the next half an hour trying to attack Marcus's mind. I was hesitant at first, despite his continual reassurances that his shield was strong enough to withstand my attacks, but by the end of the session, I'd gotten as far as making him wince. It still didn't feel like I had much control over the process. In my heart, I knew I was scared to throw my full power behind it.

"That's enough for today," he said, rubbing his temples. "I don't know about you, but my head hurts."

The dull throbbing in my skull was definitely distracting. "I can throw out the power, but I still don't feel like I can control the effects of it. It's so frustrating!"

"I know it feels like we're making slow progress, Vesper, but you *are* making progress." Marcus placed a hand on my arm. "We'll get there. I promise."

⊷⊶

"We have one week until the Games," Diana announced, stalking into the Colosseum five minutes after our training session was supposed to have started. It wasn't like her to be late, and judging from the look on her face, she wasn't happy about something. "Today, we will be fighting each other. *Properly* fighting. No holding back."

She called out names, dividing us into two groups. "For the next two hours, these are not your friends and fellow Gladiators but your opponents. Marcus and I will be on hand to intervene if any of you look to be in real danger, but don't rely on our help." Her lip curled into a cold smile. "We will be fighting outside today. Follow me."

She stalked over to a door on the far side of the Colosseum, not giving us the opportunity to ask questions. We fell in behind her as she led us out of the palace and into a deserted street surrounded by low-rise buildings. A couple hundred yards up and down the street, a thick green line had been painted on the road. I glanced over my shoulder and noticed Marcus bringing up the rear. He caught my gaze and gave me a reassuring nod.

For two weeks, I'd been training with Marcus during the day and Elan during the evening, and finally, I felt as if I was getting somewhere. Not with influencing people's minds—I was sure Elan was doing his best to help me, but I still couldn't figure that one out—but with attacking them.

The idea still made me sick. Two days ago, I'd let enough power out to knock Marcus unconscious. When he'd woken up, he'd been delighted. I hadn't. The headache I had afterward reminded me of what my powers could do and how important it was that I could control them.

At the back of my mind, Marcus's warning about the risk of holding more power than I could handle lingered. How would it feel to die like that?

Diana slammed her staff onto the ground, silencing the murmurs of apprehension. "The lines mark the boundary. You are not permitted to go into any of the buildings, but you can extend a block in that direction." She pointed to the low-rise buildings on the far side of the street. "Cato, your team starts behind the south line. Bren, you take the north line. First to get their entire team beyond the other team's line wins."

The two men grinned at each other and bumped fists.

"Loser buys the beers," Cato said.

Bren raised an eyebrow. "Hope you're feeling rich, *loser*."

Diana had made it clear we were to pull no punches. We could be hurt, or even killed. Yet they seemed to be treating the whole thing as a game. I wished I had half their confidence.

Marissa gave Cayden and me a small smile before heading off with the rest of Cato's team. I trailed after Cayden in the opposite direction until a hand on my arm stopped me. I turned and looked up into Diana's cold eyes.

"This is your last chance, understand?" she said in a low voice. "I've given Marcus, and you, the benefit of the doubt so far, but we are running out of time. If you can't come up with the goods today, we will have to change the plan."

I nodded and tried to shake off her hand, but her grip tightened, her fingers digging into my arm.

"*Don't* use that as an excuse to wheedle your way out of competing. A complete change of plan at this stage renders our chances of winning the Games pretty much zero. Do you want to watch people get hurt and die because *you* couldn't contribute?" She released my arm and stalked off.

I looked down at the white indentations on my skin. She was right. Our whole plan revolved around my ability to keep the small group of flag bearers hidden. Or, if I couldn't do that, incapacitate anyone who spotted us without drawing other people's attention. I knew Diana didn't believe in me, but Marcus did, and I didn't want to let him down.

"Hey, Vesper," Bren called from up the street. "Hurry up!"

I jogged to catch up to my team just as they reached the painted line on the road. Ty hovered in the air above me. Bren motioned for us to huddle around him.

"Cato will try and sneak around the back alleys," he said confidently. "We'll make it look as if we're doing the same but stick close to the main street. At my signal, we'll race toward the line, focusing on taking out anyone he's left to guard it."

It sounded simple. Too simple. But it seemed Diana wasn't going to give us any time for discussion.

"Ready!" she called out.

Bren glanced at me. "Ask Ty to keep an aerial lookout and let me know where Cato's people are hidden. Everyone else, keep an eye out for beasts. There are bound to be a few attracted by the noise and use of power."

Diana slammed her staff down. "Start."

I stood, my feet frozen to the ground as my team sprinted off around me. Adrenaline pulsed through my veins, making my hands shake and my mouth go dry.

Move, you idiot.

In the blur of people, I caught sight of a familiar figure and darted after it. Cayden ducked behind a small brick outbuilding. I followed.

Ty?

Up here.

I looked up to see the outline of the dragon hovering twenty feet up.

Be careful, I said. He ducked his head in response and flew off, presumably to scout out the positions of Cato's team.

The building we crouched behind was perhaps ten feet long with a battered metal door set into the wall. There was another low building a stone's throw away, behind which Thora and three others crouched. She waved for us to follow them behind the building, using it as cover. I surged forward, but Cayden grabbed my arm.

"If they saw where we hid, they'll be waiting for us to move," he whispered.

I pursed my lips. It was only a thirty-foot gap. *Had Cato's team even had time to get into position?*

Ty, can you see if anyone's watching?

There was a pause before he replied. *Not that I can see. Most of them seem to be making their way through the back streets as Bren suggested.*

I glanced at Cayden. "Ty thinks it's safe."

He took a deep breath. "Okay. Let's go together."

We burst out from behind the shelter. Cayden's powerful legs gave him a slight advantage, but I pumped my arms, desperate to keep up. Twenty feet. Fifteen. Ten. I slowed my pace to avoid slamming into Cayden and Thora, who had waited for us to come across.

That was a mistake.

My mind was hyperalert, so I sensed the pulse of energy a split second before the fireball flew toward me. I dove forward, a sharp pain stabbing through my shoulder.

Cayden caught me with a grunt and we tumbled back, falling to the ground. I lay sprawled on top of him, panting, our hearts pounding an uneven rhythm against each other.

"You okay?" he mumbled.

"I think so." My muscles felt so weak, I wasn't sure I could move.

"Do you think you could get up then? Your hair is kind of choking me."

Grit and dirt bit into my hands as I pushed myself off him, feeling heat rise to my cheeks. "Sorry."

He gave me a cocky smile. "I mean, I wouldn't usually complain about a pretty girl throwing herself at me, but I think we have other things to worry about right now."

Arrogant prince.

I'd almost forgotten he was a member of the royal family, then he had to come out with that.

"Come on, you two," Thora snapped impatiently. "Vesper, are you hurt?"

I rubbed my palms down my thighs and twisted my neck to inspect the damage to my shoulder. The fireball had burnt through my top, and the skin underneath had already started to blister. It hurt like hell, but I could still use my arm.

Pain is all in the mind, huh?

"I'm fine," I told Thora.

She searched my eyes before nodding. "Let's go."

We followed her along the length of the building and across a narrow gap to the next without incident. The rest of the group waited at the far end. Bren wasn't among them, so I guessed he must be with the other half of the group on the far side of the street.

"We're out of cover," a dark-haired man whose name I couldn't remember said to Thora. "Ready to make a run for it?"

"Hang on a sec." Thora turned to me. "Vesper, can Ty see where Bren and the others are?"

I relayed the query, and Ty said he'd find out. A moment later, I heard his voice in my head.

Bren says they're doing okay. He wants you guys to try and make it across the line. The others should be able to catch up.

I repeated his message.

Thora nodded. "We'll go as one big group. Everyone have your powers at the ready, and remember, don't be afraid to use them. How many people can you see guarding the line, Leo?"

The dark-haired man risked a peek around the corner. "Four. Mary and Jason are burners, then there are David and Marissa."

"Okay. Cayden and Leo, I want you guys to try and take the burners out. I should be able to handle Marissa. Everyone just stay clear of David, unless you want to end up in the infirmary for a week."

I remembered David as the oversized man who had what seemed like superhuman strength.

Do you need me? Ty asked

"Ty's asking if we need his help?"

"He's probably better off helping Bren," Thora said after a short pause.

I relayed the message to Ty and closed my eyes, reaching out with my power to sense who else was around us, wondering why I hadn't thought to do that earlier. "There are three people hiding on the far side of the street," I said, frowning with the effort. "A burner and two telkies, I think, though I'm not totally sure."

I opened my eyes to see surprised faces staring back at me.

"That's useful to know," Thora said. She gave me an appraising look. "Are you able to keep us updated if anything changes?"

"I'll try," I said.

Thora glanced at each of us in turn. "Everyone ready? Let's do this. *Coniuncti stamus.*"

"*Coniuncti stamus,*" we echoed.

Thora led us into the street. I felt horribly exposed, but for the first few seconds, nothing happened.

Then chaos descended.

I sensed a burst of power from the street opposite. The woman next to me screamed as she was shoved forward and thrown to the ground by invisible hands. Moments later, the air above us exploded into flames, hot sparks raining down. I patted my head frantically as they singed my hair and burned my skin, distracted by the thought that my hair could go up in flames.

"Keep moving!" hollered Thora. She ran back to pick the woman off the ground, simultaneously firing a ball of electricity across the street. It hit the corner of the building like a lightning bolt, and shards of concrete and dust rained down on the alleyway below.

I stumbled forward, trying to concentrate on pulling my power into a focal point as I'd practiced with Marcus. I sensed one of the telkies nearby and pushed out. Hard enough to hurt him, I hoped, but not hard enough to do any real damage. But I'd misjudged the strength of his shield and my power diffused over it and was pushed away. Before I could gather myself to try again, I found myself flying through the air.

The impact with the ground knocked the breath from my lungs. Dark spots danced in front of my eyes as I tried to catch my breath. Pain wracked my body, and a small moan escaped my lips.

Vesper? Ty's voice radiated concern.

I'm okay . . . I think.

I'm coming!

No—

But he'd already cut the connection.

I pushed myself up onto my elbows and looked around. A haze of smoke hung over the street. From one direction, I heard cheers; from the other, the sounds of people still fighting, but the air around me was still and silent. I suddenly felt very alone.

Gingerly, I got to my feet. Nothing seemed to be broken, but my whole body ached, and I suspected my back was one big bruise.

My footsteps sounded uncomfortably loud in the silence. Reaching out, I sensed several people ahead of me, but the members of Cato's team who'd been hiding on the far side of the street seemed to have disappeared. Did that mean they'd won?

I forced myself into a jog, smoke and a metallic taste forming an unpleasant concoction in my mouth. My shoulders and arms were peppered with tiny burn marks and bloody from the grit of the road.

In front of me, the smoke began to clear. I slowed to a walk, then halted. I was about twenty feet from the painted line, behind which Thora and the others exchanged high-fives and hugs of celebration. Bren and a few others were still missing, but it seemed as if about three-quarters of our team had already made it. I was so close.

Between me and the line stood Marissa.

A large bruise colored her left cheek and her blonde hair hung, sooty and tangled, down her back. Her face was taut, but her eyes were full of determination. She uncurled her fists, electricity sparking in the air between us.

I bit my lip, wondering if I could feign an attack and run around her. But even as I thought it, electricity flew from her fingers to form a barrier across the street between me and my teammates. No, the only way past was to take her down.

I reached out, sensing the strength of her shield, wondering if I'd be able to slip through it like Elan had been trying to teach me. But Marissa had been taught by Marcus. Her shield was strong, without any chinks or weakness.

"You can yield, Vesper, if you'd like." Her voice tremored.

Yielding wasn't really an option. It would forfeit our team's chances of winning, which wouldn't sit well with Bren—or Diana. Besides, Diana had made it clear that this was a test for me more than anyone else.

I gathered my power, focusing it into a point, and tried to judge precisely how strong a pulse I needed to pierce Marissa's shield without hurting her.

At that moment, there was a disturbance in the air above.

I'm here!

Ty's claws dug into my shoulder. My concentration flickered. Power surged through me, rushing out and down the line connecting me to Marissa.

Her eyes widened as her shield crumpled under the force of the strike. The purple sparks spluttered and died. The finish line was open to me. But I could only stare in horror as Marissa's eyes rolled back and she collapsed into a motionless heap on the ground.

22

Coffee and Cats

I SAT OUTSIDE CAESAR'S room, listening to the argument raging inside. I didn't know if they knew I could hear them, but I doubted they cared. I pulled my knees up to my chest and rested my aching head on top of them, tears soaking my legs.

Marissa had been carried to the infirmary. Thora said she was alive, but she still hadn't regained consciousness. I sent Ty with her to do whatever he could to help relieve her pain or heal her, if he were able. Part of me wanted to reach out with my mind to see if I could sense anything wrong with her, but I was afraid I'd just make things worse.

"You said she would be the key." Caesar's thin, reedy voice rose above Marcus's pleading. "You said you'd seen in the vision that she would help us win."

My head jerked up in surprise. *Marcus had a vision? About me?*

"You know the future is never one hundred percent certain, Jules. And I still do believe she *is* the key." Marcus let out an exclamation of frustration. "I just wish I knew how to train her. This is my fault, not hers."

There was a snort from Diana. "It doesn't matter whose fault it is. We have to change the plan if we are to have any chance of surviving, let alone winning."

"Diana is right, Marcus. We've given you and Vesper enough time. We have to cut our losses and move on."

"But—"

"No buts." Caesar sounded irritated. "We'll have to work with what we've got. But if she's killed that leccy, I'll have her hide. I can't believe I spent so much on her and that bloody dragon."

Guilt tore through me like a whirlwind, shredding my insides. I didn't know why I felt bad for letting Caesar down—I hated the man and everything he stood for—but I did. But overshadowing that was the guilt I felt for having hurt Marissa and failed Marcus. It wasn't his fault that I couldn't control my power. It was mine.

Where had that surge of power come from? I worked so hard to control it . . .

I was so absorbed in my thoughts that I missed Marcus's next words.

". . . sure he was part of it?" Caesar asked.

Marcus said something too low for me to catch.

Caesar let out a heavy sigh. "Well, we're running out of time. Let us know if you make any further progress with her."

Heavy footsteps moved toward the door. It opened and Marcus looked out, a flash of surprise crossing his face when he saw me sitting on the floor. He glanced back, then stepped into the corridor and closed the door behind him.

"How are you feeling?" He took in my swollen eyes and the tear stains tracking down my cheeks. "Okay, stupid question. Come on. Caesar doesn't need to see you right now. Let's go get a cup of coffee."

"You have coffee?" I couldn't hide my surprise.

Marcus chuckled. "It's a poor substitute for what you have in New Vegas, but it's coffee of sorts. Come and lend an old man a hand." He held out his arm with a smile.

I wiped my eyes with the back of my hand and got to my feet. Marcus didn't need my support to walk—he wasn't that frail—but I appreciated the gesture all the same.

To my surprise, Marcus led me not to the dining hall, but up to the living quarters. He stopped in front of a large, ornate door and pulled out an old-fashioned key. At my look of surprise, he smiled. "I know it won't deter anyone from breaking down the door, but it makes me feel better knowing my rooms have some protection from prying eyes." He pushed the door open and waved a hand. "Ladies first."

I stepped into the room, and Marcus pressed a switch on the wall behind me. A soft glow sprung from a pair of lamps set upon low tables against opposite walls, illuminating a large sitting room, with what looked to be another room through an archway on one side.

"Sit down, please," Marcus said, hurrying forward to light some of the large candles that were perched, rather precariously, on most flat surfaces. "Sorry about the mess. I'm not accustomed to visitors."

I stared around in amazement. The rooms we'd been assigned were far larger than my bedroom back home, but this was the size of a small apartment. A hodgepodge of faded, patterned rugs covered the floor, and thick curtains hung down either side of the large window. Like every other window I'd seen, it was boarded up, but there were slits cut into the boards, presumably so Marcus could look out. Battered bookcases, filled with books, lined the walls. Aside from the curiosity shop, I'd never seen so many in one place. I didn't even know there were this many books left in the world. I walked over to a leather-bound volume on a small table and ran a finger down the brittle pages.

"Careful," Marcus said sharply.

I jerked my hand away.

"Sorry. I'm a little protective about my books. They're extremely fragile."

"Where did you get all this?" I stared at the large paintings on the wall, the old-fashioned, high-backed chair that looked as if it was straight out of a documentary, and the carved wooden table next to it.

Marcus placed a kettle of water on a hotplate in a corner of the room that he appeared to use as a kitchenette. "I've collected things over the years." His eyes twinkled in the candlelight. "A little hobby of mine. It is a shame to let the relics of the past rot away entirely, don't you think?"

He didn't wait for an answer. "Now, sit down and tell me what happened."

I sank down into a squishy chair, only to leap up again when it hissed at me and a claw swiped at my butt.

"Ah, perhaps not *that* chair. Mortimer isn't too fond of strangers.

Mortimer?

I backed away from the chair. What I'd thought was a cushion was a hissing ball of fur with sharp teeth and even sharper claws. "What is it?"

"*He* is a lioncat. At least, that's what I've called him. He seems to be an evolution of the domestic cats our ancestors used to keep, but with all that hair, he does look rather like a miniature version of the lions of Africa, don't you think?" Marcus gazed at the spitting creature with a doting expression.

"He's certainly, um, intimidating," I said, rubbing my backside. Damn lioncat had torn a hole in my pants *and* drawn blood. I scowled at the creature. He barred his teeth in response.

"There, there, Mortimer," Marcus crooned, walking over and burying his hand in the lioncat's golden fur. "Vesper is a *friend*."

Mortimer let out a rumbling purr as Marcus scratched behind his ears, still eying me balefully. Not many people had cats in New Vegas—you had to have a special license for them—but Mortimer was bigger than any domestic cat I'd seen.

I walked to another chair, double checked it didn't hold any surprises, and sat down. On the hotplate, the kettle began to whistle.

I waited until Marcus had handed me a cup of coffee and sat down in the high-backed chair opposite me. The aroma of the coffee reminded me of home and tears sprang to my eyes. Dad made us coffee every Sunday morning. It was the only day we could afford to drink it, so it had become a kind of ritual. Coffee, eggs and toast.

I took a cautious sip. It wasn't quite the same, but it wasn't half bad.

"So, what happened?" Marcus said softly, taking a sip from his own mug.

I explained what I could remember. The details had already started to blur in my mind. Apart from the look on Marissa's face. I knew I wouldn't forget that.

When I finished, Marcus frowned. "You said you felt a surge of power. Was that from inside you or outside?"

"I . . . I don't know." I stared down at the black liquid in my mug. "I thought I had control, I was being so careful, but it seemed to come out of nowhere."

"And that happened when Ty arrived?"

"Yes, when he landed on my shoulder." I glanced up at Marcus. "You think perhaps it was him?"

Marcus looked thoughtful. "Possibly. I don't know exactly what powers dragons have." He waved at his bookshelf. "I've searched the archives, but the only mention of dragons is in fairy tales and stories. They seemed to appear around the time New Vegas was built. It is worth asking Ty, though. Where is he?"

"I asked him to look after Marissa."

Marcus gave me a sympathetic smile. "From what the medics told me, she's unconscious but alive, and her vital signs are good. Remember how you were knocked out after your experience in the Colosseum? It makes sense that it will take a bit of time for her body to recover."

I chewed my lip, not wanting to voice the question in my mind. *Will she ever recover?*

"You've made a huge amount of progress in controlling your power," Marcus continued. "I wouldn't be surprised if the surge you felt *did* come from Ty, whether he was aware of it or not. You said he felt your panic and came to help?"

I nodded.

"Perhaps he instinctively felt that you needed his help. I hadn't even considered this could be a possibility." Marcus's eyes sparkled. "We must ask him if he can control it and get the two of you training together. It could open up so many possibilities."

My fingers tightened around my mug. "Don't be stupid." I said bitterly. "I can't even control my own power."

Marcus's face fell. "I'm sorry. Of course, this isn't the right time." He pottered across the room and returned with a small jug. "More coffee?"

I held out my mug, feeling bad for having snapped. "So what *do* the books say about dragons?"

Marcus sat down and began to talk. From the chair opposite, Mortimer yawned, displaying a set of pointed, white teeth.

I tried to tune in to what Marcus was saying. But as hard as I tried, all I could see were Marissa's eyes, wide with shock and betrayal, as I struck her down.

23

Betrayal

I LAY ON MY bed, Ty nestled in the crook of my arm.

Do you really think it was me? Ty asked for what felt like the hundredth time.

Marcus thinks so.

I didn't know I could do that—give away my power. His faceted eyes whirred at me mournfully.

I rubbed his head and ran my hand down his long neck and between his wings. *It's not your fault. I should have been able to control it. I just wish I could influence people like Elan can. Then I wouldn't have to risk hurting them.*

Ty had returned at dinner, reporting that he'd done what he could for Marissa. He couldn't describe her condition, other than saying she was "alive, but not sleeping". From what I'd picked up from other people's conversations, she was in a coma and the medic didn't know when she would wake up or if there would be any permanent damage to her brain.

No one came to sit with me at dinner. Diana had shot me an angry look as she'd passed, but even that was better than the looks of fear I got from everyone else, as if I were a bomb liable to explode at any moment. Diana didn't seem to be scared of anyone or anything. I envied her bravery.

You should talk to Elan, Ty said. *Maybe he can explain it.*

Ty was right, but as much as I longed for Elan's comforting presence, I couldn't face explaining what had happened to him. Hearing the fear or, worse, loathing in his voice would make me crumble completely.

Go on. Ty nudged my arm with his snout. *He'll understand.*

Would he?

I lay back on my bed and closed my eyes, reaching out to Elan's mind.

Hey. What's up? He sounded surprised.

Do you have a minute?

Sure. He obviously sensed my emotions through our connection because he quickly added, *What's wrong?*

As briefly as I could, I explained what had happened in the training exercise and Marcus's view that the surge of power had come from Ty. As much as I tried to hold my emotions in check, I knew they were leaking out to him.

Have you heard of anything like that happening before?

There was a momentary pause. *No . . . At least not for certain.*

I waited, sensing there was something he wasn't telling me, but whatever it was, Elan clearly didn't want to talk about it. My heart sank.

I was thinking about a different approach to our training, he said, changing the subject. *I know we haven't gotten very far with me trying to explain how I do things, but I thought perhaps if you were able to see exactly what I was doing and the resulting action, you may have a better chance of figuring it out.*

What do you mean?

I've got a friend who's willing to help us out. I'd make him do some silly task, and you could watch and see if you can copy what I do.

I frowned. *I'm not sure I can do that from here. It's tiring enough just reaching out to you.*

That's the catch, Elan admitted. *I think it would work better if you were here—physically.*

My breath caught in my throat. He wanted me to leave the safety of Caesar's Palace and go out into the city? A ripple of unease made me shiver.

Elan caught my hesitation. *I know it's a risk for you, but I know my way around. I can meet you just outside Caesar's and take you back after. We should only be a few hours. They won't even notice you're gone.*

I considered his suggestion. It could be a trap, but why would Elan want to trap me? I was branded as Caesar's slave, and if I'd learned one thing, it was that no one messed with Caesar. Besides, I was pretty sure that if he was lying, I'd sense it.

Fine. I'll meet you outside the back entrance.

Great. Give me ten minutes.

I cut our connection and sat up, sending Ty tumbling from my chest and onto the bed. Ten minutes? He couldn't be far away then. Excitement and nerves fluttered in my stomach.

I'm going out to meet Elan, I told him. *I need you to stay here in case anyone comes to look for me. If they do, tell them I've gone to find a snack or something.*

Can't I come with you? Ty sounded like a child who'd been told he couldn't have the lollipop he wanted.

No. If they find us both gone, we're definitely in trouble.

I slipped on my boots and a lightweight hooded top, then crept from the room, leaving Ty curled up, sulking on my bed. The corridors were dark and empty as I made my way down one of the back staircases. When I got close to the back entrance, I sensed two people loitering nearby, one of them talented.

I cursed inwardly. I'd forgotten the door would be guarded.

Ty, I could do with a distraction.

Now *you need me?*

I rolled my eyes. *Please?*

You'd better bring me back something nice.

A moment later, he swooped past me and out into the corridor. There was a shout from one of the guards and the sound of running footsteps. I risked a peek around the corner. The burner had gone, leaving the other man behind. From the way he shifted uncomfortably, he was desperate for a pee.

His eyes flicked back down the corridor, then to a door a few feet away. He came to a decision and made a dash for it.

I tiptoed out and ran for the door, easing it open as a contented sigh came from the bathroom nearby. A moment later, I was through and had closed the door behind me.

Thanks, Ty. I'm out.

No problemo! Ty sounded a lot more cheerful. I guessed baiting guards was his idea of fun.

I slipped into the shadows and moved a short distance away to wait near the spot where I'd left Elan his money. My senses were on alert, and I had to restrain the power pulsing inside me.

A hand on my arm made me jump. Another covered my mouth before I could let out a squeak of alarm.

"It's only me," Elan whispered into my ear.

I relaxed a fraction. My nostrils flared with his scent. It was subtle—warm leather and musk—and disturbingly intoxicating. I struggled in his grip. He released me, grabbing my hand.

"This way."

He carefully led me between buildings and across streets, as if aware I couldn't see as well as him in the dim light. His movements were jerky, and it took me a moment to remember that he had a limp. Strange what you forgot. His hand enveloped mine, his skin rough and calloused. I fought an urge to entwine my fingers with his.

He's only showing you the way, idiot.

After perhaps fifteen minutes, Elan pushed open a battered door in what looked to have been a low-rise apartment block. Once inside, he motioned for me to sit down on a plastic chair and lit a tallow lamp he'd been carrying. I wrinkled my nose at the acrid odor.

Still standing, I looked around. "Is this your home?"

Elan snorted. "No. This is just a safe place we can use for a few hours. Jamie will be here soon."

I guessed Jamie must be his friend. I looked around the dusty room. Empty, apart from three plastic chairs and a small table Elan had placed the lamp on. He sat down on one of the other chairs. The soft light of the lamp made his warm skin glow and emphasized the shadows under his eyes. My eyes fell to his muscled arms and hands, clasped together in front of him.

When I had first landed in the city, then when I had seen him again outside the curiosity shop, he'd felt like a stranger, but now . . . now he felt different. More familiar. I could sense his mood, somehow knew that he felt as awkward as I did right now. It was as if the time we'd spent communicating telepathically had created a new type of bond. One I couldn't quite explain.

I sat down and twisted my fingers together, then let my hands fall to my side, then rested them in my lap. *Did that look dumb?*

"So, what's it like up there?" Elan jerked his head toward the ceiling. "Do you miss it?"

"New Vegas? Yes." I flushed, realizing how that must sound. "I mean, I miss my family and hot showers and things."

I felt him appraising me but dared not look up. *Why is this so awkward?*

"And the Academy?" His voice carried a familiar trace of sarcasm.

"I . . . Not really," I answered honestly. "I miss the *idea* of it, but the only time I was there was for the testing. And I'm not sure it's quite what I imagined it to be." I glanced up to find his gaze on me. A spark of amber glowed in his dark eyes.

Elan had been curious about life in New Vegas. In particular, the fact that most citizens didn't know about the talents Academy members possessed. I'd told him about the tests we'd gone through, and the outcome.

"Often, things aren't quite as they seem," he said placidly.

"How's your mom?"

"She's good."

I'd tried asking about Elan's family before, but he'd always steered the conversation to another topic. "So, she's a seer and you're a mind-talker. What about your father? Is he also talented?"

Pain flashed across Elan's face. "My father is dead," he said shortly.

I looked away, embarrassed. "I'm sorry."

We sat in silence for a moment. "So," Elan said finally, "are you feeling ready for the—"

He broke off and jumped to his feet when the sound of feet scuffing on concrete came from outside the door. A moment later, a boy of about thirteen walked in. He wore long shorts and a threadbare shirt and gazed at me with open curiosity.

"Jamie, this is Vesper. Vesper, Jamie," Elan said. "Sit down, Jamie. You weren't followed?"

"Nah. They're all out cold," Jamie said, slouching in the chair.

He's only a kid! We can't experiment on him, I said, resorting to telepathy so Jamie wouldn't hear.

You're *not experimenting on anyone*, Elan retorted. *And Jamie doesn't mind. We've done this before.*

Jamie looked from Elan to me and scowled. "Stop doing your mental talking thing. It's rude."

I stared at him. "You know when we're talking?"

"Yer eyes go funny."

I looked at Elan, who struggled to contain his laughter. He coughed and pulled a coin from his pocket, placing it onto the table next to the lamp. "Let's get started. Jamie, I'm going to get you to pick up the coin, okay? Vesper, you just watch."

Elan stared at Jamie, and I sensed a trickle of power leak out toward the boy. Jamie's eyes took on a slightly glazed look, then he reached forward and picked the coin up off the table. The thread of power retracted.

The boy blinked in confusion at the coin in his hand before grinning. "Cool."

Elan looked at me expectantly. "Did you see what I did?"

I frowned. "Kind of," I said, trying to stay optimistic. "Could you do it again?"

Elan and Jamie repeated the exercise five more times, but although it helped to see what Elan had tried to teach me in practice, I wasn't exactly sure what he was doing that I hadn't already tried.

"Do you want to see if you can try it on me?" Elan asked.

"Are you sure?"

Wasn't he worried about me hurting him?

Elan grinned, and something fluttered in my stomach. "Only if you promise to be gentle."

I swallowed, fighting the blush threatening to color my cheeks. "I'll try."

Elan's expression turned serious. He shifted his chair slightly so he faced me. "Reach out slowly, gently, and just try to insert the *possibility* of a thought that I should pick up the coin."

"Maybe this is a bad idea." I glanced around. "I don't want you to end up like Marissa."

"I'll be fine. Remember, just a trickle of power. It's hard work to control such a tiny thread, but if you have to really push, you're doing it wrong."

"Okay. I'll try." I took a deep breath and sent a thin tendril of my power weaving out toward Elan's mind.

"Fainter," he said. "I can already feel you trying to get in."

I squeezed my eyes shut and concentrated on making the tendril smaller and more transparent. Elan was right. It was difficult to keep a consistent flow of power when the thread was so small. Like trying to pour water from a bottle in the thinnest flow possible without it breaking into drips.

I let my power caress his mind, searching for a chink in his shield. Then I found it. An opening. Rather than pushing my power through, I tried to let the thin tendril ease its way in naturally, like water gravitating toward a plughole. I sent the thought with it.

Pick up the coin.

The chink in Elan's shield drew me in. His mind felt familiar, inviting. Who was this boy who had lived his whole life in this dark city, never seeing the sun, never knowing safety, security, or comfort? I teetered on the edge, driven by curiosity to slip into his mind and see what he was thinking.

About the city or about me?

Shock pulled me back as I realized just how close I'd gotten to invading his mind. Planting a suggestion was one thing, but sneaking into his mind to spy on his thoughts? How would he ever be able to trust me after that?

As I drew back, there was a gasp and a squeak from Jamie. The noise jerked me out of my trance as dread flooded through me. *What have I done?* I yanked my power back, but I still felt connected to Elan.

Power surged through me. More power than I knew I had.

My eyes snapped open and met Elan's. His face was horror-stricken.

"Stop," he said hoarsely through gritted teeth. "Let go. My power. Let it go."

What was I doing? The power coursing through my veins was intoxicating. It made me feel strong, alive, and yet . . . I saw Elan weakening before my eyes. Somehow, I was pulling his power from him.

Not knowing what else to do, I slammed my shield up, forming an impenetrable barrier between us. At once, the flood of power diminished. Elan sagged back into his chair, his face ashen.

Jamie rushed to his side. "Elan? You all right?" He glowered at me. "What have you done to him?"

"I . . . I don't know." I stared down at my trembling hands. "Elan, I'm so sorry. I didn't know I could do that."

Elan waved Jamie away and leaned forward, running shaking fingers through his hair. It made it stick up at a rough, jaunty angle, and he suddenly looked young and vulnerable.

"I'm okay, I think."

I fumbled in my pocket for the hunk of bread I'd snuck out from dinner. My hand shook as I held it out to him. "Here. Eat this."

He grabbed it gratefully and shoved it into his mouth, barely pausing to chew before swallowing.

"Thanks," he grunted, still not looking up at me.

I chewed my lip, waiting for him to recover. Tears burned at the back of my eyes. Why couldn't I get anything right? Why did I always end up hurting people?

"Okay," Elan said after what felt like an eternity. "I'm guessing you didn't do that deliberately." He eyed me warily.

I shook my head, feeling numb. "I felt myself being drawn into your mind and started to pull back. When Jamie squeaked, I panicked that I'd done something wrong. I yanked my power back, but didn't realize . . ."

"That you were drawing my power out with you," Elan finished. His lip twitched in a half-smile. "I've never heard of anyone doing that before. You are a strange one, Vesper."

Inwardly, I let out a sigh of relief. He seemed more amused than angry. At least this time, I'd managed to stop myself before I did any serious harm.

Jamie stared at me in awe. "So you're like some power vampire?"

"I guess," I said uncomfortably.

Elan picked up the coin and handed it to Jamie. "Thanks for your help."

"Anytime." The coin disappeared into the pocket of the boy's shorts. "Nice to meet you, Vesper."

"You too," I murmured as he sauntered out.

We sat in silence for a moment, the lamp flickering next to us.

"I should be going." I stood at the same moment as Elan.

"Wait." His hand brushed my arm. "Can I . . . Can I see if I can do what you just did? Perhaps I can draw power too.

Sometimes we don't know what's possible until someone shows us the way."

"You want me to let you into my mind?" I stared straight ahead, only too aware that my face was inches from his chest. The sound of my heart beating was loud in my ears.

Elan's collarbone twitched as he raised his arm and rested a hand on my shoulder. Warmth seeped through the thin fabric of my top. "Only if you don't mind," he said in a low voice.

Oh, but I did mind. I minded that he might see exactly how much I wanted to reach out and run my fingers down the strong line of his jaw. I minded that he would sense the tension pulsing under my skin, feel the peculiar mix of nerves and anticipation churning in my stomach. I minded that he would know what it meant.

Cheeks aflame, I kept my gaze straight ahead.

"Of course." My words came out as a squeak. Closing my eyes, I drew in a long breath, but the scent of sandalwood and leather made my head spin.

Focus.

"Are you ready?" Elan's voice sounded as if it came from far away.

I nodded, not trusting myself to speak.

His mental touch was light on my shield, softly probing for a way in. I could do this. All I needed to do was keep my emotions locked behind a second, inner shield that Elan couldn't access.

Vesper?

Give me a minute. Quickly, I threw up a weak inner layer to my shield, then opened a crack in the outer shield. I let a whiff of my energy leak out. *There you go.*

Elan's thread of power twisted, trying to latch onto mine but to no avail. His frustration washed over me. *It's like trying to hold smoke. Give me a bit more.*

I tried to oblige, but I couldn't let out more power without lowering my inner shield. Perhaps, if I were quick, I could do it without him sensing my thoughts and emotions.

I let the second shield fall. Power rushed out. I slammed the layers up again, but too late. Elan's surprise was a question mark between us as my feelings washed out. *Vesper, I . . .*

Digging my fingernails into my palms, I wished with all my heart that I was anywhere but here. Facing death in the Colosseum arena would be preferable to this embarrassment. Why couldn't I have been a burner or a leccy or something *normal*? Why did I have to be cursed by this stupid ability that was no help to anyone?

Elan's fingers burned my chin as he tilted my head back. When I dared meet his gaze, I saw fire smoldering in his dark eyes. A thrill of surprise rushed through me, making my mouth dry. I ran my tongue over my lips to moisten them. Cautiously, I let my senses wander. Elan's mind touched mine, then opened. For a second, I felt a surge of desire pulse along the thread that connected us. My hand found its way to his cheek. His hands dropped to my waist.

Had it been anyone else, I could have convinced myself that he was only pretending to be attracted to me. That this boy, a child of the Shadow City, was using me for some agenda of his own. But that was the beauty—and curse—of mind-talking. You couldn't lie. This feeling, this attraction between us was real.

Elan wanted me as much as I wanted him.

His lips brushed mine, the slightest of caresses that set every nerve in my body tingling. I leaned into him, hungry for more.

Vesper! Ty's voice screamed in my head. *You have to come back. Diana's—* He let out an escalating screech, which was abruptly cut off.

Shock made me jerk back. Elan's hands fell from my waist as confusion and anger flashed across his face. I stumbled backward, knocking my chair over in my haste. "I have to get back. Ty's in trouble." I started toward the door, not waiting for Elan to answer.

He caught up as I left the building and placed a restraining hand on my arm. "Wait. What did he say?"

"Just that I had to get back, and something about Diana. Then he was cut off. I think they might be hurting him." I tried to pull my arm from Elan's grasp, but his grip was firm.

"It could be a trap," he said gently. "Think about it, Vesper. They probably suspect you're out of the palace, but they aren't certain. Unless Ty told them, and I'll bet he hasn't. If you go running back, they'll *know* you ran off."

He was right. I had to think about this, or I could end up in more trouble. I looked up into his dark eyes, wishing I didn't find them quite so distracting. "What do you suggest?"

"You sneak back in a different way." He grinned. "I know a way you can get in without having to go through any of the main entrances. Follow me."

We moved faster than we had on the way out, which I was grateful for. My thoughts were clouded with worry for Ty, as well as what I'd just done to Elan. He'd said he'd never heard of anyone taking someone else's power before, and Marcus certainly never mentioned it. Was I even more of a freak than I'd thought?

"Here we go," Elan said in a low voice, stopping in the middle of a narrow street.

I looked around, confused. "What do you mean?"

He pointed to a square piece of metal set into the road. "The ancient sewer system. You can get in through the tunnels." He crouched down and pulled something from his belt, easing it under the edge of the metal plate.

I opened my mouth to protest—what was he thinking, crawling through sewers?—but a flash of power nearby caught my attention. I jerked my head up, suddenly aware that we were surrounded by minds. Talented minds.

"Elan, I—"

But I was too late.

A wall of fire exploded across the street in front of us. Elan sprang to his feet but was knocked backward as something pounced on top of him.

"No!" I lunged forward, then stopped as I caught sight of the elongated fangs inches from Elan's throat.

From the shadows, Caesar stepped out, his golden hair glowing red in the light of the flames. Diana followed, holding Ty's limp body in her hand. Behind them, lurking in Caesar's shadow, stood Marcus.

"Well, well," Caesar chuckled. "I finally get my hands on you, boy. Your father trained you well."

Elan's gaze flicked to him, eyes blazing. "You will never control me."

"I beg to differ," Caesar replied, arching an eyebrow. "I have to admit, I didn't think a pretty girl would be the key to bringing you in, but I guess we all have our weaknesses."

My hands curled into fists. Rage ignited my power. I stared at Marcus, daring him to meet my eye. *They used me.* I had confided in him, trusting him with the truth about Elan because I believed he truly wanted to help me. But he hadn't cared about any of that. All he wanted—all Caesar wanted—was to get his hands on Elan, and I had led him right into their trap.

Ty, are you all right?

He didn't move.

I pulled on all the power I had, drawing energy from deep inside and forming it into a lance, ready to strike.

Caesar's black eyes mocked me, daring me to lash out.

"Vesper, wait!" Marcus pushed past Caesar and held out his hand. "Ty is fine. He's just sleeping."

His tone was calm and soothing, as if trying to tame a wild animal. I felt his blocking powers press down on me, like a heavy blanket intended to extinguish a spark before it could burst into flame.

But the hurt of his betrayal added fuel to my fire. This was the man who'd spent hours trying to help me, who'd let me into his home and made me coffee. He made me believe I could use my talent for good.

Was it all a lie?

Inside me, power burned.

Marcus had said I was powerful. He was going to find out just how powerful I could be.

"Vesper, no!"

Elan's voice startled me, breaking my concentration. Before I could stop it, a burst of power shattered my shield. It flooded from me like a torrent, smashing through Marcus's powers and sending me reeling backward. There was a shout of pain and the sound of cursing. The flames illuminating the street disappeared, plunging us into darkness.

I fell to my knees, fighting to stay conscious.

For several long seconds, there was silence. Then the flames returned.

Marcus sat on the ground, holding his head in his hands. Caesar ignored him, fixing his cold, black eyes on me. "Take them both inside," he said, and I felt strong hands pull my arms behind my back.

Elan, I'm sorry. I didn't—

He slammed up his shield before I had a chance to finish my sentence. I opened my mouth to speak, but when he lifted his head and his eyes met mine, they were filled with such disgust and hatred, I wondered if he would ever speak to me again. Then he turned his back and let himself be taken away to Caesar's Palace.

24

Confession

M ARISSA'S FACE WAS PALE and lifeless. If it weren't for the gentle rise and fall of her chest, I'd have doubted there was any life in her. Someone had washed her face and tidied her blonde hair so it lay across her shoulders. The bed sheet had been pulled up under her arms, and I held one of her hands, as much because I felt I should as because I thought it would actually do her any good. Ty crouched on the other side of her, his neck stretched across her chest.

Is there any change?

He turned his head to gaze at me. *Her mind still feels closed.*

I had replaced Cayden at her bedside ten minutes ago. There seemed to be an unspoken schedule in place, people taking an hour shift at a time. The healer had said it was unlikely that she could sense our presence, but it felt wrong to just leave her alone. At first, I had stayed away, worried that my presence would make things worse, but even Cayden admitted that I hadn't been totally to blame for what had happened.

His words hadn't helped ease my guilt.

I glanced at the clock on the wall, the minutes dragging by. The Games were five days away. I knew Diana had come up with a different plan, one that didn't include me, and as I'd refused to go anywhere near Marcus after his betrayal, I didn't really have anything to do with my time.

Elan was locked in the underground room below the Colosseum, guarded by two of Caesar's strongest talents. I'd gone to see him yesterday, but he'd just turned his back on me and refused to talk. When I closed my eyes, I could still feel the brush of his lips on mine, but I knew there wouldn't be a repeat of that anytime soon. Maybe not ever. The thought left me hollow.

Ty had also been grumpy, ignoring me for the first twelve hours after he'd woken up. But after I'd managed to bribe the cooks into giving me a bowl of raw meat, he'd accepted my peace offering with gusto. It was a relief to know that there was someone who didn't hate me.

"Vesper? Can I come in?"

I stiffened at Marcus's voice. "I'd rather you didn't."

He ignored me and pulled up a chair on the other side of Marissa. Ty growled at him and jumped across Marissa's body to join me. Marcus looked tired, as if he hadn't slept for days. His dull skin sagged into small folds under his chin, and dark bags lined his eyes. He folded his hands on Marissa's bed and tried to meet my gaze. I stared resolutely at my friend's pale face.

Marcus was the last person I wanted to see, but I felt trapped. I couldn't really abandon Marissa just because he'd arrived.

"I want to explain," he said. "I know you must feel hurt and betrayed, but believe me, that wasn't my intention."

"Can you leave?" My words dripped acid. "I would like to spend some quiet time with my friend."

Marcus sighed. "You need to hear this, Vesper, and I knew this was the only time you wouldn't run away from me." He paused. When I didn't reply, he continued. "When you told me you'd managed to make contact with Elan, my first thought was hope. Hope he'd be able to teach you to control your powers, to succeed where I have failed."

He glanced at Marissa, and for a moment, his face was ravaged with grief.

"And I do feel like I have failed you, Vesper," he added quietly. "But I also knew that we needed both Elan and you to have any chance of winning the Games. I should have told you this earlier, but Caesar wanted it kept a secret, and to be honest, I didn't want you to feel the pressure of knowing what I know."

"I think you put enough pressure on me as it is," I snapped.

He bowed his head. "Perhaps that is true. I have never failed to train a student before, and maybe I was arrogant to believe that I would discover the secret to your powers in time. I know I have no right to ask this, but please, let me explain. Then I will leave you and Marissa in peace."

He took my silence as permission to continue.

"Some months ago, I had one of the strongest visions I have ever experienced. We were competing in the Games but losing badly. I recognized most of the people as members of our faction, but there was one girl who was a stranger to me." He glanced at me. "You. As I told you before, seeing the future is an art, not a science. I could not see what it was that you did, only that you burned brighter than anyone in that arena and were the center of everything."

I shifted uncomfortably in my chair.

"It is rare for me to see the same vision more than once," Marcus continued, "but I saw this one several times, though it played out differently each time. In the first version, you stood with Elan. The second time, you were alone. In many of the other variations, neither of you were there. I saw—" His voice broke as a shudder wracked his body. "I saw the arena filled with pain, suffering, death. Of all the visions, the one where both you and Elan were present was the only scenario in which we won. The only one in which our faction survived."

Silence stretched uncomfortably between us.

"So you think both Elan and I have to compete in order for us to win?" I asked finally.

Marcus bowed his head. "I believe it is the only way."

"And *how* do we win? What difference do the two of us make?"

"That is what I have been trying to work out ever since I saw you in Bobo's cage. In the vision, I could not even see what power you had. It was as if you were different from everyone else, yet part of everyone." He spread his hands and frowned. "I'm sure it's my lack of skill in interpreting the visions, but I still haven't been able to work out what it represented. I assumed it would become clear when we started training, but . . ."

"But then I couldn't do anything."

"It's not your fault, Vesper. We put too much pressure on you. *I* put too much pressure on you."

His sympathy and self-pity angered me. "You made me think you were trying to help me. But all you were concerned about was winning the Games."

"It's not about winning, Vesper. It's about our *survival*. The vision in which we lost . . . I have never had such an intense feeling of dread in my life, not even when they came to take Cleo away." His voice dropped to a whisper. "The Gladiators are my family. In my visions, I saw them die, again and again. I knew I had to do everything in my power to stop that from coming to pass."

He pushed himself up. "That is what I came to tell you. I know you have no love for Caesar or me, but please, think on it. Many lives rest on your decision."

He turned and began to walk toward the door, but something in his countenance made me call after him. "There's something else, isn't there? Something you're not telling me."

He paused, yet didn't reply.

I felt a spark of irritation. "If you're not going to tell me the whole truth, why bother to tell me anything at all?"

Slowly, Marcus dragged his gaze around to meet mine. His eyes were dark with sadness. "My vision ended with us winning the games. But what I could not see was whether you survived."

25

New Hope

I LAY IN BED, thinking about what Marcus had said. I didn't want to believe him. Didn't want to admit that he may have been justified in his betrayal.

Do you believe him? I asked Ty.

I think he was telling the truth, Ty replied after a moment. *But that doesn't mean he's right. He said himself that visions of the future are hard to interpret.*

So what do I do now? I thumped my fist on the bed. *I'm still no closer to mastering my powers.*

Ty uncurled himself from his usual spot by my feet and came to sit on my chest. *How did you get along with Elan? Before you got caught, I mean.*

I frowned, realizing I hadn't updated Ty on my attempts to influence Elan's mind. *I think I saw what he was getting at. I managed to get the thought into*

his head, but when I tried to draw back, I somehow pulled his power from him.

I remembered how strong I'd felt, almost as if I were on fire. "That's it," I breathed.

I sat bolt upright. Ty scrabbled at my thin vest, then toppled backward and fell onto the floor in a heap.

Some warning would have been nice. He hopped back up onto the bed. *What is it?*

I think I know what Marcus's vision meant. I swung my legs around and began to pull on my boots. *I need to speak to Elan. Can you wake Cayden*

and ask him to meet us down below the Colosseum?

Now?

Yes. Now. I stomped over to the door. *We don't have any time to waste.*

He sounds a bit grumpy, but he's on his way, Ty said a moment later.

Bren and a man I didn't know were on guard when I arrived at the door to the room where Elan was being held. Bren raised one eyebrow as I approached. "It's a bit late for you to be out and about. I thought you'd learned your lesson about wandering around at night."

"I need to speak with Elan," I said. "It's important."

Bren frowned and exchanged a look with the other guard.

"You can come in with me," I said quickly. "I'm not trying to help him escape or anything. I just figured something out and need to test it. I've asked Cayden to come down to help."

Bren's frown deepened.

"Please?" I widened my eyes in what I hoped was a convincing demonstration of innocence. "I think I can do something that could help us win the Games."

Bren glanced at his colleague, then gave a reluctant nod. "Well, okay, but we'll need to let Caesar know that you've been here."

I nodded. "If I'm right, I'll have good news for him."

Bren unlocked the door and pushed it open, handing the key to his companion. "Lock us in."

I hurried into the room. The cages were dark and empty, except for one. Electricity crackled around the iron bars, casting a pale glow over Elan, who was curled up in the far corner. I swallowed as the cages in the room brought back unpleasant memories of the short time I'd spent here. If they wanted Elan to fight for them in the Games, I wasn't sure that locking him up like a slave was going to endear them to him.

Elan stirred as we entered. I caught a flash of his eyes under a dark mop of hair before he turned away again. Bren took his stance in front of the door, and I stood as close to the cage as I dared, wondering where to start.

"Elan, I know you hate me right now, but I promise you, I had no idea what Caesar and Marcus had planned." I looked down at my hands. "They betrayed me as much as you."

He didn't move.

"I think I've worked out what my power really is."

There was a sharp intake of breath from Bren, but still, Elan didn't move. I took a deep breath. "I need you to help me test it out. Please. I don't trust anyone else."

Finally, Elan stirred, pushing himself up until he sat cross-legged. "And why do you trust me?"

Because you want to get out of here as much as me.

He seemed to consider this for a moment, then lay back down.

Elan, please.

But his mind was closed to me. An ache grew in my chest, pressing against my ribcage. Why did I always have to screw everything up? The last thing I had wanted to do was get Elan captured. The pain intensified. I had only known this man a matter of weeks—and had hated him for most of that time—but I couldn't bear the thought that he would think ill of me.

A thickness in my throat made it hard to breathe. Ty's claws squeezed my shoulder. I guessed he was trying to be supportive.

Just then, the key turned in the lock of the door and Cayden walked in. His hair was mussed and he looked half-asleep. He sauntered over to Elan's cage and peered in. "Back here again, are you? Now you know what it feels like."

"Cayden . . ." I let a warning note enter my voice. The last thing I needed was for him to antagonize Elan, however bitter he felt toward him.

Cayden glanced back at me. "What? Man can't take a taste of his own medicine?"

"Just . . . Shut up, okay?" I felt tears begin to blur my vision and blinked rapidly.

Cayden's face softened. "Sure. Sorry, Vesper." He looked around. "What's all this about?"

Quickly, I explained what Marcus had told me about his vision. "He said I was different from everyone else, yet part of everyone else. He couldn't work out what that meant, but I think it's something to do with my ability to draw power from others."

"Like what happened with Marissa?" Cayden's face darkened. "I don't see how that helps."

"What if I can give power as well as draw it from people?" I spoke faster as the thought coalesced in my mind. "If I can give others my strength—my power—it will enhance their abilities. Marcus says I'm the strongest person he's ever come across. Perhaps my ability is that I can transfer power to others."

I paused, breathless. Cayden looked confused.

"I guess, theoretically, that could work."

I whirled around in surprise at Elan's voice. He was sitting up again, looking at me thoughtfully. "But it wouldn't be easy. It's not just you who'd have to control your power. It's the person you're feeding it to."

"I know," I said quietly. "But I think I can, now that I know what I'm supposed to be doing."

I turned to Cayden and pointed to the heavy, wooden cage Marissa had been held captive in. "Can you try to lift that cage?"

Cayden snorted. "Are you having a laugh? I can't lift that."

"Just try. Please?"

His cheeks flushed. "If you're trying to make me look bad in front of your boyfriend, I want—"

"I'm not. I just need to see what you can do. And he's not my boyfriend." I dared not look at Elan, grateful that the darkness of the room hid my burning face.

Cayden turned toward the cage, his expression focused. A thin vein on his forehead throbbed and his jaw clenched. The cage didn't move an inch. After a few seconds, his shoulders sagged and he turned back to me.

"See? Even Cato would struggle with that."

"Okay. This time, I'm going to try feeding you my power." I thought for a minute. "Can you open your shield a fraction? I'm not quite sure how this works. Whether I have to push it in or you have to be open to accept it."

Cayden turned slightly pale. "Are you sure this is a good idea? You know what happened with Marissa."

"Ty gave me an unexpected surge of power that I wasn't expecting," I said, more confidently than I felt. "That shouldn't happen now."

I turned to Bren. "If anything starts going wrong, knock me out."

Bren looked taken aback.

"I mean it," I said. "I don't want to risk anyone."

That goes for you, too, Ty. Dig your claws in or something.

His talons tightened on my shoulder. *Now there's an offer I don't get every day.*

I smiled at Cayden. "Let's give it a go, okay?"

Reluctantly, he nodded. "What do I need to do?"

"Just try to accept my power rather than push it away." I closed my eyes, then reached out with a thin flow of power, just as Elan had taught me. I sensed Cayden's shield and sent a small pulse of energy out, but it just spread around the surface.

"Give me an opening," I mumbled.

I sensed his shield shift and a crack open. I let my power flow in. Just a trickle at first, then a little more.

"Can you feel it?"

"Yes, I . . . Stop there." Cayden's voice was tight with concentration.

I cut the stream of power and opened my eyes. Cayden stared at the cage again. It began to vibrate. One corner lifted perhaps an inch off the floor, then fell back down with a thud.

Cayden relaxed, a sheen of sweat on his brow. "That was amazing," he breathed. He turned to me. "Your power is so intense. For a minute, I thought it was going to overwhelm me, that I'd lose control, but once I managed to meld it with mine, I felt so much stronger."

Relief flooded through me. It worked! I didn't tell Cayden that I'd only given him a tiny fraction of the power I held inside.

"Okay. The next thing I want to try is to see if I can draw power from one person and feed it through to another at the same time."

"Like a channel?" Cayden asked.

I nodded and turned to Elan's cage. He hadn't moved, still sitting, his face in the shadows cast by the single light. "Do you mind?"

"You using me as a power battery?" He let out a mirthless chuckle. "Do I have a choice?"

My smile faltered. "Yes. I won't try it if you don't want me to."

Slowly, Elan got to his feet and padded across the cage to stand in front of me. Only the crackling iron bars separated us. Dried blood matted his hair, and a large bruise darkened his jaw in the same spot I'd run my thumb over two nights ago.

"Have they not even given you water to wash?" I whispered, horrified.

Elan just grunted in response. His eyes scanned my face, and I felt his mind fleetingly brush against mine. The sensation sent a flash of heat coursing through me.

"Fine. Let's give it a go. Just make sure you're in control, okay?"

"I promise." I hesitated. "Just don't try and push it at me, okay? Let me take it."

This time, I kept my eyes open but stared at the floor so I wouldn't get distracted. I sensed the opening in Elan's mind and, like before, sent a tendril of power toward it. When I pulled it back, nothing happened. I tried a gentle "tug". Still nothing.

Maybe try and give me a bit? I asked Elan.

A whiff of power leaked out from his shield. I latched onto it, drawing it back with me, feeling it mingle with mine. Once the connection between us was established, I found Elan's power flowed naturally to me and I could control how much of it I received by closing or widening the channel between us. Thankfully, Elan was better than me at keeping his emotions locked away, letting me concentrate on the task at hand instead of having to feel his hatred and anger.

Tentatively, I sent out a thread of power to Cayden, sensing the crack in his shield and letting my power—and Elan's—flow into him. While it took a lot of concentration to set up, once I had the two links connected, it wasn't hard to keep the power flowing.

I glanced up at Cayden. His eyes were wide and his skin almost, well . . . *Glowed* was the only way I could describe it.

"Are you okay?" My voice sounded as if it came from a different person.

"Yes. Just keep it steady." Cayden's voice rang with excitement. He stared at the cage, which slowly began to rise off the floor.

Cautiously, I fed a little more power through to Cayden. The cage rose farther and hung in the air, vibrating.

A flash of fear crossed Cayden's face. "That's enough," he panted.

I tightened the power thread slowly until it was barely a trickle, then cut it. The cage slammed to the floor.

"What's going on in there?" a voice from outside the door shouted.

Bren muttered something in response, but I was too focused on cutting my connection with Elan to listen. It took me a few attempts to figure out how to let his power go, and when it finally dissipated, I felt kind of lost.

Cayden stared at the cage. "Wow. I mean, *wow*."

I searched Elan's face. "Are you okay? It wasn't too much?"

He shook his head, a ghost of a smile crossing his lips. "No, it was fine. That was pretty amazing."

For a moment, the four of us stood in silence. Then Bren cleared his throat. "Caesar will need to know about this."

"Don't worry. I intend to tell him." I hesitated, then turned to him. "Could you just give Elan and I a moment alone?" I held up a finger. "I'll literally be one minute. I just want to ask him something in private."

"Hmm . . . Okay, but keep it quick. If you do anything stupid, it'll be me Caesar punishes," he warned.

I smiled. "Don't worry. I've broken enough rules for one day."

Cayden crossed to the door. "I guess I'll be going back to bed then. Unless you want me to stay?"

I shook my head. "No. It's probably best you get some rest. I may need you again tomorrow to demonstrate."

Cayden rolled his eyes. "Good to know I have my uses."

After he and Bren left, I turned back to Elan. "Thank you."

He grunted and turned away.

"Do you hate me?" I whispered to his retreating back.

As soon as the words left my mouth, I regretted them. *Who asks a person that? And what if he says yes?*

Elan paused. I could see the profile of his face in the dim light. "Is that what you wanted to ask me in private?"

I flushed. "No . . . I mean . . ." I waved a hand through the air. "It doesn't matter." I sucked in a breath and tried to control my pounding heart. "I wanted to ask you two things. Firstly, did Caesar do something to your father?"

Elan's jaw tightened. "What makes you ask that?"

"The way you hate him. And what he said when they . . . when they found us. About your father training you. It sounded as if he knew him." I reached out a hand, then yanked it back when a spark from the cage jumped across to my skin. "Sorry. I guess that's rather a personal question."

"My father did some work for Caesar. He didn't want to, but my mother was sick and we were tight on money. Caesar sent him down into the tunnels to find the demon. My father never returned." Elan's shoulders tensed and he cleared his throat.

"So he could still be alive?"

"No." Elan shook his head. "I . . . I followed him down. I heard him die."

"I'm sorry." My palms felt sweaty. I wiped them on my pants.

Elan shrugged. "What else did you want to ask me?"

"You heard what I said to Cayden about Marcus's vision? We need you to win the Games. Will . . . Will you help us?"

Elan let out a harsh laugh. "Why would I do that?" He whipped around and stalked over to the front of the cage. He was close enough that I could almost feel his breath on my skin. Only the crackling bars separated us. "Caesar killed my father." His voice was low and intense, hands clenched at his sides. "He took everything from me. And now you

want me to fight for him?"

I looked into his dark eyes, though his gaze burned into me. "Not for him, Elan. For us. For me." I swallowed. "For your mom."

Anger flashed in his eyes. "You leave my mom out of this."

I itched to reach through the bars of his cage, to take his hand and run my fingers over his calloused skin. I crossed my arms to distract myself from the thought.

"I know you need to get out of here," I said quietly. "But you must know there's no chance of that unless you help us. I'm going to talk to Caesar. I know how we can win, but I'll only tell him on the condition that, after the Games, he releases you."

Elan snorted. "Even if he agreed, Caesar wouldn't keep his word."

"Marcus and Diana would make him."

"Marcus? The person who betrayed you?"

I looked down at the floor, flinching at the sarcasm in his voice. Marcus's betrayal still hurt, but I believed his story. No one could fake that level of grief. "He truly believes

you and I are the key to saving the Gladiators. Once the Games are over, he's got no reason to keep you captive. As for Diana, she has this weird sense of honor. I don't think she'd go back on a bargain. And Caesar respects both of them."

Elan was silent for a moment. "You can ask him. If he agrees —which I doubt he will—then I'll fight with you."

"Great." I turned to leave, feeling slightly disappointed at his reaction to my offer. "Well, I'll let you know."

"Vesper," he called as I reached the door.

I turned to see him staring at me. Purple sparks flickered in front of his face.

"I don't hate you," he said quietly, then turned and walked to the back of his cage.

I pulled open the door and stepped out into the corridor, a smile tugging at my lips.

Bren was waiting. "Follow me. I'll take you to Caesar. I don't reckon he'll want to wait until morning."

He led me through a series of corridors to a large set of double doors guarded by a woman and a man. When they saw us approach, one of them knocked and pushed the door inward, revealing a furnished apartment. As we entered, Caesar walked in from a door at the right, tying a robe around his waist.

"This had better be worth waking me up for," he growled.

"Oh, it is," I said, feeling a sense of satisfaction at knowing something he didn't. "I know how Bellagio wins the Games. And how we can stop him."

26

The Games Begin

"**R**EMEMBER THE PLAN," DIANA instructed. "Cato's team, your priority is to find the Players and take out Damon. If Vesper's right, once he's no longer able to feed the rest of his team power, they should be easy enough to overcome."

Once I'd explained my theory about Damon's powers and Bellagio's strategy to Caesar and Diana, they'd reverted back to the original plan of splitting into two groups. Diana hadn't been convinced at first, but when I'd demonstrated how I could enhance Cayden's powers, she'd relented.

"It would explain why, individually, they seem much stronger than they should be. And why they attack in small groups rather than one big unit."

Marcus had nodded. "He can't be strong enough to boost all of their powers, but if he's able to move power between different people, it's just a case of timing and making sure they don't all attack at once. It must take a lot of skill and focus."

"They always have at least three people around him, and he keeps out of the way of the fighting as much as possible." Diana shrugged. "We've never bothered to target him, as it didn't seem worth it. Better to pick off the telkies and burners—those who seemed to pose the biggest threat."

We'd spent the last four days training. I was exhausted from long hours spent learning how to share power faster and more efficiently, but there was no time to rest. To help compensate, Marcus had fed me some of his own power just an hour before we'd left for the Games. It galled me to have to accept his help, but I knew we needed every advantage we could get. But power wasn't everything. The strain of controlling it was my limiting factor.

I adjusted the piece of green cloth around my upper arm. We all wore them, even Elan, though as far as I knew, Caesar hadn't branded him. Yet. Caesar had promised me that if we won, he'd let Elan go. I hoped he would keep that promise.

A warm breeze blew tendrils of hair across my cheek. I'd fashioned it into a tight braid, but already some unruly strands had come loose. Dust swirled into the air, hissing over the barren ridge that hid our view of the arena. I closed my eyes, picturing it as I'd looked down on it yesterday. It was how I imagined a post-apocalyptic wasteland would look. Irregular mounds and shallow valleys created a gnarled landscape scattered with the remnants of burned-out vehicles and ancient buildings, long since razed to the ground. Only the skeletal, bleached remains of trees indicated this place had once supported life.

I took a deep breath, trying to control my churning stomach. I'd been sick once this morning already but had forced down food, knowing I needed the energy.

"Nervous?" Cayden whispered.

I jumped as his voice broke the tense silence. "A bit."

He grinned. "Don't worry. I'll look after you. Just keep feeding me that juice."

Cayden had acted friendlier toward me the last few days. It helped that Marissa had finally woken up. She was still weak, but the medic didn't think there would be any long-term damage. Her recovery had lightened my spirits and boosted my confidence. I'd even caught myself fantasizing about the rewards we'd get for winning the Games—more water for drinking and washing—but had to stop myself as the image of a hot bubble bath filled my mind. That was one step too far.

Even if we were able to mess with Bellagio's plans, there was no guarantee we would win.

What I could not see was whether you survived.

A shiver ran down my spine as Marcus's words came back to me.

On my other side, Elan grunted and shot Cayden a cold look. "Yeah, and as soon as you let loose one of your fireballs, *everyone* will know where we are. If we do our job right, *you* won't have to lift a finger."

Tension radiated off Elan's body. I reached out, hesitated for a second to gather my nerves, then gave his hand a squeeze. He didn't pull away but made no move to return the gesture. I sighed inwardly as I let go. He might have said he didn't hate me, but I wasn't sure we were friends, either.

"We'll be working as a team." Thora's voice carried a trace of warning. "That's the only way we can win."

Diana had been talking to Cato in a low voice. She came over to join us. "Everyone ready?"

I nodded, straightening my shoulders. I was already sweating under the leather vest I'd been given to wear for protection, and my hand twitched toward the small water carrier attached to my belt. But I knew I had to ration it. We wouldn't get any more until the Games ended. Thora had said that some years, they'd gone on through the day and into the night.

"As soon as the bell sounds, I want Ty to go up and scout," Diana told me. "Not a moment before, or we'll be called out for cheating."

"Sure."

I relayed the message to Ty, who was perched on Cato's shoulder. Although he could talk to anyone except Diana, whose shield was impenetrable, even to him, only myself and Elan were able to talk directly to him. My role was as much to act as the communicator between the two groups as it was to feed Elan the power he needed to shield us from the eyes of our opponents.

I wish I was coming with you, Ty said mournfully.

Me too. But this plan makes sense. We'll have a huge advantage over the other teams. Just make sure you keep out of the fighting, okay?

Ty just whirred his eyes at me in response.

Caesar had to get special permission from the Gamesmasters before they'd let him in. No one had bought a creature into the Games before. After some debate, they allowed Ty to compete on the condition that he replaced a human member of the team.

A bell rang out. It tolled dolefully, as if calling mourners to a funeral. The noise reverberated in my bones.

This was it.

"*Coniuncti stamus*," Diana intoned.

"*Coniuncti stamus*," came the collective reply.

Ty launched himself off Cato's shoulder, soaring into the sky, as most of the Gladiators followed Cato up the ridge that hid our view of the arena. Diana motioned our small group to follow her. We skirted alongside the wall until we reached a channel.

Each of the factions had started at the outside perimeter of the arena, equidistant from the tower in the center. At a flat-out run, you could have crossed the distance in a couple of minutes, but the terrain was rough and uneven, and that didn't take into account the other dangers lurking in the arena and the tower itself.

What can you see, Ty?

The Sirens and the Players are both moving forward. I can't see the other two. They must be on the far side of the tower.

Can you see Damon?

There was a pause before Ty answered. *No. The Players have split up already, but I can't see him.*

I whispered this to Diana. A flash of concern crossed the older woman's face. "How many can he count?"

Fifteen, Ty said. *But everyone's splitting up now. I— A* screech of rage followed his comment.

I jerked my head toward the sky. An odd mist rolled in, blanketing the arena in a ghostly haze.

"What is that?" Cayden murmured.

"One of the Gamesmaster's surprises," Thora replied. "I guess they didn't want us getting too much of an advantage by having a dragon."

Ty?

Bloody Siren threw a fireball at me. He sounded more indignant than hurt.

I let out a sigh of relief. *Go back to Cato. You won't be able to see anything in this mist anyway.*

Diana beckoned us to crowd around her. "We'll start trying to make our way toward the tower. Vesper, you follow right behind me. If you need to speak to me, tap me on the shoulder and whisper into my ear." She glanced around. "No one else is to say anything unless it's a matter of life or death. And move quietly. Elan, you come behind Vesper. Bren, you're in the rear."

The redheaded man nodded. There was the faintest tension in his features, but he and Thora seemed relaxed compared to many of the others. I guessed they'd been through enough Games to have learned how to deal with the stress.

We set off down the narrow valley, Diana leading the way, her staff held across her body, ready to strike. I followed a couple paces behind, watching where she placed her feet on the uneven ground, trying to place mine in the same spots. The silence around us felt oppressive, and my nerves were on edge, waiting for the first scream.

I didn't have to wait long.

A strange, almost inhuman roar ripped through the silence, followed by a woman's cry. Purple sparks shot into the air, far enough away that I knew none of our faction had been hurt. A column of dust whipped across the horizon, blending into the mist hanging over the arena. From that point on, the sounds of fighting filled the air.

Through it all, Diana kept moving, slowly and steadily. We kept to the dips in the terrain, weaving between low ridges and skirting around several small ponds of stagnant water and what looked like a huge sandpit set into a long slope.

We've made contact with Bellagio's team. Ty sounded excited. *No sign of the mind-talker.*

I tapped Diana's shoulder and relayed the message. She nodded but didn't reply. Cato knew the importance of trying to find Damon as soon as possible. He didn't need reminding.

We entered another gulch, this one deeper than the last, the ridges on either side tall enough to shield us. Ahead, I caught a glimpse of the tower, mist swirling around the upper levels.

Diana motioned for us to crouch down as we approached the burned-out carcass of what looked like some kind of ground vehicle.

Where is everyone? Have we just been lucky, or are we walking into a trap?

I bit my lip, realizing that I could find out. Why hadn't I thought to sense if there were people around us before now? I cursed inwardly.

Now is not the time to be forgetful.

I sent a tendril of power out, scanning the surrounding area for any sign of people. What I found made my blood run cold.

There were two groups, six people in total, waiting on the far sides of the ridges, flanking us. They had us surrounded.

I reached out to tap Diana's shoulder, but at that moment, the vehicle in front of us exploded.

Air was sucked from my lungs as I was thrown backward. Coughing, I gasped for breath, sand and blood filling my mouth. Through the ringing in my ears, I was dimly aware of running feet, along with shouts of anger and confusion.

Bolts of purple lightning clashed in mid-air with a crack that cut through the humming in my head. I blinked and scrubbed my eyes with the back of my hand as the smoke from the explosion began to clear.

We'd been ambushed by the Sirens. I could just make out the flashes of blue on their arms. Bren, Thora, and Cayden stood back to back, fighting what seemed to be three or four assailants. Diana and Elan were nowhere to be seen.

Power. They need my power.

I forced myself onto my hands and knees, trying to catch my breath so I could focus on sending help to my friends. But just then, Thora said something to Bren and a wall of fire rose up around them. Through the flickering flames, I watched them pull back, pursued by their attackers, leaving me totally alone.

I lurched to my feet, wondering what I was supposed to do now. I could go after the others, but between me and them were four angry Sirens. Worse, I couldn't actually *do* anything to defend myself. I couldn't throw fireballs or concrete blocks. I couldn't make sparks appear from my hands. All I could do was help others to be stronger.

Damn this curse.

Are you okay, Vesper? Ty's concerned voice sounded in my head.

Yes. I just got separated from the others, I replied. *How are things with you?*

Bit tough. Still . . . not found . . . Damon. Ty sounded distracted

Stay safe. I'm going to try and find the others. I cut our connection.

Next, I searched for Elan. *Where are you?*

I felt a flood of relief through our connection. *With Diana. Where are you?*

Back in the gulch. I got separated from the others I—

"Well, what have we here." The voice was cold and calculating.

"Did Diana's little mind-talker get separated from her friends?" a second voice mocked.

"What a shame," a third woman added. "And without her dragon to protect her."

I opened my eyes and looked into the faces of Apollina's Furies. They seemed to have materialized from nowhere, though with all the confusion, they could have been right behind me and I wouldn't have noticed. I backed away. They took a step forward. I risked a quick glance over my shoulder, but the gulch behind me was empty.

I tried to remember what Diana had told me about them and put names to faces.

"You're on your own, little mind-talker," the woman with copper hair crooned. *Mara.* "Let's see how strong you really are, shall we?"

A stab of power hit my shield. I responded instinctively, grateful for the weeks I'd spent with Marcus adding layer upon layer to strengthen my mental protection. I sensed Elan pushing at my mind, but I couldn't protect myself from the Furies' attack and talk to him at the same time.

The black woman with the shaved head—Evalie—added her power and the two strands swirled together, like a drill. When they struck my shield, the bone-jarring impact reverberated around my head and my protections began to splinter.

Sweat trickled down the back of my neck as I worked to strengthen my shield, using Marcus's power as well as my own to mold the layers together into something that was hard enough to withstand the intrusion.

The third fury—a tall, lanky woman with short, brown hair—sent the first tendrils of her power out to add to the mix and my heart quailed. Then her eyes widened as she caught sight of something over my shoulder and grasped the arm of her companion.

The copper-haired woman let out an irritated click and the pressure on my shield lessoned. "What is it, Lorelei?"

The clip-clop of footsteps sounded from behind me. No, not footsteps . . . *Hooves*? A heavy musky scent reached me on the breeze, almost making me gag.

Mara slapped her hand to her mouth, retching. She tugged at her companion's arm, and I felt the pressure on my skull ease. They stepped back, slowly and fearfully.

"We'll be seeing you later," Lorelei said with a smile. "If there's anything left of you." The three of them turned and ran up the slope, disappearing over the rise.

A voice inside my head screamed at me to follow, but my feet were frozen to the ground. The musky stench grew heavier as I slowly turned around to face the beast.

It towered above me, perhaps eight feet tall. Its shoulders were huge, seemingly out of proportion to the rest of its body. Curved horns sliced through the air as it tossed its head before fixing its eyes—all three of them—on me. A thin tail swished from side to side, and a line of curved spines rose on its back. It pawed the ground, muscles rippling under its skin.

Was this the bison Marissa had faced in the Colosseum? The one who could smell fear?

"Easy there," I murmured, patting the air in front of me with my hand as if this would somehow calm the creature. I glanced over my shoulder, wondering whether to make a run for it, but I'd bet Sol's orange dragon that the beast was faster than me.

The bison snorted and steam shot from its nostrils. Throwing back its head, it let out a roar, revealing two rows of sharp, yellowed fangs.

Then it charged.

27

The Beast

T HE BEAST POUNDED TOWARD me, its huge strides quickly eating up the distance. The stench of its breath preceded it. It smelled of death. I stood fixated, unable to tear my gaze from the looming monster.

At the last minute, my brain sparked into action and I threw myself to one side, hitting the ground and rolling as the dust from the bison's passage billowed around me. My hands scrabbled across the ground, desperately seeking some kind of weapon. I curled my fingers around a couple of stones. They were barely the size of my palm and I couldn't see them making much of an impression on the creature's thick hide, but I had no other plan.

The beast's momentum had carried it past me and it skidded to a halt, circling around for another attempt. I got to my feet and weighed the stone in my hand. I was pretty sure the chances of me hitting one of its eyes were about as slim as me surviving a trampling under its hooves.

The monster bellowed, a deep-throated roar that echoed in my ears. My hand began to tremble and I gritted my teeth, willing it to stay steady. I drew my arm back. As the beast charged, I threw the stone with all the strength I could muster. It bounced harmlessly off the bison's gnarled forehead. The second stone ricocheted off its muzzle, which only served to enrage the creature even more.

I dove aside as it charged, but either I was a fraction too early or it had learned from my previous move because it kicked out one of its hind legs as it passed, catching me in the stomach.

I doubled over as I fell to the ground, clenching my jaw so I didn't cry out.

Get to your feet, dammit!

But my body wouldn't respond. I sensed the beast coming closer, sniffing the air above me. Not knowing what else to do, I lay still. Perhaps, playing dead would cause the beast to move on. That was what you were supposed to do with bison, wasn't it? Or was that bears?

The beast bellowed again, the noise rattling inside my skull. I risked a glance up, immediately regretting it. Globules of saliva dripped from its lolling tongue onto my face. I twisted to my side, fighting an overwhelming urge to vomit, and clawed at the ground to try and pull myself away, though I knew the gesture was futile. Its breath was hot on my neck.

There was a flash of movement out the corner of my eye. The beast's head jerked back, and it let out a deafening roar. Not a roar of victory but a roar of pain.

It turned, nearly trampling me under its hindquarters, its tail slicing through the skin on my arm as it turned to face this new threat.

Strong hands grabbed my shoulders, pulling me roughly along the ground. Elan's mind touched mine. *Are you okay?*

I think so, I replied, one hand still clutching my stomach. The sharp pain had faded to a dull ache.

He helped me to my feet, placing my arm around his shoulders and looping his arm around my waist. He began to half pull, half carry me up the slope toward the crest of the ridge.

"Wait!" I pulled back and turned to see what had happened to the beast.

Black blood streamed from several deep gashes to its hindquarters and it dragged one of its back legs awkwardly, as if it were broken. Diana danced around the creature, running forward to jab her staff into its belly before darting back as its massive head turned to snap at her. A pointed blade glinted from one end of the staff.

"We have to help her."

"With what?" Elan growled. "Our minds?"

Just then, the creature snarled and lunged, snapping its jaws shut on Diana's leg. She fell to the ground with a grunt of pain, then bought her staff down hard on the beast's muzzle, causing it to release its grip and rear back. It screeched in anger and pain.

Diana's eyes met mine. "Run, you idiots!"

I let Elan pull me up over the crest of the ridge and down the other side, our feet skidding and sliding in the sand. At the bottom of the slope, I pulled him to a halt. "We can't just leave her there."

Elan glanced back, his chest heaving from exertion. "What can we do? She's a better fighter than both of us together."

Ty! Need you here—now. Diana's being attacked.

I sensed a flash of surprise.

On my way.

I shook off Elan's arm and tried to run back up the slope, my feet scrabbling for purchase.

"What are you doing? She told us to run."

"She has the flag," I panted. "Without that, we can't win." *That, if nothing else, should convince him to help.*

Elan cursed and followed me up the slope. We crested the ridge to see Diana hauling herself to her feet. She stood on one leg, swaying slightly, the other hanging like a dead weight, blood flowing from a deep wound on her thigh. Yet she grasped her staff firmly in her hands as she stared the beast in the eye.

"You've got to hand it to her," Elan murmured. "The woman never gives up."

The creature eyeballed her, then lunged and grabbed the staff. Diana yanked it back, trying to twist it from the beast's grasp, but her weight was no match for the power of its jaws. She didn't let go, though, not even when it tossed its head, cartwheeling her through the air.

I glanced around, searching for a weapon, but there was nothing. Then Elan's words hit me. I could knock out a human, even a talented person, with my mind. Surely I could do the same to a beast?

I closed my eyes, feeling the well of power inside me. Drawing on a fraction of it, I threw it like a spear toward the bison's mind.

It let out a bellow of pain and reared back, shaking its head and pawing at the ground. Released from its grip, Diana fell back to the ground. With a roar almost equal to that of the beast's, she pushed herself up onto her good leg and plunged the pointed blade of the staff into the bison's exposed throat.

Black blood flowed out. The beast writhed and threw its weight forward, forcing Diana to her knees. Still, she did not relent. It opened its jaw to roar, but all it could manage was a gurgle as it shook its head in one last defiant gesture before collapsing to the ground, trapping Diana under its massive bulk.

I ran down the slope, but Elan was faster. He wedged his shoulder under the beast and, with a grunt of exertion, heaved upward. It was just enough that I was able to pull Diana free.

The warrior's face was pale, her golden hair stained with the dark blood of the creature she'd killed. I scanned her body anxiously, my heart sinking as I saw the red blood pulsing from her leg. Elan quickly ripped off part of his shirt, which I used to bind the wound.

"It's not far to the arena perimeter," I told Diana. "We'll get you out as quickly as we can."

Her hand grasped my arm, fingers digging into my skin. "No. Leave me . . . You have to go on."

I stared at her in horror. "Don't be stupid."

Diana pushed herself up onto her elbows, her face twisting in pain at the movement. "I can get myself out." She fumbled inside her vest and pulled out a tattered piece of green cloth, shoving it into my hands. Her bloody fingers left black smears on the fabric.

"Take it, Vesper," she said hoarsely. "Find the others. Do whatever you have to, just get that flag up the tower. And remember to watch your back."

Breath hissed through her teeth and she squeezed her eyes shut. Stretching her right hand out, she groped along the ground. Silently, Elan fetched her staff and placed it into her grasp.

Do you still need me? Ty flew down to land on the ground beside me.

I looked down at the bloodstained flag in my hands, feeling the weight of the responsibility that had been passed to me. Ty twisted his neck, gazing at Diana, then extended his head so it rested on her arm.

She gave a sharp intake of breath, then the tension in her face relaxed a fraction. "He really can take away pain," she murmured.

I nodded. "He can go with you."

Diana shook her head. "You need him here." She gave a wan smile. "I'll be all right. I've had worse."

She looked down at Ty and gently pulled her arm from under his head. "Thank you, dragon," she said quietly. Her expression turned stern as she glanced up at me and Elan. "Now, go. You can't have much time left. *Coniuncti stamus.*"

I shoved the flag inside my vest and stood. Elan hesitated, then reached down to squeeze Diana's shoulder. "Good luck. You'll be needing another tattoo now."

Once we reached the crest of the ridge, I looked back to see Diana, standing on one leg and leaning heavily on her staff as she limped in the direction of the perimeter wall.

"*Coniuncti stamus,*" I whispered into the air.

There was no way she could have heard me, but Diana looked back and a faint smile crossed her face as she ripped the green armband from her arm and raised it in salute. Then she turned and continued her journey alone.

28

Confrontation

I TURNED BACK TO survey the arena. The mist had lifted slightly. The echoing sounds of fighting must have been coming from the valleys between the ridges because from our vantage point, the arena seemed to be deserted.

"So, what do we do now?" Elan asked.

Ty, can you scout?

The dragon nodded and launched himself off my shoulder. He returned a few minutes later. I winced as his claws dug through the thin leather of my vest.

The Venetians and Ragazzi are busy fighting each other, though both are close to the tower, he reported. *The rest of your group were forced to flee, but they injured a couple of the Sirens badly enough that they're out of the Games. They're heading this way now.*

What's Cato's team up to? Elan asked.

Still battling the Players.

And Damon? I sent.

There was a pause before Ty replied, sounding triumphant. *I found him. He and a couple others are hiding behind some concrete blocks in a valley the other side of where Cato's fighting. Cato doesn't have anyone available to attack them.*

He's having a hard enough time just holding off the rest of Damon's force. They need my help.

I exchanged a look with Elan. "Let's go," he said.

After giving us rough directions through the maze of valleys, Ty flew off. It wasn't hard to figure out where our team was, though. We just had to follow the sounds of fighting.

"Keep your shield tight and *don't* reach out to him," Elan murmured as he quickly limped through the rough terrain. "Hopefully Damon is fully occupied with the rest of his team, but the closer we can get to him without him detecting us, the better."

"Good idea."

I'd been about to reach out with my mind to see if I could sense the mind-talker and confirm Ty's report. Now I realized how stupid this would have been. If he even sensed my mind touching his, he'd suspect something. Surprise was our only advantage, even if that meant sacrificing some of our ability to communicate. We'd have to rely on Ty's eyes to guide us.

Elan, whose senses were sharper than mine, pulled me back behind the dubious shelter of a vehicle's shell a second before I heard footsteps approaching. I eyed the hunk of metal warily, remembering the explosion of the last one we'd encountered.

Moments later, Bren rounded the corner, followed by Cayden and Thora. I burst out from behind the wrecked vehicle and rushed over to my friends. Bren's face sagged in relief.

"Good to see you," he said gruffly. His gaze passed over Elan, who walked toward us, and scanned the landscape. "Diana?"

"She's alive . . ."

Thora caught my hesitation. "But?"

"She's badly wounded," Elan said. "Killed a bison, though." It was the first time I'd ever heard anything approaching admiration in his voice.

"What about the flag?" Bren asked in a low voice.

I pulled the fragment of fabric out from under my vest and his face relaxed. "Do you want it?"

He covered my hand, pushing it back under my vest. "No, you keep it hidden. That way, the opposition won't know who's got it."

Of course. They don't even have to take out the whole team to make us lose. Just whoever has the flag.

I grinned, a thought striking me.

"What?" Elan asked.

"Damon may be the key to Bellagio's strategy, but as the most heavily guarded person on their team, I bet he has their flag."

Thora glanced at me in surprise. "You're probably right. I hadn't thought of that. Do you know where he is?"

I nodded. "Ty said he's hiding just on the other side of the ridge from where Cato's fighting. We thought we'd sneak up on them. He's only got a couple of guards."

Thora nodded. "Lead the way then."

We crept close to the fighting until a call from Ty made me raise my hand. "Ty thinks they're just over this ridge," I murmured.

Bren motioned for us to retreat ten paces and huddle around him. "We'll use the cover of the ridge to attack," he whispered. "I don't think Elan's mind tricks are likely to work on Damon, so I need you both to boost our powers so we can take out the guards and bring him to us."

We both nodded, knowing he was right.

Elan took my hand, the contact helping us forge a stronger mental connection. His touch sent a spark of something else tingling up my arm, which I tried my best to ignore. I reached out for his power and drew a small thread to join with my own. Then I reached out to Thora, Bren, and Cayden, forming a link with each of them until I was at the center of a web of power. I marveled at how much progress I'd made in controlling and using my power in the past few days, having finally discovered what I was good at.

I opened my eyes. "I'm ready."

We crawled up the slope and crouched just below the ridge. Bren motioned us to stay back and crept the final few feet to peer over the top. After a moment, he returned. "There are three figures crouched behind some concrete blocks," he whispered. "I don't think they saw me."

"Did you see Damon?" Thora asked.

Bren shook his head. "He must be in the middle. The other figures hid him. They're keeping watch. Ready?"

We all nodded. Adrenaline coursed through my veins and I took a deep breath, trying to calm myself. I couldn't lose control. Not when I was connected to so many people.

Bren raised five fingers to count us down.

Thora attacked first, launching a bolt of electricity at the nearest figure, who cried out and crumpled to the ground. I felt a pull on my power as Cayden toppled one of the concrete blocks, exposing the group's hiding place. I stared at the two figures who turned to look at us. The hairs on my neck prickled.

Something was wrong.

Thora gasped at the same moment that it clicked what I was seeing. The men wore red armbands. The red armbands of the Ragazzi, not the purple armbands of the Players.

But if they were Ragazzi, then where was Damon?

Remember to watch your back.

I whirled around, but before I could shout a warning, I was thrown back. I tumbled down the far slope, feeling the threads of power between me and the others snap as my concentration splintered.

I heard Elan shout my name and felt the heat as Bren threw up a wall of flames. Footsteps pounded on the earth and Elan grabbed my arm, dragging me to my feet as he passed. The color drained from Bren's face with the effort of holding the wall of fire in place.

"Can't hold much longer," he hissed through gritted teeth.

"Behind the blocks!" Thora shouted. She turned and looked me straight in the eye. "Vesper, we need your power. Can you make the links again?"

I nodded, though I wasn't sure. My mind was a turmoil of conflicting thoughts and emotions. Damon had set a trap and I had led my friends straight into it.

How had he known? How had he set things up so perfectly?

We ducked down behind the remaining concrete blocks, next to the two men with the red armbands. They were both wounded, and their companion, whom Thora had struck with the lightning bolt, lay motionless. The rise and fall of his chest indicated he was alive. None of them were in any position to be a threat to us.

"What happened to you?" Cayden muttered.

"We got separated," one of them said through chattering teeth. "The Players told us to huddle behind here and that if we moved, they'd kill us." He gave Thora a malicious look. "Haven't you got better things to do than attack the wounded?"

Thora ignored him. "Vesper, you ready?"

I closed my eyes and reached out to my companions, forming the connections that allowed me to move power between us. My body shook as I forced air into my lungs to try and calm my mind.

Control. Control.

"Vesper," Thora said in a voice low enough that only I could hear. "We need to disable Damon, even if that means killing him."

I stared at her, eyes wide. "No. I can't do that. I won't."

"You have to. He's got a bigger force than us. I don't know where Cato and his team got to, but we're outnumbered. We can hold them off for a time, but we can't defend you and Elan *and* attack them *and* take Damon down." Thora's face was hard. "*He* is the key to all of this. You may not be able to influence his mind, but with our power, you can hurt him."

Before I could reply, Bren gasped out a warning. "It's coming down."

He slumped forward as the wall of fire flickered and died. For a moment, there was silence. Then, through the dust swirling around the crest of the ridge, the Players emerged. Damon stood at the center of the line, his face and clothes remarkably clean given the dust and chaos around us. A cold smile split his face as his eyes found mine.

But it was not his smile that sent a dagger of fear stabbing through my heart. It was his power.

He was ablaze with it. The threads of energy connecting him to his companions fluxed as he channeled power between the members of his team. Individually, they may have been of average ability, but together, they were strong. And at the center of them, like a spider in its web, Damon stood, smiling, as if this was all just a game.

Thora was right. My power was only a fraction of what Damon held. Unless we took him out, we wouldn't have a chance of defeating the people around him.

But with that much power, how could I hope to harm him?

Unless . . .

Marcus had assumed I could influence minds, overlooking my true strength. Had I overestimated what Damon could do? Perhaps he could only channel power, not use it.

Does he have the power to kill?

"Now, Vesper!" Thora cried.

Elan's power surged through me. I swayed slightly as I fought to control it, then slowly drew more power from each of my friends until the energy I held pulsed through my veins and I could barely breathe. I burned as brightly as the strongest torch in the blackest night, yet I still held back.

Please, Vesper. I've seen what he's done. He is a cruel man who will kill us if he gets the chance.

Elan's words were a seductive whisper in my mind. They gave me permission to strike, alleviating the guilt of what could happen. Damon threatened my friends, my own life. I couldn't let him hurt us.

From deep inside me, that nagging voice reminded me of the consequences of releasing too much power.

It would be a painful death.

But this time, I refused to listen. Gritting my teeth, I dug my fingernails into my palms to remind me what pain felt like and began to draw my power together into a point. I let the fear I held inside me flow away as, like a knight with his lance, I launched my power toward Damon.

29

Losing Control

DAMON'S SMILE WAVERED FOR only a second before he responded.

Our power streams collided, sending a shockwave back toward me that caused my grip on the energy flooding through me to falter. A hot breeze coated my mouth and tongue with dust as I struggled to maintain my focus. It was like pressing the tip of a stylus against a second one suspended in mid-air. If I released the pressure or relaxed for even a second, my stream of power would collapse and Damon's strike would hit home. And unless I could cut the connections to my friends, his power would flow through me to them, striking all of us down in one blow.

I bit down on my lip, the copper tang of blood filling my mouth as I drew up more power from the well inside me. Already, I felt tired, spent, empty. As Damon pushed back, his power thread lengthened and mine slowly wore down. I drew more energy from Bren and Thora, knowing they were the strongest, but I could sense Bren's power was almost drained, having used so much to keep up the wall of flames.

Gradually, inexorably, Damon pushed closer.

I felt Elan take my right hand, Thora my left, but it was as if the sensations belonged to a different person. I could spare no thought to speak to them. My entire focus was on maintaining the line of power and holding Damon off as long as possible. My body trembled with exertion, nausea rising in my throat, but my gaze did not leave him.

We're going to die.

I couldn't see any way around it. We didn't have the power to push Damon back. Marcus had told me I was powerful, and I had believed him, but now I saw how foolish I had been. I wasn't strong enough. Without something to distract Damon, it was only a matter of how long we could hold on. And that time would be measured in minutes, not hours.

Then, just as spots danced at the corner of my vision and the energy streaming through me began to waver, Damon screamed.

My power surged forward as the resistance disappeared. It drained from me until my legs collapsed. For a split second, I gazed into an empty, never-ending blackness.

I reached out, grasping at my power like a drowning sailor reaching for a lifeline, fighting to draw it back into me. Strong arms held me up. Slowly, it began to fill me. I greedily pulled in more, not realizing I was too tired to control it. Like a deluge of water, it streamed into me, and I cut the power connections to my friends as I fought to contain it.

Control. Control.

Damon screamed again. Dragging my gaze from the ground, I looked up and saw Ty hovering over him. Blood streamed down Damon's face and arms from deep scratches. Around him, power pulsed an irregular rhythm as he fought to keep it flowing while fighting off the dragon attacking him. I didn't have to be a genius to realize he was treading a fine line between control and chaos.

It was the same tightrope that I was walking.

Ty dove again, his claws aimed at Damon's eyes. Damon raised his arm, but it was too late.

In that single moment when Damon's concentration finally broke, he lost control.

Marcus had said the most dangerous thing that could happen with a person's power was for them to hold onto too much and lose control when using it. If the person didn't black out, their power would destroy them—and the people around them. And that was only one person's power, not the collective power of five individuals.

Instinctively, I threw out the power roiling inside me. Not in attack, but in defense, creating the largest shield I could imagine to encompass my friends.

The world exploded.

Damon's power slammed into my makeshift shield like a tidal wave. When I felt it buckle, I frantically drew on the last vestiges of power inside me to throw more energy into the shield. As quickly as I could build new layers, the outside ones crumbled under the onslaught. My command of my power began to fade, the tightrope between control and chaos swaying beneath me.

And then, as quickly as the power had struck, it disappeared.

My shield collapsed around us as my strength gave out and I fell into unconsciousness.

❧ ❧

When I opened my eyes, Elan's concerned face swam above me. My senses returned. Sandalwood, leather, and musk filled my nostrils. I felt strong arms wrapped around me.

Elan's arms.

A dopey smile spread across my face.

"Vesper?" His eyes searched mine. His face was lined with exhaustion and sweat plastered his dark hair to his brow.

"Hmm?"

Elan's brow furrowed. "Are you . . . okay?"

He didn't *look* like someone who hated me. In fact, there was a spark in his eyes, a fire that told me something quite different. Perhaps he was going to kiss me again. I half-closed my eyes in anticipation.

"Try sitting up." Elan pulled me—rather hastily, I thought— up into a sitting position.

I groaned, and not just from the loss of his touch. It felt like Thor himself pounded his hammer inside my skull. I hadn't had this bad a headache since my first experience in the Colosseum.

"What in the name of the gods just happened?" Bren breathed.

I blinked, trying to focus on the scene in front of me. "Damon?" I croaked.

"Neither he nor the rest of his team are going anywhere," Thora said flatly.

When I could finally see straight again, I saw what she meant.

The Players lay scattered across the side of the dune, some motionless, some moaning. Damon lay at the center of them, his glassy, lifeless eyes staring up at the sky.

The burst of power had exploded from Damon like ripples from a stone thrown into water. My shield had protected my friend but next to us, the Ragazzi lay unconscious.

A shout from behind made us turn. Cato stumbled down into the valley. Burns covered one side of his body, but as he surveyed the scene in front of us, a ghost of a smile flickered across his face.

"Well, that was harder than I thought it would be," he said as he got closer.

Bren pushed himself to his feet and clapped his friend on the shoulder. "Did you feel it?"

"Feel it?" Cato replied. "It knocked half of us—and them—out. What the hell happened?"

"I'm not quite sure," Thora said, giving me an odd look. "But right now, we need to move. Vesper, you still have the flag, right?"

Although I heard her words, I couldn't reply. Among the still forms littering the ground, my gaze lit on a smaller body. So small, it was easy to miss under the dust and sand.

It can't be.

"No!" The cry ripped from my throat.

I dragged myself to my feet and stumbled forward. With every step, my eyes confirmed what my heart wanted to deny. Falling to my knees, I reached down and plucked him from the dirt as gently as if he were the first flower of spring. He felt so light in my arms. So fragile.

Ty? Please, answer me.

But there was no reply. No rise and fall of his chest under my hand. A tear leaked from my eye, then another and another until there was a constant trickle that washed away the sand coating the small dragon's scales, making them glint with life.

He had always wanted to be brave.

"You stupid dragon," I muttered, scrubbing at my eyes. "You were supposed to stay with Cato."

Carefully, I folded Ty's wings in so they rested on his back.

I didn't rescue him from that shop for this.

"He's still there." A hand rested on my shoulder. "His mind, Vesper. I can still feel it. He's still alive."

I dragged my gaze from Ty to stare up at Elan, wondering if this were another lie to make me feel better.

Elan shook his head. "I can sense a glimmer of power. He's strong, Vesper. Stronger than you think." He reached out, and I let him take Ty from my hands. He cradled him like a baby. "We need to go."

I stared at him uncomprehendingly.

"The flag, Vesper. We may still be in time."

"To win?" I asked, my voice bitter. "Does that even matter?"

"Of course it matters. You want all this to have been in vain?" He strode away from me. Not knowing what else to do, I followed.

Thora and Cato conferred in low voices. They glanced up as we approached. Thora's eyes softened as she took in Ty's limp form. From over the ridge, what remained of Cato's team trickled down.

I stared down at the ground, feeling as if I could lay down on the packed earth and sleep for a week. From the look of the people around me, none of them felt much better.

"Last we heard, the Ragazzi and the Venetians were bogged down, fighting each other," Cato said as everyone gathered around. "I'm not sure what happened to the Sirens, but it's a fair bet they've taken advantage of our fighting to get ahead. Our focus now is on getting Vesper and the flag to the tower." He jabbed a finger in the direction of the tall structure poking over the ridgeline.

"You two, scout ahead," Thora instructed, pointing at two of the fresher looking members of the group. "Everyone else, form a protective group around Vesper. I know we're all tired, but this is the final push. Drink your water, if you haven't already, and eat something to boost your power reserves. We move in thirty seconds."

I tugged the small water carrier from my belt, having forgotten about it until now. The warm liquid tasted faintly metallic and did little to sate my thirst, but at least it moistened my dry mouth and made the jerky we'd been given a little more palatable.

"Do you really think he'll be okay?" I asked Elan, staring down at Ty. He still looked lifeless.

"I don't know."

I reached out and stroked Ty's head, then glanced up at Elan. "Are *you* okay?"

He nodded, though his face was drawn. "When Mom told me about the vision she had of you, she also said you'd be the death of me." He gave me a crooked smile, and something in my heart melted. "I'm not sure whether she was joking."

"Time to go!" Thora called.

We formed a ragged group and set off up the nearest ridge. The mist began to lift as we crested the rise, and for the first time since the Games began, the top of the tower came into view. Cato let out a string of curses as the people in front of me slowed. Figures stood on top of the tower. As we watched, a blue flag, the color of the sky above New Vegas, rose jerkily up the tallest flagpole.

The Sirens had made it.

They had won the Games.

30

The Tower

I STARED AT THE flag rippling in the breeze, the Sirens' dagger emblem striking at my heart.

We had failed.

My eyes fell on Ty, cradled in Elan's arms. My small friend, with a heart the size of the fearsome beasts he dreamed of being. Tentatively, I reached out with my power, feeling the faint spark that Elan had mentioned deep inside Ty's mind. I clung to it like a lifeline because the alternative, knowing that he died for nothing, was too much to deal with.

"Are you okay carrying him?" I asked Elan.

"Sure. Why wouldn't I be?" He caught my glance down at his leg and scowled. "I might have a limp, but it doesn't mean I can't run." His tone was scathing.

I bit my lip. "Sorry. I didn't mean—"

A hand on my arm pulled me forward. "Keep going!" Thora shouted. "It's not over yet."

Hope flickered in my heart. She was right. We hadn't won, but we hadn't lost—yet. If we could get our flag up on the second flagpole, we would still get control of one of the water wells. Ty's sacrifice would not have been in vain.

Cato urged us into a run, or at least what would have been a run if we weren't all exhausted and injured to various degrees.

"Diana's gonna be so mad," Thora muttered as she paced beside me.

"What's she got against the Sirens?" I panted.

"Don't you know?" She glanced at me, seeing my head shake. "Apollina is Diana's sister."

I gaped, nearly tripping. Apollina and Diana were sisters? But Diana always seemed as if she hated the Sirens, and from the way I'd caught Apollina looking at her, the feeling was mutual. What could cause such hatred between siblings?

I pushed the thought to the back of my head to consider after all this was over.

We closed the distance to the tower without challenge. When we were fifty feet away, Cato muttered something to the woman next to him, who shot a fireball at the door, blowing it in. Cato charged through, the rest of us hot on his heels.

The tower was larger inside than it appeared from the outside. There were no rooms, just a staircase winding its way around a central atrium that got progressively smaller higher up. Smoke tainted the air, the after-effects of the firebomb that had blown open the door, but that wasn't the only sign of destruction. The stone walls were blackened, and the staircase was far from intact. As our group began to ascend the stairs, I saw the body of one of the Sirens, legs sprawled at an unnatural angle, lying in a pool of her own blood. I wondered how many others hadn't survived the Games.

"Come on, Vesper." Thora tugged my arm, pulling me away from the grotesque sight. I stumbled after her, my muscles screaming as I ran up the stairs.

There was a shout from Cato, who had pulled ahead, taking the steps two at a time. Glancing up, I caught a flash of red and three figures, seemingly motionless, on the stairs.

The Ragazzi. But why aren't they moving?

As we rounded the corner of the stairs to start up to the next level, the answer to my question became clear.

There was a gaping hole in the staircase. Coming down, it may have been possible to gain enough momentum to clear the gap, but moving upward, I couldn't see how anyone would be able to jump over it safely.

The Ragazzi seemed to be conferring. One of them pulled back and pressed himself into the wall as Cato approached. With a shock, I recognized Aidan. The other two glanced at the man bearing down on them and seemed to come to a decision. They raised their arms in the air and stepped back, their faces downturned in shame.

Cato ignored the men, his long legs eating up the final few steps to the gap. When he reached it, he leapt into the air.

My heart skipped a beat, and beside me, I heard Thora's sharp intake of breath. We both stopped, unable to look away.

But in the moment I expected him to fall, Cato flew. He landed neatly two steps up from the gap and grinned down at us.

"Hurry up!"

"Show off," Bren muttered behind me.

"He used his powers to fly?" Cayden panted.

"Yes. It's his party trick." Bren sounded disgusted and relieved at the same time. "But don't you try it. It's taken him years to master."

Cato ordered a couple of people to escort the Ragazzi out of the tower. I gave Aidan a weak smile as he passed, but either he didn't see me or he was scared of returning it because he kept his head down.

Thora pulled me forward. I'd barely had time to notice that I was on the edge of the gap before I felt an odd sense of weightlessness and looked down to see my feet hovering a foot off the stairs. There was a sickening moment when I had an uninterrupted view through the gap to the base of the tower, then I safely landed behind Cato on the other side. He still wore his customary grin, but up close, I saw the strain on his face.

"Have you any power left?" he muttered in a voice too low for the others to hear. "I'm not sure how many I can bring across."

I still felt weak, but the water and jerky had helped. "A little," I replied.

I placed my hand on his back to make it easier to form a connection and opened a thin channel between us, pushing as much of my power as I dared toward Cato. He let out a small sigh of relief.

"Thora!" he called.

Thora flew across the gap as calmly as if it were something she did every day. "We need Elan," she murmured, "in case the Furies try any of their mind tricks."

Cato nodded and shouted to Elan, who jerked his head up in surprise. He turned to Bren and tenderly placed Ty's limp body into the stocky man's arms. Bren said something that I didn't catch, and Elan nodded, running one finger over the rounded protrusions on Ty's head before turning back to us and nodding.

"More power if you have it, Vesper," Cato muttered. He grasped the thick banister against the wall with one hand, and slowly, Elan was lifted off the stairs.

He was heavier than me and Thora, and Cato's body began to tremble with effort. I tried to feed him more power, but I couldn't widen the channel any more without draining myself completely.

Elan moved slowly—too slowly—across the gap. When he was halfway over, he stopped, suspended in mid-air. An anxious look crossed Thora's face as she looked from Cato to Elan.

"Take my power, Vesper," she whispered into my ear. But I shook my head, unable to open a channel with her without letting go of the thin stream of power I currently fed Cato.

Cato's jaw clenched, his fingers white on the banister. I saw the tension on Elan's face and the fear he was trying to hide. He began to move again, closer, until he was almost within spitting distance. Then Cato's power snapped.

A scream broke free from my lips as Elan plummeted down. At the last minute, Cato reached out and grabbed his wrist. If it had been anyone else, Elan's weight would have pulled them both down into the void, but Cato managed to hold on just long enough for Elan to pull himself up and get hold of the edge of the stairs. A minute later, he stood behind me, breathing heavily.

Cato bent over, swaying slightly, his breath coming in short gasps.

Elan grasped his arm. "Thank you."

Cato glanced up at him and grinned weakly. "Let's hope we don't run into any other issues."

We started up the stairs, moving steadily, yet cautiously.

"Do we have to cross the gap on the way back?" Elan asked in a low voice as we made our way higher.

Thora shook her head. "Not if we get the flag up. As soon as both flags are up and the bell rings, that's the end of the Games. The Gamesmasters will make sure we get down safely."

"That's a relief," Elan said, though I couldn't tell whether he was being sarcastic or not.

"Let's just hope the Sirens let us up and don't play any mind games," Cato growled.

His words rang in my mind as we approached the trapdoor leading onto the roof. It was closed, but sensing the tendrils of power from mind-talkers on the other side, I was under no illusion that our arrival was a surprise.

"There are four of them," Elan murmured. "The Furies and one other."

Thora nodded and pressed a finger to her lips. She pointed at herself, up at the trapdoor, then at Cato, Elan, and finally me, indicating the order we were to come up. We nodded in agreement.

Thora crept up the final stairs and crouched below the trapdoor. I sensed the pulse of power a split second before she blasted the door open. Thora sprang through, disappearing from view. Cato ran up and launched himself through the opening. There was a cry from above and a hiss of sparks. Elan followed, leaving me alone on the stairs.

I turned and looked back down to the base of the tower where the Siren lay sprawled. A wave of dizziness washed over me, and I had to grasp the banister to steady myself.

"Vesper, come on!" Cato called.

I shook myself out of my daze and pulled myself up through the trapdoor. The three Furies stood against the battlements, Elan and Cato in front of them. Cato held a metal pole, and Elan grasped a knife, though I'd no idea where they'd gotten them. From the look on Elan's face, the Furies weren't just standing placidly, but we didn't seem to be in any imminent danger.

"Quick, Vesper," Thora said. I turned to see her crouched, her arm around the throat of a young woman with distinctive red hair.

"Daria?" I stared at her. She suited the Siren's look, though the dirt smeared across her face and her ruffled hair was a far cry from the poised student I remembered from the Academy.

Thora jerked her head to the left. "The flag."

In the center of the roof, two flagpoles rose high above the battlements. At the top of one, the Sirens' flag fluttered in the warm breeze. I moved toward the second pole, pulling the piece of green fabric from my vest, and reached out for the attachment points, my fingers fumbling with the clips in my haste.

You could just let it go.

I paused, the clip halfway to the small loop on the flag. Where had that thought come from?

Let it fly away on the breeze. It would look pretty, no?

I dropped the clip and stood there, holding the flag out in my hand. The laurel wreath fluttered as the wind snatched at the green fabric. It *did* look pretty.

Vesper, no! Elan's voice roared in my head.

I jerked as if awaking from a dream and looked around, catching the eye of the copper-skinned Fury, whose lips curled into a smile.

Go on. Let it go.

I gritted my teeth. *No!* I shot back, putting as much force behind the word as I could.

The woman flinched, her face tightening as my strike hit home. Quickly, I turned back to the flagpole and clipped the flag to the lanyard. The thin cord bit into my palms as I yanked on it, pulling the green flag of the Gladiators up into the sky.

The moment it reached the top of the flagpole, a bell rang.

I crumpled to the ground, my whole body shaking.

It was over. We'd done it.

There was a ragged cheer from the arena below. Thora relaxed her grip on Daria's throat and helped her sit up, patting her shoulder companionably. Daria didn't return the gesture. She just looked relieved that it was over.

"Congratulations," Evalie said, inclining her head to Cato. "It was a good fight."

Cato nodded and lowered the metal bar he'd been holding. "Congratulations," he replied, though I could see he struggled to get the word out. We may not have lost, but neither had we won, and I could see that grated on him.

I pushed myself to my feet, just as Elan came over. "You okay?" he asked.

I nodded. "You?"

"I've felt better." He smiled ruefully. "But I've also felt worse."

We stood there awkwardly for a second. Then Thora and Cato came over and gave me a hug, so it seemed natural when Elan wrapped his arms around me.

I held onto him for a fraction of a second longer than I should, my face buried in his chest, inhaling the smell of sweat, leather, and the underlying scent of *him*. When he pulled back, I had to swallow down my disappointment.

I turned to Thora. "What happens now?"

"I'm hoping the Gamesmasters do something to fix that staircase," she said, "and then we can—"

An explosion ripped through the air, swallowing her next words. I pushed past Elan and hurried over to the battlements, leaning out to see what was going on. There was a second explosion, closer this time, and smoke filled the air. Too much smoke for the size of the explosions.

"What are the Gamesmasters playing at?" Elan came over to stand beside me.

"Not the Gamesmasters." Cato pointed up. "Pods" he said, pointing up.

Elan ducked as another explosion shook the tower. "What are they doing attacking us?" He tugged at my vest to pull me away from the edge, but I couldn't move. I stared at the sky. The pods were silver—the color of the Royal Academy. But why would they be here?

From the ground below, shouts and screams filtered up. A few fireballs and bolts of electricity flew into the sky, but they all fell short or bounced harmlessly off the surface of the pods.

I leaned out farther, trying to see if Bren, Cayden, and the rest of our team were okay. Then the tower took what must have been a direct hit. The building shook, stone falling from the battlements, and I felt the wall holding me back crumble. For a second, I teetered on the edge. A hand grabbed at me, but I slipped through their fingers and started falling.

Air rushed up around me, tearing the breath from my lungs, making it impossible to scream. Time seemed to slow as I saw the faces of my friends turned up toward me, shielding themselves from the debris raining down.

I am going to die.

The thought struck me with a quiet certainty. I closed my eyes and prayed it would be quick.

When I hit the ground, I didn't feel the impact, which I thought was odd. I had braced myself for pain, but I just had this floating sensation, as if I were lighter than the air around me.

Is this what happens when you die?

I opened my eyes. I *was* floating, perhaps twenty feet above the ground. I searched the ground below me for my body but couldn't see it. Bren stared up at me, mouth hanging open. Then I realized that I wasn't just floating. I was rising.

Invisible hands twisted my body in mid-air so I stared up at the dark belly of the pod drawing me in.

31

Home

THE FIRST FACE I saw when I opened my eyes was my mom's.

She let out a choked sob and flung herself toward me, pulling me into her arms. I could feel her heart beating through her thin jacket. Honey and vanilla filled my nostrils. She smelled so sweet. So clean.

Maybe I *was* dead.

But the dull throbbing of the pod told me otherwise. I gently eased myself out of my mother's grasp and looked around. Guardians and Peacekeepers surrounded us. They looked at me warily, and two of the Peacekeepers kept their weapons trained on me, their faces grim. I almost laughed. What did they think I was going to do? I didn't have enough strength in me right now to put up a shield, let alone attack them.

The pod was dimly lit, and I couldn't see anything through the porthole windows except dark clouds. I stared around in confusion, trying to figure out how I had gone from falling to my death to being safe inside an Academy pod. And, more importantly, why?

Just then, my stomach lurched. For a moment, I felt strangely detached from myself, separated from the core of my being. But as soon as I identified the feeling, it was gone. Next to me, a Guardian shuddered.

"W-what's going on?"

My mother cradled my face. Her hair was pulled back into a loose knot, her eyes red-rimmed, lines of grief and worry on her forehead that I was sure hadn't been there when I'd left. She smiled at me through the tears that welled up in her eyes. I felt her reassurance seep into me.

"Oh, my child," she breathed. "I'm so glad you're alive. I didn't know if—" Her voice broke and she moved her hand impatiently to wipe away a tear before returning it to my shoulder, as if she couldn't bear to let me go, even for a second. "Are you hurt? You're so skinny!"

I shifted on the uncomfortable floor of the pod and winced. "Not really," I said quickly, seeing the flash of concern in my mother's eyes. "Just cuts and bruises." *And a pounding headache*, I didn't add. "Where are we going?"

"To the Academy."

I turned to the Guardian who had spoken, a tall woman with short, brown hair. I didn't recognize any of the people in the pod, but now I knew what they could do—that each of them had a hidden power—I knew I could never look at them the same way again.

"Then home," Mom said, turning my face to hers again. "We've missed you so much."

I stared at her, my mind still foggy. What was she doing here? And why had I been plucked from the city below to be taken home? In all my conversations with Marcus and the others, none of them had ever mentioned the Guardians picking people up. Elan had said it was impossible to return home, and I got the impression that if anyone knew a way up to the towers, it would be him.

The thought of Elan sent a flutter of anxiety rushing through my chest. Had he been thrown off the tower, too? He had been right beside me when the explosion had hit. I bit my lip.

"Did you pick anyone else up?"

"That's not your concern," the Guardian replied stiffly.

Anxiety tightened my belly, but I had no time to consider the implications of the Guardian's comment as at that moment, the pod touched down. The doors swished open. I blinked as a blinding light filled the pod.

"Have you got her?" a man asked.

"Yes," the Guardian replied, holding up an arm against the light. "Stop blinding us with that thing. Did the other pod pick up h—"

"Yes," the man said curtly, cutting her off. The lights drew back and we were allowed to exit the pod.

The evening sky was dark, made even more so by the floodlights dazzling the transporter deck. I scrubbed my eyes with the back of my hand to try to stop them from watering, but the dirt on my skin just irritated them more. I guessed my eyes had gotten so used to the gloom of the city below that they'd have to adjust to the normal lighting of New Vegas.

It hit me then that I was home. But why? And who—

"Vesper!"

I turned toward the familiar voice and saw Cayden being helped out of a second pod beside us. I made a move toward him, but my mother's hand on my arm held me back. She nodded to a tall man, flanked by a quartet of guards, waiting to one side.

He was a few inches taller than Cayden but had the same dark blond hair and sky-blue eyes. I had almost forgotten that Cayden was royalty, but the presence of his father is a stark reminder that he and I came from very different places.

The crown prince stepped forward and pulled Cayden into a hug. They stood there, clasped in an embrace, for several long seconds.

I glanced at the third pod, which had just landed, but the figures spilling from its belly were all dressed in gray uniforms.

I turned to my mother. "Is this it? You only rescued us?"

My mind flashed back to one of the first things Cayden had said to me when we'd been taken in by Caesar.

I made a bargain with your sister . . . Father will find a way to get us out of here.

Was that why I had been rescued? Had Layla somehow persuaded the crown prince to rescue me as well as his son? I scanned the faces of the gray-uniformed people around us, but I didn't see my sister anywhere.

When my mother didn't answer, I turned to follow her gaze. Cayden and his father were walking over. A flash of anxiety washed over me. Was I supposed to curtsy? Or bow? We had been in the Shadow City so long that I'd completely forgotten about Cayden's royal status.

Cayden answered my unspoken question by closing the distance between us and pulling me into a rough hug. "I'm glad you're okay. I saw you fall from the tower . . ." He stepped back, suddenly awkward.

Cayden's father inclined his head toward us, and I suddenly realized that I'd not even acknowledged his presence. I hurriedly executed a half-bow, half-curtsy that I was sure made me look like an out-of-sync puppet.

"There's no need for that, Vesper," he said with a wry smile. "I'm just glad you're both safe."

He turned to his son. "I made the Academy rerun the test footage and watched it myself. The results got mixed up. You should never have been sent down there in the first place." He let out a long sigh and rested his hand on Cayden's shoulder. "At least we managed to get you back."

"But how did you know where to find us?" Cayden asked.

The crown prince smiled. "Your microchips, of course."

Of course.

Every citizen in New Vegas had a tiny microchip implanted under their skin. It held our identity records and, I guessed, tracked our movements, though it wasn't something I had ever really thought about before.

But that would mean they knew we were alive down there . . . Have they been watching us all this time, waiting to see if we'd survive?

I felt a surge of anger, but it quickly dissipated. I was too tired to figure this out right now.

"You will both start at the Academy in the morning. But first, a night at home." He smiled kindly at me. "I'm sure your parents will be relieved to have you back."

My mother's grip tightened on my arm. "Thank you," she whispered.

The crown prince's gaze slid to hers. For a fraction of a second, something passed between them. Then he nodded awkwardly and turned to leave. "Cayden, shall we go?"

Cayden's eyes met mine. I could tell he was thinking the same thing I was. "What about the others who were thrown down there, Father?"

His father cleared his throat. "I'm sorry, but there was no doubt as to their test results."

I thought of Shui, cowering in the corner of her cage, and Aidan, his face ashen and hands raised as he pressed his back to the wall of the tower.

How could either of them be considered a danger to society?

"You're wrong," I said.

There was a sharp hiss of breath from my mother. The crown prince paused.

"They're just kids," I said. "Like us. They haven't done any —"

"I'm sorry, Your Highness." My mother's voice overrode mine as she grasped my arm, pulling me away sharply. Her nails dug into my skin so hard, they made my eyes water. "She's just tired and has been under a lot of stress. She doesn't mean it."

I glanced at her in surprise, struck dumb by the fear in her eyes.

The crown prince gave a curt nod. "We have all been through a lot. But you would do well to remember, Miss Rodriguez, that today, you have been given a second chance at life."

He turned and walked away stiffly. After casting a sympathetic and confused glance in my direction, Cayden followed. I let my mother pull me over to where a small taxi pod waited.

"Come on, Vesper. Let's go home."

The second I walked through the front door, my father was on me, wrapping both me and my mother in a giant hug. When I managed to extract myself, I saw he was crying. The sight made tears of my own spring into my eyes.

I had never seen my father cry. Not even when Layla had graduated or Sol had been born.

When we parted, Mom waved her hand at us to keep the noise down. "Sol is asleep. I didn't want to keep him up, in case . . ."

In case the rescue didn't work out.

The unspoken words hung between us.

I nodded. "Layla?"

"She's at the Academy. You'll see her tomorrow when you enroll." My mother's smile seemed slightly forced as her eyes scanned mine anxiously. "Fergus is there, too. His parents were delighted when he got accepted. You may have to take some extra classes to catch up, but you're so smart, I know it won't take you long. Just remember to do everything they tell you. They'll be keeping a close eye on you."

My eyes widened as the true meaning of her words hit home. *She knows what the Academy really is. She knows about our powers. But how is that possible?*

I looked at my father, wondering if I'd been wrong all along. Maybe this was something all adults knew and they just kept it from us when we were young. But his face was open, hiding nothing. I knew him well enough to know that he believed me to be a normal girl who had just been the victim of some horrible mistake.

I turned back to my mother, intending to question her further, but she gave the slightest shake of her head and patted my arm.

"Shower, food, then bed," she said quietly. "Everything else can wait until morning."

"I saved some of my special chili for you," my father said happily. Like my mother, his face had more lines and his hair more gray than I remembered, but he couldn't keep the grin off his face as he led me into the main room of our apartment and retrieved a bowl from the food heater. "You look half-starved. Eat first, then you can clean up."

I nodded, a wave of exhaustion overcoming me as the aroma of the chili filled the small room. The rich spiciness smelled of home. It was a smell I never thought I'd experience again. A hard lump formed in my throat, and I had to drink the glass of water Dad placed on the table in front of me before I could trust myself to swallow the food. But once I started, I couldn't stop, shoveling the food into my mouth as if it were the first meal I'd had in weeks.

It *had* been a long time since breakfast.

When I finished, my father took the bowl away, and Mom escorted me into the small bathroom, then helped me strip and step into the shower. She sucked in a breath when she saw the brand on my arm, but didn't say anything. As she turned to pick up my clothes, I caught the glint of tears in her eyes.

I wasn't sure that the regulation two-minute water allowance was going to make much of a dent on the dirt ingrained into my skin and hair, but when the flow of water stopped and I stepped out, my mother gently pushed me back in. "Dad skipped his shower today, so you can go again."

Grateful, I stepped back into the small cubicle and washed my hair again, running detangling cream through the knots. It was, without a doubt, the best shower I'd ever had.

When I stepped out, Mom stood there with a warm, fluffy towel. I looked around for my clothes.

"They're on the way down to the incinerator," she said, wrinkling her nose. "I wasn't sure even I could get the stains out to reuse them."

I felt a mix of relief and disappointment. My final connection to the Shadow City thrown into the trash.

A shiver ran through me as my mother squeezed the water from my hair. "Time for bed. You're safe now."

As I followed her out of the bathroom, I felt a weight lift from my shoulders at her words. Finally, I was safe.

Finally, I was home.

32

Choices

I AWOKE IN A cold sweat, my bedsheet tangled around my limbs. For a moment, I was disorientated, part of my consciousness still back in the dream. I'd been in the arena at the moment Ty dove down from the sky to attack Damon. Except this time, I saw the explosion of power as if I were above it, watched it ripple outward and cause people to fall to the ground, clutching their heads or collapsing into unconsciousness. I'd seen Ty thrown twenty feet like a rag doll to crumple to the ground.

I sniffed and wiped at the tears trickling from my eyes, gulping in air. Elan had said his mind still had a spark of life, and dragons were powerful, weren't they? In the stories I'd heard, I was sure they'd been hard to kill. Perhaps Ty would be okay.

But I would never know.

I rolled over and reached for the glass of water by my bed. It tasted odd, until I realized that was because it tasted of nothing at all. I must have gotten used to the strange aftertaste of the water in the Shadow City. A dull pounding echoed in my head, and I stifled a groan as I swung my legs over the edge of the bed and stood. Moving as quietly as possible, I crept out of the room to fetch a headache pill from the small stash my mother kept in the kitchen, then refilled my glass of water. I stood for a moment, staring out the glass doors at our small garden-yard. The clock on the wall read 03:00. Still a few hours before the city awoke and a new day started. A few hours until I would start my new life at the Academy.

I padded back to my room and lay down again, but sleep would not come. Instead, my mind returned to the events of the day before.

Cayden had always protested his innocence and insisted he'd done nothing in the test that could have justified sending him down to the city below. Perhaps he had been right. Perhaps there was some plot against the royal family.

But I knew what I had thought when they'd shown me those images of the so-called criminals and the small boy. I had been angry. I had criticized the society's values. Not out loud, but loud enough for the Guardian reading my thoughts to hear. They were right to have thrown me out.

No, not right. Thinking differently doesn't make someone a criminal.

Except in New Vegas.

I bit my lip. The tone of the crown prince's voice implied that I *had* failed the test, but for some reason, I'd been given a second chance. A chance Daria, Aidan, and Shui wouldn't get.

The society said only criminals were banished to the city floor. But my friends weren't criminals. If they fought and hurt others in the Games, it was only to ensure their own survival. Sure, there were some bad people down there—I shivered at the memory of Bobo and the slavers—but not *everyone* was the same.

The Gladiators had welcomed me, in their own way. They had given me a home.

A position at the Royal Academy was all I'd ever wanted. It was what I'd spent years working for, sacrificing my leisure hours and sleep. It would give my family the security I so desperately craved for them. It would mean my father wouldn't have to work into old age just to pay for a cruddy bed in one of the homes where the old went to die.

I should be happy I'd been given a second chance. But all I felt was shame.

Shame that I was up here when my friends below were hungry and in pain. Shame that I would become part of a system I wasn't sure I believed in anymore. Shame that I would have to wear a mask for the rest of my days and pretend I was a model citizen who believed in the ideals of New Vegas.

I *did* believe people deserved safety and security. But not if this was the price.

Before I could really think about what I was doing, I jumped out of bed and pulled on an old pair of pants and a top. I stuffed some spare clothes into a small backpack and looked around my tiny room.

What was I thinking?

I can't leave my family again.

But how could I stay and live the rest of my life as a lie?

I understood now why Marcus had fled the Academy after his lover's death. Understood why, despite the horrors and dangers of the Shadow City, Thora, Bren, and Cato expressed no desire to return to New Vegas. I still didn't know the full truth of what the Academy was, but I knew that it wasn't what I had believed it to be.

I took a deep breath and closed the backpack. I would leave a note for my parents. They'd understand. They had to. This wasn't like last time when they thought I was dead. I would explain everything so they'd see that this was the right choice—the *only* choice I could make. Hadn't Dad always talked about honor? Surely this was the honorable thing to do.

In the dim light, I ran my fingers over the holoprints pinned to my wall. A family shot, taken last Christmas, Layla grinning as she dug her finger into my ribs to make me double over in laughter. One of me with Fergus and Lainey, taken on the night of school prom. I bit my lip, wondering where they were now, and felt a pang of longing to go back to those days, just a few months earlier, where everything had seemed so simple.

I yanked the snapshots from the wall and slipped the one of my family into my pocket. Looking down at the picture of Fergus and Lainey, I hesitated. Somehow, I felt closer to my new friends than to those I had grown up with. They were part of my childhood, part of a time when we were blissfully ignorant of the truth of the world we lived in.

I crumpled the holoprint in my hand. That world was closed to me.

But as I opened my hand to drop the crumpled print into the trash, something made me pause. My fingers closed again and I shoved the crumpled ball into my pocket before turning and slipping silently from the room.

I didn't have much of a plan, other than to somehow steal a pod and take it down to the city below, but my powers already felt stronger, rejuvenated by food and rest. As I tiptoed past Sol's room, a noise from inside made me pause.

I couldn't leave without at least seeing my baby brother.

To my surprise, when I silently opened his door, Sol was sitting up in bed. His face lit up when he saw me, glowing in the warm light of the dragon-shaped nightlight by his bed. I hadn't seen it before and wondered if he'd been having bad dreams since I'd been gone.

"Vesper! I knew you would come home."

"Shush." I placed a finger to my lips, quietly closed the door behind me and moved over to the bed. "Don't wake Mom and Dad."

His gaze took in my clothes and backpack and he frowned. "Are you going away again?"

I hesitated, not sure what to tell him. I didn't want to lie, but I also didn't want to be the one to tell him I was going away again, for good this time.

The thought made my confidence waver. Maybe leaving wasn't the right decision.

"I just had a dream about you," Sol said quietly.

I wrapped my arm around his thin shoulders and pulled him in for a hug. "Oh yes? What was I doing?"

"You were scared. You were fighting something, but I couldn't see what it was. And you didn't have any weapons . . ." His voice trailed off in puzzlement. "There was a man helping you. A big man with black hair and a limp. He wore a t-shirt with a snake on it."

My breath hitched and my fingers tightened on Sol's shoulders, though he didn't seem to notice. "This man . . . Did he have a name?"

Sol shook his head. "I'm not sure, though you liked him very much."

I swallowed, my mind racing. Sol had never met Elan, never even seen him. How could he have dreams about him? Unless . . .

The thought was too much for me to face.

"Have you had any other strange dreams recently, Sol?" I asked carefully.

"I always have strange dreams," he said wistfully. "Mom says I shouldn't talk about them, but I'm sure she won't mind me telling you." His dark eyes met mine. "Sometimes they're good dreams, like when I saw you coming home. There was a dragon in that one." His voice rose in excitement.

I gestured at him frantically to keep his voice down.

"Sorry. It wasn't a *proper* dragon anyway because it was so small and couldn't breathe fire. You were in some big battle with a lot of other people." He frowned. "I can't quite remember what happened next, but then angels came down and brought you back home to us."

He smiled up at me, his face awash with the innocence that only a child who didn't understand what he was could have.

"Impossible," I whispered.

Marcus had assured me that talents only became apparent when children reached puberty. Even then, their power would only be activated if they had an extremely traumatic experience, like Marissa had. Nothing like that had happened to Sol, but what else could his dreams be but a seer's visions?

I felt the blood drain from my face. What would happen to Sol if the Guardians found him? They'd take him to the Academy, wanting to know why his powers came through so young. Maybe they'd experiment on him to find out what made him different.

Ow! You're hurting me.

Sorry. I forced myself to relax my grip on his shoulders.

Sol snuggled into me. *That's better.*

I froze, only just realizing that he hadn't spoken the words aloud. Not only was he a seer, he was also a telepath. Dual powers were rare enough, but Sol was only six!

Ice seeped through my veins as I looked down at my brother, who'd wrapped his thin arms around my waist. He yawned, his eyelids fluttering as sleep began to claim him, and something in my heart cracked.

What do I do?

My first instinct was to take him with me. Down in the Shadow City, he'd be safe from the clutches of the Guardians. But I immediately berated myself for the thought. How could I even think to take a child down there? It was too dangerous. But I didn't know what the Academy would do. Would they experiment on him, then discard him on the city floor anyway, telling our parents there had been an "accident"?

Panic choked my throat, clouding my thoughts. My mind sped through all the possible scenarios, none of them good. Either I left my brother here and prayed he wouldn't be discovered, or I stayed and tried to protect him for as long as I could. But once I was trapped inside the white tower of the Academy, there would be little I could do to help him.

Unless I can figure out how the Academy really works. And the truth about why I was brought home from the Shadow City.

I pried Sol away from me and shook him gently. He blinked up at me sleepily, puzzled.

"Sol, listen to me carefully. Mom was right. You can't tell anyone about the dreams, okay? Not even Layla or Dad."

He nodded, confused but compliant.

I gave his arms squeeze. "And you must never tell anyone, not even Mom, that you can talk to me . . ." *Like this. Okay?*

He nodded again.

"Promise me, Sol." I looked around wildly, my eyes alighting on the row of dragon toys in a place of pride on his shelf.

"Promise me on your orange dragon."

His eyes widened, the enormity of what I asked hitting home.

I stroked his cheek and forced a smile onto my face. "Please, Sol. It's important."

"I promise, Vesper," he said seriously.

I pulled him to me, trying to project love and reassurance. I blinked away tears as I stared at the dragons on his shelf. I was faced with an impossible choice, and whether I decided to stay or go, there would be consequences. Not just for me, but my family and friends.

Elan's face appeared in my mind, accompanied by an overwhelming sense of loss. If I stayed, I would never feel the touch of his mind again. Never know whether he had meant everything I had felt when we kissed. And Ty. He would think I left him, abandoned him. If he were even alive.

And if he weren't, he died for me.

A solitary tear trickled down my cheek.

Sol wiggled uncomfortably under my arm. "Vesper?"

"Yes?"

"In my dream, you had a dragon. I know Mom and Dad say dragons don't exist." He paused. "But do they, Vesper? Do dragons exist?"

I clutched him to me again, feeling his small heart beat against mine as my tears soaked his hair. "Yes, Sol. Yes, they do. And they're not all bad. Some of them are *good* dragons."

***

Sign up to my newsletter to be the first to hear when the next book in The Shadow Academy series releases. You'll also get a free copy of Crown of Darkness, the prequel to my Dark Enchanted Courts Series.

Sign up here: https://www.subscribepage.com/alisonfantasy

If you want more in this world, read on to find out about my next Shadow Academy release – *Trial by Fire.*

Vesper & Elan

Coming Soon...

WOULD YOU BETRAY YOUR friends for freedom? As the daughter of one of the richest magnates in New Vegas, Daria was born into wealth and privilege. When she fails a mysterious test, she's torn from her life of luxury and banished to the city floor to die. Instead, she discovers a dark, underground world she never knew existed.

Daria is sold to one of the factions who control the Shadow City. They want her for her power—the power to control fire. Branded a Siren, she's doomed to a life of servitude.

But Daria will not give up her freedom that easily.

She knows it will take all her cunning and strength to find a way back home. But when the ghosts of her past rise up to haunt her, Daria realizes that the choice between freedom and slavery is not as simple as it seems.

Life is not just about survival.

It's about deciding who you want to be.

***

Find out more about Daria's induction to the Sirens in Trial by Fire, coming soon!

The Shadow City – Who's Who

GLADIATORS

Jules Caesar – *faction leader, enjoys intimidating people*

Marcus – *blocker and seer, loves coffee and books*

Diana – *a famed hunter, Apollina's sister, only member of the Gladiators who doesn't carry Caesar's brand*

Vesper – *mind-talker and empath, loves hot showers, hates rats*

Cato – *telky, hates the Sirens for killing his partner in the Games*

Thora – *leccy, Bren's partner*

Bren – *powerful burner, Thora's partner*

Cayden – *grandson of the King of New Vegas, telky, dropped in the Shadow City with Vesper*

Marissa – *leccy, dropped in the Shadow City with Vesper*

Ty – *tiny dragon, loves stealing other people's dinners, hates people commenting on his small stature*

Nimra – *Caesar's pet beast, resembles a sabre-tooth tiger, would quite happily eat Ty for breakfast if it wasn't for his scales*

Mortimer – *Marcus's lioncat pet*

SIRENS

Apollina – *faction leader, leccy, Diana's sister, likes to be the center of attention*

Mara – *mind-talker, one of Apollina's furies*

Evalie – *mind-talker, one of Apollina's furies*

Lorelei – *mind-talker, one of Apollina's furies*

Daria – *burner, dropped in the Shadow City with Vesper*

PLAYERS

Bellagio – *faction leader, unknown power, likes expensive suits*

Damon – *mind-talker*

Shui – *water weaver, dropped in the Shadow City with Vesper*

RAGAZZI

Nero – *faction leader, telky, Venilia's brother*

Aidan – *burner, dropped in the Shadow City with Vesper*

VENETIANS

Venilia – *faction leader, wind and water-weaver, Nero's sister, flirts with anything on two legs*

UNAFFILIATED

Bobo – *eccentric slaver who captures those banished to the city floor and sells them as slaves to the factions*

Elan – *mind-talker, born and brought up in the Shadow City, grumpy until you get to know him*

Eben – *shopkeeper, collects and sells antiques*

Remo – *Head Gamesmaster, runs the Games in exchange for water and a tithe from each faction*

Afterword

I had planned for this book to be a focused, "to-market" book rooted in the conventions of a specific genre. However, as with many of my writing aspirations, this didn't go quite to plan, and what emerged from my befuddled brain was instead a mashup of all the things I love best about my favorite books. Friendship, teamwork and found family. A far-future dystopian setting, but with a fantasy flair. Supernatural powers and strange monsters. And, of course, a dragon.

It may not be "to market" but I had a blast writing it and I fell head over heels in love with the characters. I hope that if you're reading this, they found a place in your heart, too.

While the towers of New Vegas stemmed purely from my imagination, there are elements of the Shadow City that were inspired by modern-day Las Vegas. We were lucky enough to visit the city briefly some years ago, enabling me to combine our holiday with a bit of book research. The Colosseum today is an entertainment venue of a less brutal sort, but a few of the details of Caesar's Palace are taken from its real-life counterpart. Apollina's motorcycle caught my eye in Treasure Island, and I couldn't resist including it in this book. And, of course, the factions are inspired by the rival casinos of modern-day Las Vegas.

I did much of the plotting for this book on a long mountain bike ride in Kielder Forest, Northumberland. More specifically, on the very long ascent up wide gravel tracks and paths that we cycled up to get to the start of the swooping singletrack that would lead us back down to the lake. There's something about having your lungs burn and your

legs ache that takes your mind to a different place. I'm pretty sure my uphill slog was nothing compared to one of Diana's training sessions, but it inspired the scenes in the Colosseum and Diana's story. The descent, while a lot of fun, did not seem nearly long enough to justify the effort put in to get to the start!

Anyway, I digress…

Writing and publishing a book is never a solo effort and I have some very special people to thank for their help in getting The Shadow Games published. Firstly, my beta readers: Clare, Rhiannon, Anni, Isabel and Candy. You never fail to pick up on loose threads and always help me wrangle my early drafts into shape. Thanks also to my editor,

Kim Young, for speedily working her magic and making sure none of my Britishisms made it into the final draft.

The gorgeous cover for the ebook and paperback versions was designed by the talented Jay of https://coversbyjuan.com/. The character art of Vesper and Elan in the paperback version was created by Keni Aryani, and prints along with additional swag and signed paperbacks are available to buy from my shop (alisoningleby.com).

Huge thanks to Krista and Elle for support, friendship and laughs during the ups and downs of 2019. We did it together!

Final thanks, as always, go to my wonderful family. To my husband, who is my biggest supporter, my firstborn who is always missed, and my rainbow baby who is my greatest joy.

The Shadow Games was first published in the Cursed Lands box set, which hit the USA Today bestseller list when it launched in May 2019. I had planned to re-release it later that year, but sadly, a tragic event in my personal life sent my writing plans spinning off the rails for a good while and it spent two years buried in the files on my computer.

I hesitated about re-releasing the book before I had written the sequel, but I felt that Vesper, Ty, Elan and their friends deserved to be out in the world for readers to read, not languishing on my hard drive. I'm really excited to continue their adventures and write the stories of some of the other characters who had less of a starring role in this episode. (Please tell me I'm not the only one who wants a Diana/Apollina story?!)

If you want me to hurry up and get the second book written, then please leave a review for The Shadow Games on whichever retailer you bought it from. More reviews = more pressure for me to write!

Until next time,

Alison x

About the Author

Alison Ingleby is a *USA Today* bestselling author of sci-fi and fantasy fiction. She loves writing cross-genre books featuring complex characters, twisting plots and fast-paced action with a dash of romance.

When not writing, Alison enjoys reading, drinking tea and spending time outdoors. She lives in Yorkshire, England, but her heart loiters by the sea in north-west Scotland.

You can find out more about Alison on her website: https://alisoningleby.com/

By Alison Ingleby

The Wall Series

A dark, gritty young adult dystopian series with a dash of romance.

Expendables

Infiltrators

Defenders

Liberators

Outsider (free prequel)

Dark Elemental Courts Series

A fae urban fantasy series with magic, snarky sidekicks and enemies to lovers romance.

Fae's Destiny

Fae's Downfall

Fae's Defeat

Crown of Darkness (free prequel)

Short Stories & Novellas

The Faerie Flag

Red Sun Rising: A Story from the Alteruvium Expanse

Dystopian Dreams *(free short story collection)*